Midnight Crossroad

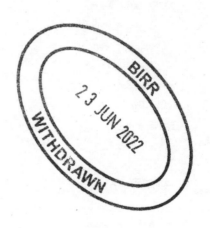

BIRR

23 JUN 2022

WITHDRAWN

Also by Charlaine Harris from Gollancz:

SOOKIE STACKHOUSE

Dead Until Dark
Living Dead in Dallas
Club Dead
Dead to the World
Dead as a Doornail
Definitely Dead
All Together Dead
From Dead to Worse
Dead and Gone
Dead in the Family
Dead Reckoning
Deadlocked
Dead Ever After
A Touch of Dead
After Dead
The Sookie Stackhouse
Companion
The Sookie Stackhouse novels
are also available in three
omnibus editions

HARPER CONNELLY

Grave Sight
Grave Surprise
An Ice Cold Grave
Grave Secret

The First Aurora Teagarden
Omnibus
The Second Aurora Teagarden
Omnibus

The Lily Bard Mysteries Omnibus

Wolfsbane and Mistletoe
(co-edited with Toni L.P. Kelner)
Many Bloody Returns
(co-edited with Toni L.P. Kelner)
Crimes by Moonlight
Death's Excellent Vacation
(co-edited with Toni L.P. Kelner)
Dead But Not Forgotten
(co-edited with Toni L.P. Kelner)

Midnight Crossroad

CHARLAINE HARRIS

GOLLANCZ
LONDON

Leabharlann

Class: F

Acc: 14/1558

Inv:

Copyright © Charlaine Harris, Inc. 2014
All rights reserved

The right of Charlaine Harris to be identified as
the author of this work has been asserted by her in accordance
with the Copyright, Designs and Patents Act 1988.

First published in Great Britain in 2014 by Gollancz
An imprint of the Orion Publishing Group
Orion House, 5 Upper St Martin's Lane, London WC2H 9EA
An Hachette UK Company

A CIP catalogue record for this book is available
from the British Library

ISBN 978 0 575 09284 6 (Cased)
ISBN 978 0 575 09285 3 (Export Trade Paperback)

1 3 5 7 9 10 8 6 4 2

Printed in Great Britain by
Clays Ltd, StIves plc

The Orion Publishing Group's policy is to use papers that
are natural, renewable and recyclable products and made from
wood grown in sustainable forests. The logging and manufacturing
processes are expected to conform to the environmental
regulations of the country of origin.

www.charlaineharris.com
www.orionbooks.co.uk
www.gollancz.co.uk

As always, this is for my readers.
I hope you like this new world and its people.

ACKNOWLEDGMENTS AND THANKS

My thanks to Dr. Karen Ross, Dr. Ed Uthman, the Reverend Gary Nowlin, Ellen Dugan (witch and writer), and Mike Meyers, the owner of Purple Heart Pawn. All of you helped me in the writing of this book. If I have made mistakes, they are mine alone. And, as always, thanks to Dana Cameron and Toni L. P. Kelner (aka Leigh Perry), for aid and support above and beyond the call of friendship. Paula, I really appreciate your reading the hate mail so I don't have to wade through it. Joshua, I couldn't have a better agent. You and the staff of JABberwocky are my agents of S.H.I.E.L.D. Hal, thanks for staying calm.

You might pass through the town of Midnight without noticing it, if there weren't a stoplight at the intersection of Witch Light Road and the Davy highway. Most of the town residents are very proud of the stoplight, because they know that without it the town would dry up and blow away. Because there's that pause, that moment to scan the storefronts, maybe three cars a day do stop. And those people, more enterprising or curious (or lower on gas) than most, might eat at the Home Cookin Restaurant, or get their nails done at the Antique Gallery and Nail Salon, or fill up their tanks and buy a soda at Gas N Go.

The really inquisitive ones always go to Midnight Pawn.

It's an old building, the oldest building in town. In fact, it was there before the town grew up around it, before there were two roads to intersect. The pawnshop, situated at the northeast corner of the intersection, is stone, like most buildings in Midnight. Rock is easier to come by than timber in West Texas. The colors—beige, brown, copper, tan, cream—lend a certain charm to any house, no matter how small or ill-proportioned. Fiji ("Feegee") Cavanaugh's cottage, on the south side of Witch Light Road, is a prime example. It was built in the nineteen thirties; Fiji ("I'm named for the country; my mom and dad liked to travel") doesn't know the exact year. Her great-aunt, Mildred Loeffler, left it to Fiji. It has a stone-flagged front porch big enough for two large urns full of flowers and a little bench. There's a low wall all around it, and rock columns hold up the porch roof. The large living room, across the whole front of the building, has a fireplace on the right side, which Fiji uses in the winter. The living room is now a shop/meeting place where Fiji holds her classes. Fiji is an avid gardener, like her great-aunt before her. Even at the beginning of fall—which is only a date on the calendar in Texas; it's still hot as hell—the small front yard is overflowing with flowers, in large tubs and in the ground. The effect is charming, especially when her marmalade cat, Mr. Snuggly, sits like a furry statue amongst the roses, the ice plants, and the petunias. People stop and look, and read the prim, small sign that says THE INQUIRING MIND on the top line, followed by Classes for the Curious, every Thursday evening at 7:00.

The Inquiring Mind, most commonly known as Fiji's house, is on the east side of the Wedding Chapel and Pet Cemetery, run by the Reverend Emilio Sheehan. The Wedding Chapel is open (that is, unlocked) twenty-four/seven, but the sign at the gate of the fenced cemetery behind the chapel informs mourning pet owners that funerals are by appointment. Though his business is to the east of the Davy highway, the Rev's home lies to the west, to the right of the Home Cookin Restaurant, which is past the closed hotel and the closed hardware store. The Rev's house is similar to Fiji's, but it's older, smaller, and has only sparse grass in the little front yard. It is also in no way welcoming or charming, and he has no cat.

But back to Midnight Pawn, the largest occupied building in Midnight. The pawnshop has a basement, sort of, which is unusual in Texas. Digging through the rock is a job for the stout of heart, and the original owner of the pawnshop was a formidable individual. That basement is only partly under the ground level; the windows of the two apartments peek out above the hard-baked dirt like suspicious prairie dogs. Most of the time, the prairie dogs' eyes are shut, since the windows are heavily curtained. The main floor, up a set of six steps at the entrance, is the pawnshop proper, where Bobo Winthrop reigns by day. He has an apartment above the shop, a big one, taking up the whole floor. There are only light curtains over the windows in his personal space. Who is there to look in? There's nothing else that tall for miles. Bobo bought the house next door in a parcel with the pawnshop. It's intended for the owner to live in, but at the time he bought the place, Bobo thought he would be just as happy over the shop. He planned to rent the house for extra income. He did some necessary repairs and advertised for years. But no one wanted to rent the house until now.

Today, the house has a brand-new tenant. Everyone in Midnight (except the Reverend Sheehan; who knows what he thinks?) is excited because the new resident is moving in.

Fiji Cavanaugh peeks out from behind her lace curtains from time to time and then commands herself to go back to work behind the glass shop counter, which is filled with New Age–type merchandise: glass unicorns, fairy bookmarks, dolphins galore on every conceivable item. On the lower workspace built in behind the high counter, Fiji is mixing an herbal compound that should confound her enemies . . . if she had any. She is fighting the impulse to dig into the Hershey's Kisses she keeps in a bowl on the counter for her customers. (Her customers just happen to like Fiji's favorite candy.)

Across Witch Light Road, at Midnight Pawn, Bobo walks down

the enclosed staircase from his apartment. At the pawnshop level, he has choices. There's a door to his left leading out to the driveway. There's a short open stairway down to the tenants' floor. And there's an inner door to the pawnshop on his right. Bobo should unlock it and enter, since the pawnshop has been closed since Lemuel went to bed a whole two hours before, but Bobo ignores it. He chooses the outer door, relocks it when he's outside, walks across the graveled driveway leading to the rear of the pawnshop, then over a little strip of downtrodden grass, then across the rutted driveway of the house next door, to offer help to the newcomer, a short, slim man who's unloading boxes from a U-Haul truck and sweating profusely.

"Need a hand?" Bobo asks.

The new tenant says, "Sure, some help would be great. I had no idea how I was going to get the couch out. You can take the time from the store?"

Bobo laughs. He's a big golden guy in his thirties, and his laugh is big and golden, too, despite the lines in his face and the expression of his mouth and eyes, which is mostly sad. "I can see if a car pulls in and walk back into the shop in less than thirty seconds," he says. In no time he's lifting boxes and putting them where the labels say they should go. Most of the boxes have "Living Room" scribbled on them, and they're heavy. The bedroom boxes are not so numerous, nor the kitchen boxes. There's furniture to move, really old furniture that wasn't that nice to begin with.

"Yeah," Bobo says, surveying the interior of the U-Haul. "You would have been up the creek without another pair of hands."

Joe Strong, with his little Peke on a leash, strolls over from the Antique Gallery and Nail Salon. He, too, offers assistance. Joe looks like his name. He's muscular in the extreme, and tan, though thinning brown hair and the lines around his eyes hint that Joe is older than his body suggests. Since Joe's obviously a great box lifter, the new tenant accepts his help, too, and the job goes faster and faster. The Peke, Rasta, is tethered by his rhinestone leash to the front post of the porch, and the new tenant unearths a bowl from a "Kitchen" box and fills it full of water for the dog.

Looking out her front window, Fiji wonders if she should go over to help, too, but she knows she can't carry as much as the guys. Also, Mr. Snuggly has an ongoing feud with Rasta; he would be sure to follow her if she crossed the road. After an hour of inner debate, Fiji decides that she will carry over lemonade and cookies; but by the time she gets everything assembled, the men have vanished. She steps out onto the street to see them heading down to the Home Cookin Restaurant. Apparently, they're taking a lunch break. She sighs and decides to try again about three o'clock.

As the small party walks west on the north side of the road, they pass the pawnshop and cross the intersection. The Davy highway is wider and well paved, the newcomer notices. They pass Gas N Go, waving at the middle-aged man inside. Then there's an alley and another vacant store, and next they'd reach the Antique Gallery and Nail Salon. But instead, they cross Witch Light Road to get to Home Cookin. The newcomer has been taking in the vacant buildings.

"Are there more people?" the newcomer asks. "Than us?"

"Sure," Bobo replies. "There are people strung out along Witch Light and a few on the Davy highway, and farther out there are ranches. We see the ranch families and workers now and then. The few other people who live close, the ones who don't run ranches, work in Davy or Marthasville. The commute is cheaper than moving."

The new tenant understands that the core group of people in Midnight is *very* small. But that's fine with him, too.

When the men (and Rasta) come into the restaurant, Madonna Reed looks up from the infant carrier atop the ancient Formica counter. She's been playing with the baby, and her face is soft and happy.

"How's Grady?" Joe asks. He brings the Peke in with him without any discussion, so the new tenant realizes Joe must do this often.

"He's good," says Madonna. Her smile switches from genuine to professional in a wink. "I see we've got a newbie today." She nods at the new tenant.

"Yeah, I guess we'll need menus," Bobo says.

The newcomer looks politely from Madonna to the other men. "You must come here often," he says.

"All the time," Bobo says. "We may only have one place to eat fresh-made food, but Madonna's a great cook, so I'm not complaining."

Madonna is a plus-size woman with an intimidating Afro. Perhaps her ancestors were from Somalia, because she is tall, there is a reddish cast to her brown skin, and her nose is thin and high-bridged. She is very pretty.

The newcomer accepts his menu, which is a single-sided typed sheet in a plastic envelope. It's a bit battered and obviously hasn't been changed in some time. Today is a Tuesday, and under the heading "Tuesday" he sees he has a choice between fried catfish and baked chicken. "I'll have the catfish," he says.

"What sides with that?" Madonna asks. "Pick two out of the three. The catfish comes with hush puppies." The sides for Tuesday are mashed potatoes with cheese and onions, slaw, and a baked apple with cinnamon. The new guy picks slaw and an apple.

They're sitting at the largest table in the restaurant, a circular one set in the middle of the small room. It seats eight, and the newcomer wonders why they're at this particular table. There are four booths against the west wall, and two tables for two against the front window, which looks north over Witch Light Road. After looking around, the new guy doesn't worry about hogging the big table any longer. There's no one else in the place.

A short Hispanic man walks in, wearing a crisp striped sport shirt and immaculate khakis with a gleaming brown leather belt and loafers. He's probably forty. He comes over to the table, kisses Joe Strong on the cheek, and slips into the chair by him. The new customer leans over to give Rasta a scratch on the head before he reaches across the table to shake hands with the new guy. "I'm Chewy Villegas," he says.

Not Chewy . . . Chuy. "I'm Manfred Bernardo," the new guy says.

"Did Joe help you get settled?"

"I'd still be moving furniture and boxes if he and Bobo hadn't shown up. There's not that much more to go. I can unpack in increments."

Chuy bends down to pet the dog. "How's Rasta been?" he asks his partner.

Joe laughs. "Ferocious. Scared Manfred to death with his vicious fangs. At least Mr. Snuggly stayed on his side of the road."

Though Chuy's eyes are marked by crow's feet, his hair does not show a trace of gray. His voice is soft and has a very slight accent, maybe more a careful choice of words, that indicates he was not originally from the United States. He seems to be as muscular as his partner.

A man in his sixties enters, an electronic chime on the door announcing his arrival. Like Chuy, he's of Hispanic origin, but otherwise the two men are nothing alike. The newcomer is cadaverous, and his skin tone is much darker than Chuy's caramel. There are deep creases in the older man's cheeks. He's maybe five feet five inches in his cowboy boots, and he's wearing a white shirt and an ancient black suit with a black Stetson. His only adornment is a string tie with a hunk of turquoise acting as a clasp. The older man nods politely at the group and goes to sit by himself at one of the small tables at the front window. He removes his hat, revealing thinning black hair. Manfred opens his mouth to ask him over, but Bobo puts a hand on Manfred's arm. "The Rev sits alone," Bobo says in a low voice, and Manfred nods.

Since he's sitting facing the window, Manfred can see a fairly steady stream of people going in and out of the convenience store. The two gas pumps are out of his range of sight, but he assumes that each person going into the store has a vehicle that is getting filled. "It's a busy time at the Gas N Go," he comments.

"Yeah, Shawn and Creek never come in for lunch. Sometimes for supper," Bobo says. "Creek has a brother, Connor—he's fourteen? Fifteen? He's at school in Davy."

"Davy is north of here?"

"Yes. A ten-minute drive. Davy's the county seat of Roca Fría County. The town's named for Davy Crockett, of course. 'Crockett' was already taken."

"So I'm guessing you're not from around here, either," says Manfred.

"Nope." Bobo doesn't amplify. This is a big clue, to Manfred. He's thinking it over when Madonna emerges from the kitchen to carry a glass of water over to the Rev and take his order. She's put glasses full of ice and pitchers of tea and water on the big table already.

Then Manfred spies a woman walking on the old sidewalk across Witch Light Road. She's passing the Antique Gallery and Nail Salon, though she barely glances at the CLOSED FOR LUNCH sign in the window. She's a showstopper. She's easily five foot nine, she's wearing jeans that show she is slim without being gaunt, and her orange sweater clings to square shoulders and thin, muscular arms. Though Manfred vaguely feels she should be wearing four-inch heels, she's not. She's wearing battered boots. She's got on a bit of makeup, and she's decorated with silver earrings and a silver chain.

"Damn."

He's not aware he's said it out loud until Bobo says, "Be very afraid."

"Who is she?"

"She rents one of my apartments. Olivia Charity." Manfred is pretty sure that Olivia Charity is not the woman's real name. Bobo knows her true name, but he's not going to voice it. Curiouser and curiouser.

And then Manfred realizes that all morning, throughout the camaraderie of unloading the van, neither of his companions asked the obvious questions. *Why are you moving to such a godforsaken place? What brings you here? What do you do? Where did you live before?*

And Manfred Bernardo realizes he's moved to the right place. In fact, it's just like he belongs here.

1

Manfred succeeded in getting his computer equipment set up in less than two days. He started catching up on his websites Thursday afternoon. Time was money in the psychic business.

He was able to roll his favorite chair right up to the large L-shaped desk that dominated what should have served as the living room, the room facing Witch Light Road. His computer equipment was set up there, and there were filing cabinets that rolled under the desk, though most of his files were online. Aside from the computer desk and chair, in an alcove there were two padded chairs with arms. He'd arranged them facing each other over a small round table, just in case he had a client in his own home who wanted a palm or tarot reading.

This seemed like the obvious and best use of the biggest room, to Manfred. He had no sense of decorating, but he had a great sense of utility. The big room had windows on three sides, all covered with ancient blinds. The blinds were useful but depressing, so he'd put up curtains to camouflage them. The ones he'd hung at the front were forest green and gold, the ones at the side overlooking the driveway were paisley patterned, and the set facing the next house to the east (which was empty) were solid red. Manfred thought the result was cheerful.

He'd placed his grandmother's love seat and an easy chair in the former dining room, along with the TV on its stand, and he'd jammed Xylda's little dinette set into an alcove in the kitchen. His bedroom, which was reached through a door in the west wall of the kitchen, was very basic. With Bobo's help, he'd assembled the double bed and made it up with sheets and a bedspread. The bathroom off it, the only one in the house, was also basic, but large enough. There was a toolshed in the backyard, which he hadn't investigated. But he'd taken the time to make an exploratory trip to the biggest grocery store in Davy, so there was food in the refrigerator.

Manfred was satisfied that he was set up in his new place and ready to go back to work.

The first website he visited was the one dedicated to "Bernardo, Psychic and Seer." His publicity picture was half of the home page. He was wearing all black, naturally, and he was standing in the middle of a field with lightning coming out of his fingers. (Every time he admired the Photoshopped bolts, he thought of his lightning-struck friend, Harper.)

Bernardo, Psychic and Seer, had gotten 173 e-mails during the days he'd been busy with the move. He checked them quickly. Some of them were of the spam variety, and he quickly deleted them. Four were from women who wanted to get to know him intimately, one similar message was from a man, five were from people who thought he ought to go to hell, and ten were from people who wanted to know more about his "powers." He referred them to his biography, largely fictitious and obviously prominent on his home page. In

Manfred's experience, people were endlessly prone to ignore the obvious—especially people who were seeking help from psychics. Out of the 173 messages, he would answer the rest, but in his estimation there were only nine that might lead to money.

His duty done by the Bernardo visitors, he checked his "The Incredible Manfredo" website. If you used your credit card (or PayPal) to give fifteen dollars to Manfredo to answer your question, he would reply. The Incredible Manfredo was adept at discerning this answer "from beyond" and relaying that answer to the questioner over the Internet. The beyond was "the place from whence he received his awesome powers." Many seekers were attracted to the Incredible Manfredo, a dark-haired, dramatically handsome man in his forties, judging by the picture on the website. He had 194 questioners lined up, and these people had paid. Responding to these took quite a bit longer, and Manfred thought about his replies carefully. It was impossible to use his true gift over the Internet, but he did use a lot of psychology, and he thought a television doctor could not have done better. Especially since most of the answers could be made clearer in a subsequent query for another charge of fifteen dollars.

After he'd spent three hours working on the "Incredible" website, Manfred made his third stop of the day, at his professional Facebook page under his full name, Manfred Bernardo. The Facebook picture was much slicker and played up his pale face, his platinum spiked hair, and the multiple piercings on his face. Tiny silver rings followed the line of one eyebrow, his nose was pierced, and his ears were scattered with silver rings and studs. He couldn't stomach gauges, but he'd had his rook pierced. He looked very dynamic, very intense. The photographer had worked well with him.

There were lots of messages and comments on his last posting, which read: "I'll be out of touch for a few days. It's time for me to retreat and meditate, to tune my psyche for the jobs ahead. When I'm back in touch with you, I'll have some amazing news."

Now Manfred had to decide what the amazing news would be. Had he received a great revelation from the spirits of those who'd passed beyond? If so, what would it be? Or maybe it was the right moment for Manfred Bernardo, Psychic and Seer, to make some personal appearances. That would be some amazing news, all right.

He decided that now that he was in Texas, fresh territory, he *would* schedule some one-on-ones, for a few weeks from now. These were taxing, sure, but he could charge a lot more for them. On the other hand, there was the expense of travel. He had to stay in a very good hotel, to reassure the clients that they were getting their money's worth. But it would feel good to touch the flesh a little, get the spark going again. He'd learned everything about the psychic business from his grandmother, and she'd believed in the power of personal attention.

Though Xylda had loved the concept of easy money to be made online, she'd never adapted to it; and really, she'd been more of a performance artist. He grinned as he remembered Xylda's appearances in front of the press during the last big murder case she'd worked. She'd enjoyed every minute of the publicity. Most grandsons would have found the old lady a source of acute embarrassment: her bright dyed hair, her flamboyant clothes and makeup, her histrionics. But Manfred had found Xylda a fountain of information and instruction, and they'd adored each other.

For all Xylda's fraudulent claims, she'd had flashes of the real thing. Manfred hoped she'd never realized that he was much more gifted than she'd ever been. He had a sad suspicion that Xylda had known this, but they'd never done more than refer obliquely to it.

Now they never would. He dreamed of her often, and she talked to him in those dreams, but it was more of a monologue than a dialogue.

Maybe she would pop up in one of his séances.

On the whole, he hoped she wouldn't.

2

A few days later, Bobo Winthrop was thinking about his new tenant when Fiji came into Midnight Pawn. Bobo was sitting in a comfortable chair probably crafted sometime around the turn of the century. It was made of dark, ornately carved wood with faded crimson velvet cushions. He'd been sitting in this chair for a month now, and he would miss it if the owner ever came back to redeem it. Of course, the guy should have taken it down to the Antique Gallery and Nail Salon, but he hadn't wanted to deal with "fruitcakes," as he'd so charmingly termed Joe and Chuy. After looking at the chair for twenty-four hours, Bobo had positioned it in front of one of the wooden posts that went from floor to ceiling. He'd put an old table by it. The chair seemed at home in the maze of the pawnshop, and he was not instantly visible from the front door.

"Bobo?" Fiji called. "You here?"

"In my chair," he said, and she began working her way through the furniture and assorted items that had been left there over the years. Away from the front windows, the pawnshop was dim and dusty, with a lamp left on here and there to guide the visitor.

Bobo was pleased to see Fiji. He liked her freckles and her gentleness and her cooking. It didn't bother him that Fiji said she was a witch. Everyone in Midnight had a past, and everyone had a freaky side. Some showed it more than others. Backlit by the daylight streaming in the big front window, Fiji picked her way carefully through the decades of accumulated items that filled Midnight Pawn. She smiled when she reached Bobo.

"*Hola*, Fiji!" Bobo said, flipping a hand toward the rocker that he'd favored before he'd tried out the velvet chair.

She smiled even more happily after his greeting and sat her generously curved derriere in the rocking chair. "How are you, Bobo?" she asked, a little anxiously.

"Good. And yourself?"

She relaxed. "Fine as frog's hair. What are you thinking about today?"

"My new neighbor," Bobo said promptly. He had never lied to Fiji.

"I took him some lemonade and cookies," she said.

"What kind of cookies?" Bobo asked, because to him that was the important point.

She laughed. "The sand tarts."

Bobo closed his eyes in exaggerated longing. "You have any left over?"

"I might have kept some back, after I had a good look at him. He didn't look like much of a cookie eater." In fact, Manfred's thin body had made Fiji all too conscious of her own curves.

Bobo slapped his stomach, which was still quite flat. "Not my problem," he said.

"No, it's not," she said dryly. "I'll bring 'em over later." Then she paused, just on the verge of saying something else.

"Out with it," he said.

"I recognized him," she said. "Manfred."

His brilliant blue eyes opened wide. "From where?"

"From the newspapers. From *People* magazine."

Bobo sat forward, his lazy contentment destroyed. "Maybe you better tell me," he said, but he didn't sound excited. "I'm surprised you didn't come over before."

"I'm sorry," she said. "I . . ." She stopped dead.

"What?"

She looked as though she wished she'd sink through the floor. "You've had enough to deal with since Aubrey took off."

"You really don't need to coddle me, Feej," he said. "Women leave guys every day. I felt pretty damn bad about it, but she's gone and I haven't heard from her. Aubrey's not coming back." He forced himself out of the abyss always waiting to swallow him. "So what's the deal with Manfred?"

"Okay, then," Fiji said, shrugging. "He's a psychic."

Bobo began to laugh. "A phone psychic? No wonder he was so interested in the phone and Internet situation here. He must have asked me a dozen questions. I couldn't even answer all of them." Midnight was very fortunate in getting excellent cell phone service and Internet service, purely by chance. A division of Magic Portal, a major Internet gaming company, was located just close enough.

Fiji's lips tightened. "Ha-ha," she said flatly. "Listen, I know you're not a computer person, but Google his name, okay? You know how to Google, don't you?"

"I just put my lips together and blow?" Bobo said.

Fiji caught the reference, but she wasn't in the mood for jollity. "Bobo, he's the real deal." She wriggled uneasily in her hard wooden rocker. "He'll know stuff."

"You saying I have secrets he might reveal?" Bobo was still smiling, but the fun had gone out of his eyes. He combed his longish blond hair back with both hands.

"We all have secrets," Fiji said.

"Even you, Feej?"

She shrugged. "A few."

"You think I do, too?" He regarded her steadily. She met his eyes.

"I know you do. Otherwise, why would you be here?" Abruptly, Fiji heaved herself out of the rocker. Her back was stiff, as if she intended to march out of the store. But instead, as he'd known she would, she wandered through the pawnshop for a minute or two before she left. Fiji always found it impossible to leave without looking at the pawned things in the store . . . on counters, on shelves, in display cases. Countless items, once treasured, sat in weary abandonment. Bobo was surprised to see her face turn a bit sad as she reached the door and cast one look back over her shoulder.

Bobo imagined that Fiji was thinking he fit right in.

3

Manfred worked every waking hour for the next few days to make up for the time he'd lost moving. He didn't know why he felt impelled to work so hard, but when he realized he felt like a squirrel at the approach of winter, he dove into making the bucks. He'd found it paid to heed warnings like that.

Because he was absorbed in his work and had promised himself to unpack three boxes every night, he didn't mingle in Midnight society for a while after that first lunch with Bobo, Joe, and Chuy. He made a couple more grocery and supply runs up to Davy, which was a dusty courthouse town—as bare and baked as Midnight but far more bustling. There was a lake at Davy, a lake fed by the Río Roca Fría, the slow-moving, narrow river that ran northwest–southeast about two miles north of the pawnshop. The river had once been much wider, and its banks reflected its former size. Now they sloped down for many feet on either side, an overly dramatic prelude to the lazy water that glided over the round rocks forming the bottom of the bed.

North of the pawnshop, the river angled up to hug the western side of Davy and broadened into a lake. Lakes meant swimmers and boaters and fishermen and rental cottages, so Davy was busy most weekends year-round and throughout the week in the summer. Manfred had learned this from reading his Texas guidebook.

Manfred had promised himself that when he felt able to take some time off, he'd hike up to the Roca Fría and have a picnic, which the guidebook (and Bobo) had promised him was a pleasant outing. It was possible to wade the shallows of the river in the summer, he'd read. To cook out on the sandbars. That actually sounded pretty cool.

Manfred's mother, Rain, called on a Sunday afternoon. He should have expected her call, he realized, when he checked the caller ID.

"Hi, Son," she said brightly. "How's the new place?"

"It's good, Mom. I'm mostly unpacked," Manfred said, looking around him. To his surprise, that was true.

"Got your computers up and running?" she asked, as though she were saying, "Have you got your transmogrifinders working?" That shade of awe. Though Manfred knew for certain that Rain used a computer every day at work, she regarded his Internet business as very specialized and difficult.

"Yep, it's all working," he said. "Are you okay?"

"Yeah, the job is going all right." A pause. "I'm still seeing Gary."

"That's good, Mom. You need someone."

"I still miss you," she said suddenly. "I mean, I know you've been gone for a while . . . but even so."

"I lived with Xylda for the past five years," Manfred said evenly. "I don't see how much you could miss me now." His fingers drummed against the computer table. He knew he was too impatient with his mother's bursts of sentimentality, but this was a conversation they'd had more than once, and he hadn't enjoyed it the first time.

"You asked to live with her. You said she needed you!" his mother said. Her own hurt was never far below the surface.

"She did. More than you. I was weird, she was weird. I figured it would suit you better if I was with her."

There was a long silence, and he was very tempted to hang up. But he waited. He loved his mother. He just had a hard time remembering that some days.

"I understand," she said. She sounded tired and resigned. "Okay, call me in a week. Just to check in."

"I will," he said, relieved. "Bye, Mom. Stay well." He hung up and went back to work. He was glad to answer another e-mail, to respond to a woman who was convinced that he was both talented and discerning, a woman who didn't blame him forever for doing the obvious thing. In his job, he was nearly omnipotent—he was taken seriously, and his word was seldom questioned.

Real life was so different from his job, and not always in a good way. Manfred tugged absently on his most-pierced ear, the left. It was strange that he seldom got a reading on his mother. And really strange that he'd never realized it before. That was probably significant, and he should devote some time to figuring it out. But not today.

Today, he had money to make.

After another hour at his desk, Manfred became aware he was hungry. His mouth started to water when he wondered what was on the restaurant menu this evening. He'd checked the Home Cookin sign, so he knew the place was open on Sundays. Yep, time to eat out. He locked up the house as he left. As he did so, he wondered if he was the only one in Midnight who locked doors.

Before he could give himself the treat of a dinner he hadn't cooked, he had to perform his social duty. He looked both ways on Witch Light (nothing coming, as usual) and crossed to Fiji's house. He'd been eyeing her pink-flowered china plate and her clear plastic pitcher in a guilty way since he'd washed them. He'd enjoyed the cookies and lemonade, and the least he could do was walk across the street to return Fiji's dishes.

The previous Thursday evening, he'd taken a break from work to watch the small group of women who came to Fiji's "self-discovery" evening. Manfred had recognized the type from his own clientele: women dissatisfied with their humdrum lives, women seeking some power, some distinction. There was nothing wrong with such a search—in fact, people searching for something above and beyond the humdrum world were his bread and butter—but he doubted any of them had the talent he'd seen lurking in Fiji when he'd opened the door to find her standing there in jeans and a peasant blouse, a plate in her left hand and a pitcher in her right.

Fiji was not what he thought of as his "type." It didn't bother him at all that she was older than he was; he found that suited him just fine, as a rule. But Fiji was too curvy and fluffy. Manfred tended to like hard, lean women—tough chicks. However, he had to appreciate the home Fiji had made for herself. The closer you got to the stone cottage with its patterned-brick trim, the more charming it was. He admired the flowers that were still burgeoning in the pots and barrels in Fiji's yard, despite the fact that it was late September. The striped marmalade cat known as Mr. Snuggly displayed himself elegantly under a photinia. Even the irregular paving stones leading to the porch were laid in an attractive pattern.

He knocked, since Fiji's place wasn't open on Sunday.

"Come in!" she called. "Door's open."

A bell over the door tinkled delicately as he went in, and he saw Fiji's unruly head suddenly appear over the top of the counter.

"Hi, neighbor," he said. "I came to return your stuff. Thanks again for the cookies and the lemonade." He held out the plate and pitcher, as if he had to provide evidence of his good intentions. He tried not to stare too obviously at the shelves in the shop, which were laden with things he considered absolute junk: books about the supernatural, ghost stories, and guides to tarot readings and dream interpretation. There were hanging sun catchers and dream catchers. There were two mortar-and-pestle sets that were pretty nice, some herb-gardening guides, alleged athames, tarot cards, Ouija boards, and other accoutrements of the New Age occultist.

On the other hand, Manfred liked the two squashy flowered armchairs sitting opposite each other in the center of the floor, a magazine or two on the small table between them. Fiji stood up, and he saw she was flushed. It didn't take a psychic to tell she was really irritated about something.

"What's wrong?" he asked.

"Oh, this damn spell," she said, as if she were talking about the weather. "My great-aunt left it to me, but her handwriting was atrocious, and I've tried three different ingredients because I can't figure out what she meant."

Manfred had not realized that Fiji openly admitted she was a witch, and for a second he was surprised. But she had the talent, and if she wanted to lay herself open to judgment like that, okay. He'd encountered much weirder shit. He set down the plate and the pitcher on the counter. "Let me see," he offered.

"Oh, I don't mean to trouble you," she said, obviously flustered. She had on reading glasses, and her brown eyes looked large and innocent behind the lenses.

"Think of it as a thank-you note for the cookies." He smiled, and she handed over the paper.

"Damn," he said, after a moment's examination. Her great-aunt's handwriting looked like a dirty-footed chicken had danced across the page. "Okay, which word?"

She pointed to the scribble that was third on the list. He looked at it carefully. "Comfrey," he said. "Is that an herb?"

Her eyes closed with relief. "Oh, yes, and I have some growing out back," she said. "Thanks so much!" She beamed at him.

"No problem." He smiled back. "I'm going down to Home Cookin for dinner. You want to come?"

He'd had no intention of asking her, and he hoped he wasn't sending the wrong message (if a casual dinner invitation could be the wrong message), but there was something vulnerable about Fiji that invited kindness.

"Yeah," she said. "I'm out of anything remotely interesting to eat. And it's Sunday, right? That's fried chicken or meat loaf day."

After she locked the shop (now Manfred knew he was not the only one who continued his city ways) and patted the cat on its head, they walked west. Manfred had gotten into the habit of casting a glance down the driveway that ran to the back of the pawn-shop. Though his view wasn't as good from the south side of the street, he did it now.

Because he was an observant kind of guy, Manfred had noticed soon after he'd moved in that there were usually three vehicles parked behind Midnight Pawn. Bobo Winthrop drove a blue Ford F-150 pickup, probably three years old. The second car was a Corvette. Manfred was no car buff, but he was sure this was a classic car, and he was sure it was worth huge bucks. It was usually covered with a tarp, but Manfred had caught a glimpse of it one night when he was putting out the trash. The Vette was sweet. The third car was relatively anonymous. Maybe a Honda Civic? Something small and four-door and silver. It wasn't shiny new, and it wasn't old.

Manfred hoped the hot chick, Olivia, drove the Vette. But that would be almost too good, like pancakes with real maple syrup *and* real butter. And who was the second tenant? Manfred thought the smart thing to do would be to wait until someone volunteered the information.

"How do you get enough traffic through the store?" he asked Fiji, because he'd been silent long enough. "For that matter, how does anyone in Midnight keep a business open? The only busy place is the Gas N Go."

"This is Texas," she said. "People are used to driving a long way for anything. I'm the only magical-type place for—well, I don't know how big an area, but big. And people crave something different. I always get a decent crowd on my Thursday nights. They come from forty or fifty miles away, some of 'em. I do some Internet business, too."

"You don't sell love charms or fertility charms out your back door?" he asked, teasing.

"Great-Aunt Mildred did something like that." She looked at him with an expression that dared him to make something of it.

"I'm cool with that," Manfred said immediately.

She only nodded, and then they were at the restaurant. He opened the door for her, and she went in ahead of him, her expression somewhat chilly, as far as Manfred could interpret it.

Home Cookin was almost bursting with activity this evening. Joe and Chuy were sitting at the big round table. There was a husky man with them, someone he hadn't met, jiggling a fussy baby. Manfred noticed cars far more than he did babies (and shoes and fingernails), but he thought this infant was the same size as the one he'd seen the first time he'd been in Home Cookin. That made the chances good that this was Madonna's baby; he figured the man was Madonna's, too.

As the electronic chime sounded and the door swung shut behind them, Manfred looked to his right. The two tables for two by the front window were occupied, and one of the four booths on the west wall. Reverend Emilio Sheehan (the Rev) sat by himself at his usual table, not the one next to the door but the second one. And his back was to the entrance, a placement that practically screamed "leave me alone." This evening he had brought a Bible to read. It lay open on the table before him. Two men, not natives of Midnight, were at the table closest to the door. They were preoccupied with their drinks and menus.

Though Manfred was sure he hadn't met all the townspeople, he knew the family sitting in the U-shaped booth was also just passing through. The four of them looked too . . . too shiny to be residents. Mama had subtly streaked hair, breast implants, and expensive-casual slacks and sweater. Dad was wearing rich-rancher clothes (gleaming leather boots and a pristine cowboy hat). The kids—a boy about three or four, a girl maybe two years older—were looking around them for something to do.

"Excuse me!" the mother called to Madonna, who was pouring tea for Chuy. "Do you have some colors or games for the children?"

Madonna turned to regard her with astonishment. "No," she said. After she put the tea up on the counter, she vanished into the kitchen.

The mom gave the dad a significant look, as if to say, *I don't like this, but I'm not going to rile the natives.* Manfred deduced it was some planning error on the dad's part that had led to this unlikely family eating dinner at Home Cookin. He did not think the dad was going to get to forget about it for a couple of days. However, the family cheered up when Madonna brought out their dinner plates on a huge tray. The food looked good and smelled wonderful. Madonna had help tonight: Manfred caught a glimpse of someone moving around in the kitchen when the swinging doors were open. As the family began to eat, the restaurant grew quieter.

Manfred and Fiji had taken seats at the big round table—he in the same chair he'd had before, facing the front door, and Fiji by the man holding the baby, with an empty chair or two between her and Manfred. Maybe she was more steamed about his selling-spells remark than he'd thought. Joe and Chuy said hello to Manfred, but they could hardly wait to tell Fiji about a woman who'd brought in an old book for Joe to look at. Manfred gathered that the book was an account of witches in Texas in the early part of the twentieth century.

Madonna's man was putting a bib on the baby and seemed pretty busy with the process, so Manfred put off introducing himself. While he waited, he evaluated the newcomers by the door. The two strangers at the small table fit in a bit better than the affluent family. They were both wearing worn jeans and T-shirts. Their boots were scuffed. The taller of the two, a dark-haired man, was wearing an open plaid sport shirt over his tee. His beard and mustache were neatly trimmed. The smaller man had medium brown hair; he was clean-shaven. Manfred set them in their early thirties.

The opening of the two swinging doors into the kitchen attracted Manfred's gaze. He only had to turn his head to the right to see the girl who emerged from the kitchen carrying two salads. Manfred's attention was instantly riveted. His eyes followed her as she crossed the room to the two men by the door. She set the salads in front of them, returned to the counter to get two packages of dressing, and took the packages back to the table along with a basket of crackers. Manfred knew the people at his table were talking, but they might as well have been making paper chains for all he knew.

Fiji was talking baby talk to the child, so Manfred leaned to his left. "Chuy, excuse me. Who's that? The girl serving?"

After a moment, it dawned on Manfred that the conversation at his table had stopped. He looked at Chuy, beside him, then at Fiji,

Joe, and the dark man with the baby. They were all regarding him with some amusement.

"That's Creek Lovell," Chuy said, his grin broadening.

"Her dad owns the Gas N Go on the other corner," Fiji said. "By the way—Manfred, meet Teacher." She nodded at the dark man.

"Good to meet you. How's the little . . ." And he stopped dead. For the life of him, he couldn't remember if the baby was a boy or girl. "Grady!" he said triumphantly.

"Good save, man," Teacher said. "Till you have 'em, they're hardly top of your list. Yeah, this is Grady, he's eight months old, and I do handyman work. So if you need some home repairs, give me a call."

"Teacher can do anything," Joe said. "Plumbing, electric, carpentry."

"Thank you, my friend," Teacher said, with a blinding smile. "Yes, I'm a handy guy to have around. I help Madonna out here, and every now and then I work for Shawn Lovell over at the gas station, when he just has to have a night off. And I fill in for Bobo, too. Call me if you need me." He fished a card out of his pocket and slid it across the table to Manfred, who pocketed it.

"I'm not good with anything but the most basic hammer jobs myself, so I'll be doing that," Manfred said, and then reverted to a more interesting topic. "So, how old is Creek?" he asked. His attempt to sound casual was a dismal failure; even he knew that.

Joe laughed. "Not old enough," he said. "Or, wait, maybe she is. Yeah, she graduated from high school last May. We gave her a gift certificate to Bed Bath and Beyond, so she could get stuff for her dorm room. But apparently she's not going to college, at least not this semester. You know why, Fiji?"

Fiji's forehead wrinkled. "Something was wrong with their loan application, I think," she said, shaking her head. "Something didn't come through with the financing. She's still hoping that'll get straightened out, even if her dad's lukewarm about her leaving. I feel bad for Creek; she didn't go to college, her puppy got killed, and her dad watches every move those kids make. A girl as young and smart as Creek doesn't need to be hanging around Midnight."

"True," Manfred said. Though height was not a major issue with Manfred, he was pleased to note that Creek was at least two inches shorter than he was. Her black hair was just down past her jawline, all one length, and it swung forward and backward with every step she took. Her skin was apparently poreless and clear, her eyebrows smooth dark strokes, her eyes light blue.

She was not really thin. She was not really curvy. She was just right.

"A word to the wise," Chuy said. "Don't let Shawn see you looking at his baby girl that way. He takes his job as her dad pretty seriously." All the men at the table were smiling, and even Fiji looked amused.

"Of course he does," Manfred said, breaking himself out of his trance. "And I don't mean any disrespect," he added. Was it disrespectful to hope someday he would be naked with Creek Lovell? And was it even more disrespectful to pray that it would be sooner rather than later?

"How old are you?" Joe asked.

"Twenty-two." Almost twenty-three, and it felt strange to try to minimize his age, rather than stretch it.

"Oh." Joe digested that. "You're closer to her age than anyone in town." He met his partner's eye. Chuy shrugged. "May be a good thing," he said. "Manfred, keep in the front of your mind the fact that all of us like the girl and none of us want her hurt."

"It's at the top of my list," Manfred said, which was not completely true. The way she walked, smooth and even, *that* was at the top of his list of things he noted about Creek Lovell. He reminded himself that she could have attended her senior prom only months ago . . . which went some way to quell the involuntary physical reaction he had when he watched her cross the room. *Some* way.

It was not quite full dark outside, and the family of outsiders had finished their meat loaf and fried chicken. The little girl was beginning to pick on her younger sibling, and the mom was casting desperate looks toward the kitchen. Madonna was cooking, to judge from the sounds of pots and pans and the sizzle of frying, and Creek hurried out with the plates for the two men sitting together. She put them down, gave the men an impersonal smile, and scurried over to the booth to take the payment tucked into the black plastic folder the dad was extending.

Just after the sun set, the bell over the door chimed as Bobo walked in with a man Manfred had never seen. As Manfred had noted before, his landlord was lucky enough to have a pleasing color palette; his hair was golden blond, his eyes were bright blue, his skin was a golden dusky tan. And he was tall, robust. His companion was more like—Bobo bleached and dried and shrunken. Instead of blond, his hair was platinum: the same shade as Manfred's, but the newcomer's hair was natural. His eyes were a pale, pale gray. His skin was . . .

"White as snow," Manfred whispered, remembering the old fairy tale Xylda had read to him. "His skin was white as snow."

Joe glanced at Manfred and nodded. "Be cool," he said, very quietly. "That's Lemuel."

Manfred planned on being cool as cool could be, since he wasn't sure exactly what Lemuel was—but no one had given Nice Normal Family the same memo. The children fell silent as the newcomer glanced around the room. He smiled at the children, who looked terrified. At least they were too frightened to speak, which was almost certainly a good thing. The two visitors kept their eyes down on their plates after a quick glance upward, and they very deliberately did not look up.

The Rev didn't even stop reading his Bible.

"This is beyond weird," Manfred said in a voice no louder than a whisper, but the bleached man looked at him with a smile.

Good God, Manfred thought. He had a ridiculous impulse to jump to his feet and interpose himself between the bleached man and Creek Lovell, but it was really fortunate he didn't act on that. Creek returned with the family's change, and after she placed it on their table, she flung her arms around the bleached man's neck—which Manfred wouldn't have done for any amount of money—and said, "I haven't seen you in so long, Uncle Lemuel! How are you?"

Released from their table by Creek's return, the mom and dad gathered all their belongings and shepherded the two kids, still openmouthed and staring, out the door of the Home Cookin Restaurant as quickly as possible. Manfred followed them with his eyes. Once outside, the mom stood on one side of the car, gripping the daughter's hand, the dad on the other side with the boy in his arms. They spoke to each other briefly and intensely across the hood of the car before piling in and speeding away.

"Uncle" Lemuel (if he was Creek's uncle, Manfred was an insurance salesman) gingerly embraced the girl and gave her a kiss on the hair. Lemuel was not any taller than Manfred, and even more slightly built, but his presence was bigger than his body. The eye could not pass over Lemuel; it was caught and fascinated. Manfred thought, *I could have skipped getting all this body art if I'd dyed myself dead white,* but he knew that he was simplifying.

The two strangers by the window had finally looked up now that

Lemuel's back was to them. They looked determined not to flee or flinch. The scene seemed frozen for a long moment, and then Lemuel's eyes met Manfred's and held. It was like being fixed in place by an icicle.

Bobo started forward, gently nudging his companion, and the connection was broken. *Thank God*, Manfred thought, an acknowledgment he didn't make very often.

In seconds Bobo and Lemuel had seated themselves, Lemuel at Manfred's right and Bobo in the seat between Lemuel and Fiji. *I can almost feel the cold coming off him*, Manfred thought, and turned to look welcoming. He registered that the girl Creek had hustled over to ask the two men by the door if they needed anything, before pausing by the Rev's table. After that, she buzzed over to find out what Bobo would like to drink, and Manfred got to enjoy her nearness, but his pleasure was muted by Lemuel's proximity.

After opting for sweetened iced tea, Bobo said, "Lemuel, meet the newest guy in town. Manfred Bernardo, meet my basement tenant, Lemuel Bridger."

"Pleased to meet you," Manfred said, extending his hand. After a slight pause, Lemuel Bridger gripped it. An icy chill ran up Manfred's arm. He had to fight an impulse to yank his hand from Lemuel's and cringe back in his chair. Out of sheer pride, Manfred managed to smile. "Have you lived here long, Lemuel?"

"Almost forever," the pale man answered. His eyes were fixed on Manfred, intense with interest. "A real long time."

His voice was not anything like Manfred had expected. It was deep and rough, and Lemuel's accent was just a bit unfamiliar. It was definitely a western accent, but it was like a western accent interpreted by someone from another country. Manfred was on the verge of asking Lemuel if he'd been born in America, when he remembered that asking personal questions was not the style in Midnight—and he'd already asked one. Lemuel released his hand and Manfred lowered it into his lap casually, hoping the feeling would come back soon.

"How are you going with your box schedule?" Bobo asked Manfred. "Still opening three a day?" He was smiling a nice warm smile, but Manfred knew that Bobo was not a happy man in his heart.

"I have a day left," Manfred said. (He'd realized long ago that most often you had to react to what was on the surface.) "Then I'll be done. My bad luck that all my files and paper stuff must be in one of the last three boxes."

"You don't go by what's in them?" Joe said. Creek was smiling, just a little, to Manfred's pleasure.

"Nope. I just open the next three boxes in the stack," Manfred confessed. He could read the complex of thoughts on Fiji's face: She had the impulse to tell him she would have helped; she had the awareness he didn't need or want her help; she made the decision to keep her mouth shut.

His grandmother had taught him how to read faces, and because of his natural aptitude, it hadn't taken long to develop his skills. While Fiji was an easy subject, and Bobo, too, Creek had depths and undercurrents. Joe and Chuy registered as agreeable and warm, but reserved. Lemuel was as opaque as a wall. Manfred struggled not to turn to his right to stare at his new acquaintance.

Lemuel, meantime, seemed just as interested in Manfred as Manfred was in him. He stared at Manfred's eyebrow, the one that had so many rings in it that the hair was hard to see. Since a few of Manfred's tattoos were visible in his short-sleeved T-shirt, Lemuel spent some time examining those, too. Manfred's right arm was decorated with a large ankh, and his left with a lightning bolt, his newest embellishment.

"Did that hurt?" Lemuel asked Manfred when the conversation about the weather and Manfred's move had been exhausted.

"Absolutely," Manfred said.

"Did you need to get 'em for your job, or you just like 'em?" The pale gray eyes in the snow-white face were fixed on him with curiosity.

"A combination," Manfred said. He felt compelled to be honest. "They're not exactly necessary for my job, but they make me stand out more, seem more interesting and alien, to the people who hire me. I'm not just another smooth con man in a suit." It felt strange to be telling so much truth.

Lemuel waited, obviously aware he'd not gotten the whole answer. Manfred felt like he'd lost the brakes on his conversational car as he continued, "But I did pick symbols I liked, ones that had a personal meaning. No point in getting tattooed with dolphins and rainbows."

From Fiji's sudden, deep flush, Manfred was sure she had a little dolphin tattooed somewhere and that she had felt very dashing at getting inked. He liked the witch a lot, but he couldn't seem to avoid stepping on her toes.

To Manfred's relief, Creek came to take their order, and not only did he get to break eye contact with Lemuel, he got to look at Creek some more: a win-win situation.

Like everyone else, he glanced at the door when the bell tinkled.

Olivia Charity had arrived. It was interesting, when Manfred thought about it later, the difference between Olivia's entrance and Lemuel's. Or maybe it was not the entrance that made the difference—both of them had just walked in, no posing, no attitude. It was the reaction of the Home Cookin patrons. When Lemuel had joined them, wildness and death had walked in the door, though the drama inherent in that statement made Manfred uncomfortable. When Olivia stepped inside, it was sort of like the first appearance of Lauren Bacall in an old movie. You knew someone amazing and interesting had entered the room, and you knew she didn't suffer fools gladly.

Olivia registered everyone in the diner as she strode to the round table. Manfred didn't think she missed a thing. As she took the chair opposite him, the one between Chuy and Teacher, he stared. It was the first time he'd seen her up close. Her hair was a reddish brown, almost auburn, but he suspected that was not her natural color. Her eyes were green, and he was sure they were colored by contact lenses. She was wearing ripped jeans and a brown leather bomber jacket that looked as soft as a baby's cheek, and underneath it she wore an olive green T-shirt. No jewelry today.

"You're the new guy, right?" she said. "Manfred?" Her voice was not a western voice; if he'd had to guess, he'd have said Oregon or California.

"Yep. You must be Olivia," Manfred said. "We're next-door neighbors."

She smiled and immediately looked five years younger. Before the smile, Manfred would have estimated her age at maybe thirty-six, but she was not that old, not at all. "Midnight is so small that everyone here is a neighbor," she said, "even the Rev." She inclined her head toward the old man, who had not turned to look to see who had come in.

"I've never talked to him." Manfred glanced at the Rev. The small man had put his big hat on the other side of his table while he ate, and the overhead lights glinted off his scalp. But there were only a few strands of gray in the remaining hair.

"You may never talk to him," she said. "He likes to keep his thoughts and words to himself." And because Manfred was watching Olivia so closely, he noticed that while her head was turned in the Rev's direction, she was actually looking at the two men by the door.

Then she glanced at Lemuel. Their eyes met, and she gave a tiny tilt of her head in the direction of the strangers' table.

The strangers were studiously minding their own business, but in a way that seemed a little too obvious to Manfred.

Creek hustled out of the kitchen then. "Sorry, Olivia, I was getting another meat loaf out of the oven," the girl said. While Olivia was choosing her food, Manfred realized that while everyone else at the table had ordered, Creek had not asked for Lemuel's selection. Manfred opened his mouth to say something about the omission, then thought the better of it. Lemuel would speak up if he wanted something. Manfred was fairly sure Lemuel did not eat, anyway.

It wasn't long before Madonna and Creek brought out the plates. Teacher had finished feeding Grady some plums from a Gerber jar, and he handed the child over to Madonna, who carried him off into the kitchen while the people of Midnight enjoyed their meal. Manfred, who had never been too particular about food, was deeply impressed with Madonna's cooking. After a lot of meals spent by himself, he actually enjoyed passing salt and pepper, butter, and rolls. The flurry of little activities that constituted a communal meal felt pleasant.

He also liked watching Creek move around the room, though he warned himself not to look at her too often. He didn't want to be creepy.

Olivia talked about an earthquake in East Texas, Fiji commented on how late the county garbage truck had been this past week, and Bobo told them a man had come in the afternoon before, trying to pawn a toilet. A used one.

Because he was curious about the two strangers, Manfred cast a glance in their direction several times during the meal. Since he was facing their table, he could do that without being obvious. They had ordered coffee and dessert (cherry pie or coconut cream pie), and they were *lingering*. In Manfred's experience, silent men didn't dawdle over food. Talking women might, talking men maybe. Silent men paid and left.

"They're watching someone here, or they're waiting for something to happen," he murmured.

"Yes, but which?" Lemuel replied, in a voice so low it was almost inaudible.

Manfred hadn't been aware he was speaking out loud, and he had to check his startle reflex. He choked on a bite of yeast roll, and Lemuel offered him a drink of water, his eyes distantly amused.

Everyone at the table tried to look away discreetly while Manfred recovered himself. It was a relief when he could say, "Went down wrong. Fine in a second!" so they could all relax and resume their conversations. A cold hand against the back of his neck was a help, oddly, and the fact that Creek looked concerned as she carried the empty bread basket back to the kitchen.

Yeah, Manfred thought. *'Cause choking guys look soooo cool.*

"What do you think?" Lemuel said, in the voice that nearly wasn't there.

Manfred turned his head a little to look into the eyes that were exactly the color of—wait, he nearly had it—the color of snow and ice melting over asphalt, a cold gray. "I thought they must be watching you or Olivia," he said, though he couldn't get as close to silent as the creature next to him. He managed well enough that Joe (to his left) didn't hear him but kept up his conversation with Chuy about Chuy's cousin's upcoming visit.

"That's what I thought, too," said Lemuel. "Which one of us is the target, do you reckon?"

"Neither," Manfred said, in a normal voice, and then hastily looked away and brought his volume down to extra-low. "They're watching Bobo. They're interested in you and Olivia because you're his tenants."

Lemuel did not reply. Manfred was sure he was chewing over this idea, seeing if it could be digested.

"Because of Aubrey, maybe," Lemuel said, just when Manfred was sure the topic was concluded.

"Who's Aubrey?" Manfred asked blankly.

"Not now," Lemuel said. He tilted his head very slightly toward Bobo. "Some later time."

Manfred patted his lips with his napkin and put it by his plate, which was still half full. He'd eaten enough. He wondered if Lemuel would suddenly pounce on the two strangers and kill them in some horrific way. Or maybe Madonna would charge out of the kitchen with a cleaver in her hand and fall upon them.

It seemed possible in Midnight.

"Ridiculous," he muttered.

"What?" said Chuy, across Joe.

"The amount I've eaten is ridiculous," Manfred said. "You'd think I was a starving dog." Too late, he noticed his half-full plate contrasted with Chuy's empty one.

Chuy laughed. "I always figure if I only eat here two or three times a week and I'm careful all my other meals, I'm okay," he said. "And you'd be surprised how many times I have to lift things in the store . . . plus, taking turns with Joe walking the dog, and doing yard work. I keep telling myself I need to start jogging, but Rasta won't pick up the pace when we're out." And Chuy was off and running . . . about the dog.

Once Rasta was the topic of conversation, Manfred didn't have to say a word. He'd observed that a small percentage of pet owners are simply silly about their pets, especially the owners who don't have human kids in residence. Part of that silliness lay in assuming other people would find stories about the pet as fascinating as the owner did. But (Manfred had always figured) there were a lot worse things to make false assumptions about.

For example, he found it far more pleasant to think about a little fluffy dog than to wonder what two strangers were doing at Home Cookin. Two *lurking* strangers. And it was far better to consider Rasta's history of constipation than the cold hand gripping his own under the table. When Joe turned to ask Chuy a question about a television show they'd watched, Manfred was left alone with his acute anxiety.

He didn't want to offend the terrifying Lemuel, but he wasn't used to holding hands with a guy. Manfred liked to think of himself as cool and comfortable with all sexual orientations, but the grip Lemuel had on his fingers was hard to interpret. It was not a caress, but it didn't seem like a restraint, either.

So Manfred took a sip of his water left-handed and hoped his face wasn't all weird.

"Manfred," Fiji said, "do you watch a lot of television?"

She was trying, very kindly, to draw him back into the conversation, since Joe and Chuy had transitioned from the dog's bowels to an argument about *Survivor* with Teacher.

"I have one," Manfred said.

Even Olivia laughed, though Manfred noticed that while he'd been preoccupied with Lemuel, she'd edged her chair out from the table, perhaps so she could rise quickly. She'd also told Joe and Chuy she sided with Teacher on the *Survivor* issue (whatever it was), and she'd angled her chair to align with Teacher's, so she could see the men by the door without turning her head too much.

"She has a gun," Lemuel said in that voice that was audible to Manfred alone.

"I figured," Manfred said. He was feeling unaccountably tired. Suddenly he figured it out. "You *leeching*?"

"I'm sorry, yes." Lemuel turned his head to look at Manfred. His flaxen hair brushed his collar. "I am a bit unusual."

"No shit," Manfred muttered.

Lemuel smiled. "Absolutely none."

"Don't they have a bottle of blood here for you? Wouldn't that help?"

"I can't tolerate the synthetics. They come up as fast as they go down. I can drink the real stuff in any method of delivery. Energy is just as good."

"You got enough, now? Think you can let go?"

"Sorry, fellow," Lemuel whispered, and the cold hand slid away.

Manfred thought, *I feel like a pancake that's been run over by a tank.* He wasn't sure he could get up and walk out of the restaurant. He decided it would be a sound idea to sit right where he was for a few minutes.

"Drink," said the sepulchral whisper, and Manfred carefully reached for his glass of water. But the white hand interposed a glass of a dark beverage full of ice. Manfred put it to his lips, discovering the glass contained sweet tea, very sweet tea. Normally he would not have been interested, but suddenly that seemed like exactly what he'd been longing for. He drank the whole thing. When he put down his empty glass, he caught sight of Joe's startled face.

"Thirsty," he said brusquely.

"I guess so," Joe said, looking a little puzzled and concerned.

Manfred felt much better after a moment or two.

"Eat," whispered Lemuel. Though his hands were still a little shaky, Manfred now finished his dinner completely. His plate was as bare as Chuy's.

"I got my second wind," he said sociably to Chuy and Joe (though why he had to cover for Lemuel, he couldn't have expressed in words). "I think I missed lunch, too. I'm going to have to watch that."

"I wish skipping meals was my problem," Joe said, patting his gut. "The older I get, the more my metabolism slows down."

That sparked a discussion about treadmills that engaged the whole table. Manfred was only obliged to look attentive. He wanted to leave, so he could get back to his house and think about what had just happened—decide if he was angry at Lemuel "borrowing" from him, if he was cool with it, or if he should make an "okay for one time but don't do it again" speech. At the same time, he was sure he needed to sit for a while longer.

Everyone at the table had finished eating now, and only Bobo ordered coffee. Teacher ordered cherry pie, and at Lemuel's urging Manfred got the coconut pie. Creek brought it to him. She was as pleasant with him as she was with everyone else—no more. *But no less,* he told himself.

Well, he hadn't ever imagined it would be easy to make an impression on her, even though he was the only male close to her age in Midnight. A girl as amazing as Creek would know she had plenty of options just down the road.

And that was what flipped him over to the "cool with it" option about the incident with Lemuel. Creek liked Lemuel well enough to call him "Uncle." So she wouldn't be disposed to date anyone who publicly freaked out about Lemuel being an energy-sucking vampire.

Manfred was relieved to find a practical reason for doing what he instinctively felt was the right thing. After all, if you live next door to an apex predator, you shouldn't go around poking him with a stick.

Fiji rose to depart, and a chorus of protests went up. (This group was as clannish as it was disparate, Manfred thought.) "Guys, I have to get home and feed Mr. Snuggly," she said, and there was a collective groan. She raised her hands, laughing. "Okay, it's a silly name, but I inherited the name along with the cat," she said. "I think he's gonna live forever."

Bobo, Chuy, and Joe began a mild argument about how long Mildred Loeffler had owned Mr. Snuggly before she passed away. Fiji lingered long enough to chip in some solid information. The vet's records indicated that Mr. Snuggly had lived with Mildred for a year before her demise, that he had been a kitten when Aunt Mildred had taken him in for his first shots; that set the cat's age at four years. "So Mr. Snuggly's in the prime of his life," she finished, and putting a careful ten dollars by her plate, she left.

There seemed to be no moon that night. The plate glass windows were filled with blackness. "Should I walk back with her?" Manfred asked in a low voice. "Or would that be, you know, sexist?"

"That would be sexist," Olivia said. She smiled around the table. "But I'll step outside to watch until she gets to her house."

Manfred didn't believe for one minute that Olivia's real purpose was to ensure Fiji's safe journey back to her cottage. Fiji was safe, and Olivia knew it. Manfred was sure Olivia was going to the door to examine the two strangers more closely.

What a complicated evening it had turned out to be. "Is every evening here like this?" he asked Lemuel.

"Oh, no, never before," Lemuel said. He seemed quite serious.

Joe and Chuy had been arguing over whose turn it was to walk Rasta, whom they'd left at home, so they didn't hear Lemuel's remark. But Bobo looked at him quizzically. "Something wrong?" he asked.

"Don't worry," Lemuel said. He smiled at Bobo. Most people would have found this terrifying, but Bobo smiled back, perfect white teeth flashing in a tan face. Bobo would be comfortably handsome the rest of his life, Manfred realized, and tried not to be envious.

The Rev made a silent departure, leaving his plate quite clean and not waving good-bye to anyone. As he passed Olivia at the door, he patted her shoulder. Olivia did not speak, nor did he. After she'd stood in the doorway for approximately the time it would take for a woman to get to her cottage after crossing the Davy highway, Olivia returned to the table.

The two men by the door had eaten all their pie and drunk all their coffee. Creek had come by the table twice to see if they needed anything else, and she'd left the bill between them on her second pass. Still the two were exchanging idle comments, as if they'd realized they had to justify their presence at the table.

Finally, Madonna came out of the kitchen and rang the bell on the counter. "Guys and gals, I love being a social center for this little town, but I need to get Grady and Teacher home, and I need to watch me some television. So you all clear out and let us close up."

You can't get any more straightforward than that, Manfred thought.

Those who hadn't paid got out their wallets. Manfred noticed that the two strangers paid Creek in cash before they slipped out the door, watched closely by Olivia, Lemuel, and Manfred.

"They're all wrong," Manfred said to Lemuel. He watched as Olivia left the diner by herself, moving quickly and neatly.

Lemuel's snow-slush eyes regarded him briefly. "Yes, young man, they are." Madonna was standing by Teacher, holding Grady, who was heavy-eyed. Lemuel rose and stepped away to pat the baby on the head. Grady didn't seem to mind Lemuel's chilly touch; a pat on the head and a smile was all it took to make the baby gleeful. He stretched out a little hand to Lemuel, who bent to give it a quick kiss. Grady waved his arms enthusiastically. Lemuel drifted closer to the door. Though Manfred hadn't noticed Madonna and Grady tense at Lemuel's attentions, he did notice when they relaxed.

Abruptly, Manfred felt foolish. Why had he been so concerned? Two men he'd never seen had eaten in a restaurant and lingered in a somewhat odd way. Lemuel had held his hand. Why should he worry about either of those things?

As Manfred rose to take his own departure, a bit shakily, he thought about his sudden change in attitude. Had his physical proximity to Lemuel affected his judgment? Was his reversion to "everything is probably okay" a valid viewpoint or some kind of mild euphoria induced by Lemuel's leeching?

Lemuel turned to give Manfred one last enigmatic look before he left the Home Cookin Restaurant.

Bobo, exchanging good nights with Joe and Chuy, seemed oblivious to any undercurrent in the evening . . . and so did the rest of the Midnight people. The strangers had (Manfred assumed) piled into their pickup and driven off, never to be seen again. But as Manfred walked past the area between his house and the pawnshop, he saw that the anonymous silver car was gone.

He suspected strongly that Olivia Charity was following the strangers.

And he thought, *It would be interesting to know why they were here. And why Lemuel is different from other bloodsuckers. And—who's Aubrey?*

Then Manfred reminded himself that he was here to work, and to work hard. He was planning for his future. The problems of these people were not his problems.

But he thought about those people until he went to sleep that night, all the same.

4

Two mornings after that, Fiji sat on her small back porch, look-ing at the herb garden with some satisfaction. She'd put in an hour's work this morning before breakfast, and she felt satisfyingly relaxed and pleased with her labors. She was wearing her oldest jeans and a torn sweatshirt stained with the results of a long-ago painting project, its sleeves hacked off to elbow length. In her sta-dium chair, her feet propped up on her weeding stool, Fiji was utterly comfortable. She had a big mug of tea and a blueberry scone on the little table beside her.

This was as good as it got, and she had a whole hour and a half before the shop opened to enjoy it.

If she hadn't felt so content and comfortable, she'd have gone in to get her camera to take a picture of the cat. Mr. Snuggly was curled picturesquely on a flat paving stone. The slanted morning sun warmed his striped orange fur to show up golden against the green of the plants and the dark brown of the stone.

She couldn't be bothered to get up. She took a mental picture, to hold forever. She surveyed the pile of weeds with some satisfaction. "I'm just amazing," she told Mr. Snuggly, who looked up at her without moving his head.

"Yes, you are," said Bobo, and Fiji jumped and made a sound like "Eeep!"

"Sorry," he said, his smile dazzling. "I didn't mean to scare you. I knocked on the shop door, but when you didn't answer, I figured you were back here. Want me to go away?"

Fiji *never* wanted Bobo to go away. Keeping him from knowing how much she craved his company was her problem, not how to get rid of him. "No, fine, come sit," she said, mortified at how lame she sounded. "Want a cup of tea? A scone?" She had had plans for the second scone, but she would gladly give it to Bobo. Maybe not the one sitting on her plate, but the second one . . . sure.

"That would be great, if you have extra," he said hopefully, and took the second chair after Fiji removed her gardening gloves from the seat. Once inside, Fiji flew around her little kitchen. It only took a moment to prepare his tea and to arrange his scone on a little plate with a pat of margarine and a knife to spread it.

"You do everything nice," Bobo said, looking at the pale green cup and dish.

Fiji glanced down at her paint-stained sweatshirt. "Not everything," she muttered.

Her guest took a big sip of his tea and a bite of the scone. "How's your house?" he asked, after he'd had a good look at the garden and the cat, appreciating both. "You need anything fixed?"

He's so damn nice, she thought. *Why didn't I get a fixation on a plain man?*

She scoured her mind for some fix-it job for Bobo. "The Formica on my kitchen counter," she said. "There's like a strip around the edge of the counter? And it's getting loose at one end. Probably you just glue it back on, right? With superglue?"

Bobo brightened. "Hot glue would be better. Got a hot glue gun?"

"I don't think so," Fiji said. "I'm not too crafty." *In any sense,* she thought, with some regret.

"I'll bring mine over," he said. "I have to track it down. I'll call."

"That's well worth the scone." She made herself relax, tilting her head back and closing her eyes. She had to teach herself not to tense up when Bobo was around. "I'm so glad it's cooling off in the daytime. At least a smidgen. You know what we ought to do? We ought to plan a citywide picnic day, now that it's slightly less brutal weather."

"Citywide?"

"Yes." Fiji was firm. "*Townwide* sounds too podunk; *hamletwide* sounds too precious. Everyone in Midnight, even the Rev, should come. We'll all bring some food, walk over to the Río Roca Fría, and have a fall picnic. The restaurant is closed on Monday. So are the pawnshop and the salon. A potluck picnic would be fun."

"You think Shawn and Creek and Connor would come? Shawn's open every day."

"Surely Shawn could do without Creek for a couple of hours, and Connor could get out of school a little early? Or maybe Teacher would stay at the gas station. There's not *ever* a time when *everyone* is off work. I thought about Sunday, but that's Madonna's big day at Home Cookin, and Rev would never come then, though his service is over early. Starts at nine thirty, but he's usually done in half an hour."

"He has a church service? Where?"

"In the chapel," she said, astonished that no one else in Midnight seemed to have learned this. "Where else? He has a nondenominational service in there every Sunday morning."

Bobo gaped at her. "I had no idea. And it's not on the sign. Does anyone ever go to it?"

"I do, pretty often. Though I'm not exactly a Christian. Once in a blue moon, someone else will come, someone he's helped. But hold on, we've gotten off topic. Let's circle back around to the picnic plan."

"That might be a nice outing. I haven't hiked over there in a long time. Since . . ." His voice trailed off.

Since before Aubrey left you. She restrained herself from gritting her teeth and growling. "We ought to do it. That would be nice for the new guy. Manfred."

"You like him?" Bobo asked.

Fiji looked at him uncertainly. Was Bobo teasing her? Did he seriously believe she would enjoy, at twenty-eight, having a crush on the new kid in school?

After a second, she decided there were no overtones. Bobo was making a casual inquiry . . . at least, she was fairly sure. "He seems okay," she said. "Unusual job, unusual guy. Lemuel sure took a shine to him."

"Really?" Bobo looked surprised. "Huh. That's good, I guess."

She nodded. "I thought so."

"Too bad Lem can't go to the picnic, then." Bobo appeared to be considering. "Nah, we couldn't have it at night," he concluded. "There's no light out there at all. Even if we went on a full-moon night, it would be too dark to hike out there. Picnics are a daytime thing."

"So we just need to pick a day and ask people," she said. "What about next Monday? A week from yesterday? I'll ask around."

"Sure, great," Bobo said. He did seem to be a little happier. "I can bring the beer and some soda." He looked down at his watch. "I better go open the store. Not that anyone hardly ever comes in this early."

"Lem still working five nights a week?" Midnight Pawn was open from nine in the morning to six at night, then eight at night until six in the morning, six days a week. It was closed for twenty-four hours on Sunday. On Monday, Teacher took the day and Olivia took the night shift, if it suited them, but more often than not the pawn-shop was closed on Monday. That gave Bobo and Lemuel two days and nights off.

"We're thinking of hiring someone," Bobo said. "This piecing Monday together as we go is getting old. We need someone reliable, someone who can maybe come in at other times when we're busy. But yeah, Lemuel is always there five nights. Sunday and Monday nights off."

"I wonder what Lemuel does when he's not working," Fiji said. "On his times off." There was a moment of silence. "Better not to know, I guess."

"Yeah. Better not."

Fiji hesitated. She wanted to ask, *Did you ever wonder if he knew anything about what might have happened to Aubrey?* But she didn't speak. *He would have asked Lemuel if the thought had occurred to him, because he's just that transparent,* she thought.

After Bobo went back to Midnight Pawn, Fiji propped her feet up again with a sigh, though it was more regretful than contented. In a moment, she'd have to give up her garden and her comfort and get cleaned up for work, but usually work was enjoyable, if not exactly fun. And she had the picnic to look forward to. But her thoughts about Aubrey had stirred up an unpleasant nest of feelings.

Fiji had not liked Aubrey Hamilton; in fact, she'd loathed her with an intensity almost amounting to hate. Guilt stirred in Fiji's gut as she remembered all the bad energy she'd sent Aubrey's way. Had she ever wished Aubrey was gone, never to be heard from again? Sure, many times . . . in fact, every time she'd watched Aubrey cling to Bobo's arm and rub herself all over him. And then Aubrey had actually done just that. She'd disappeared.

Because most of the residents of Midnight were quite perceptive, Fiji had never discussed Aubrey with any of them, before or after the vanishing. She knew her dislike would be easy to read . . . if they hadn't picked up on it already. Instead, she'd cast a spell. If it worked, everyone in Midnight should have been able to perceive Aubrey's true nature; but if the other Midnighters had suddenly opened their eyes to Aubrey's awfulness, not one of them had mentioned it.

And now no one would, because Bobo was miserable that Aubrey had left him, and everyone loved Bobo.

Fiji frowned at Mr. Snuggly. For the first time, she realized that in her thoughts she'd been putting Aubrey in the past tense. Bobo might be grieving because she'd left him, but Fiji could tell he also lived in anticipation of the day when Aubrey would return to her senses and come back to Midnight, to Bobo.

Fiji didn't believe that was going to happen. She didn't think she'd ever see Aubrey again.

As it turned out, she was wrong.

5

Manfred's cell phone rang early Saturday morning. "Manfred," said Fiji's voice. There was a *whoosh* in the background, and Manfred peered out his front blinds with his phone to his ear, to see her standing in her yard with her own cell phone, a truck running between them and making her hair even more tousled by the wind of its passing. "The Rev needs a witness. You want to come over to the chapel?"

"Right now?" Manfred looked at the "reading" he was typing onto the screen. *I sense you are involved in great turmoil right now. The way will be made clear. You will get a sign in the next three days pointing the way to the solution to your problems. In the meantime, be careful whom you trust with your secrets. Someone close to you does not wish you well.* Since he'd had no clue about Chris Stybr (sometimes he had a genuine impression about the seeker, but this Chris could be a man or a woman or a hermaphrodite for all Manfred knew), he'd had to resort to the tried and the very likely true.

"Well, they want to get married now, so yeah," Fiji said, with more than a touch of impatience. "If you can come?"

"On my way," Manfred said. Typing swiftly and accurately, he created another sentence of bullshit (*You will be interrupted in a task unexpectedly*) and sent it off. Then he was out the door, locking it behind him as he always did. He looked both ways, just in case, but as usual there was not a car in sight on Witch Light Road. Even Fiji had vanished. He'd pulled on a hoodie; it was just cool enough that another layer didn't seem ridiculous. Manfred craved the hint of fall. He had no idea what the Rev needed, but he was so curious about the older man and his chapel that he found himself a little excited by the summons.

He mounted the rickety wooden steps of the Wedding Chapel (defiantly constructed of wood and painted white, except for the double doors, which were brown) and stepped inside for the first time. The floor was constructed of boards, too, recently painted battleship gray. There were four long benches at the front of the chapel, which must serve as pews. They were white like the walls. Against the rear wall, there was an altar, a simple table with a picture mounted above it. Instead of Jesus being surrounded by little children, he was standing in the midst of a throng of animals. Manfred was both fascinated and curious.

A small cluster of people turned to look at him. The Rev, in his customary black suit and white shirt (complete with hat and bolo tie), held up his hand in blessing. Manfred found this disconcerting. The Rev's narrow, lined face was dominated by small eyes overhung by shaggy brows. It was hard to tell because of the brows, but Manfred thought the Rev's eyes were weirdly yellowish. The old man was holding a Bible and a pamphlet. There was a lectern at his side, and on it was a white certificate.

Fiji was wearing a long brown skirt and she'd pulled on a patchwork sweater over a turquoise T-shirt. She looked exactly like a mildly eccentric young woman who claimed to be a witch.

At a quick glance, he knew he hadn't met the wedding couple before. They were both in dire need of an orthodontist, and they were painfully young. Her hair was a pleasant light brown, and his was a few shades darker. They looked poor and terrified at their own daring . . . yet excited and happy. All at the same time.

As Manfred joined the little group, he nodded to the Rev, who nodded back. Without further ado, the Rev opened the pamphlet and began to read a very bare-bones marriage service. The depth and richness of his voice was a shock to Manfred, who'd expected something much rustier. "Lisa Gray, Cole Denton, you've come here to be joined in holy matrimony in front of these witnesses . . ."

In wavering voices, the two impossibly young people pledged to take care of each other for the rest of their lives. When the Rev had pronounced them man and wife, the kids kissed each other and smiled, full of a foolish happiness. From the fit of the bride's tight jeans, Manfred suspected there was another person present in utero.

Manfred joined Fiji in clapping enthusiastically, and he was smiling because the kids were smiling; but his inner cynic gave this marriage two years, at most. *I'm the Scrooge of weddings*, he thought. Well, his mom hadn't set a very good example; he'd never met his father. In fact, he didn't know who his father was.

The Rev didn't seem to be troubled by any doubts. He showed them their wedding certificate after he'd signed it. "I'll mail this to the county clerk right away," he assured them. "Go in peace, to love and serve the Lord."

Wasn't that from the Episcopalian prayer book? Manfred wondered. He'd been to church a few times with his mom.

"Thanks, Reverend Sheehan," said the girl, and her face passed into prettiness as she gave the old man a hug.

"We're really grateful," said the boy, and shook the Rev's hand with enthusiasm. He bashfully handed the minister a ten-dollar bill.

"Thanks, son," said the Reverend Emilio Sheehan, with genuine gratitude.

Then the young married couple left for whatever honeymoon they could manage, and the occasion was over. Fiji raised her hand in farewell. Manfred duplicated her gesture as he, too, turned away. He'd have liked to manage a conversation with the Rev, but the minister didn't seem as interested in Manfred as Manfred was in him. Manfred took a moment to study the license on the wall, which proclaimed that Emilio Sheehan was ordained by the Church of the Ark of God to perform weddings in the state of Texas. So, this was the real deal. Manfred felt subtly reassured.

As he left the chapel, which was all of twelve feet wide and fourteen feet deep, he walked slowly to take a longer look around. He realized he was in an old building, at least in American terms. Except for the benches, the wood of the building was roughly cut, and when he looked at the planks closely, he could see that the nails holding them together were old and irregular. The heat was apparently provided by a wood-burning stove at the front of the church. To cool the space in the summer, there were fans hanging down from the ceiling, so there was electricity. There was not a closet or a bathroom: one room was what you got.

Manfred and Fiji descended the wooden steps, both watching their feet with some care because the boards shifted a little. Manfred cast a glance under the structure. Mr. Snuggly was peering out at him, and he waved at the cat. Mr. Snuggly pointedly looked in another direction. A pebble path ran the short distance to the rutted driveway, which led past the chapel to the gate in the fence surrounding the pet cemetery.

Manfred glanced behind him to see if the Rev was also leaving the gloomy building. But the door had fallen back into place, and it did not reopen. Did the old man stay there all day in the bare room, waiting for whoever might come? How did he keep from madness?

"So, you do that often?" he asked Fiji, because he didn't want to think about the Rev going mad.

Fiji smiled. "Nah. And usually, when he asks me, I call Bobo and he walks over. But I could see he had a pawnshop customer this morning, so I called you. I hope you don't mind."

"No," Manfred said, surprised to discover that was the truth. He hastened to add, "Some days I might be too busy, though."

"Gotcha." She turned to go back to her house. Manfred saw that Mr. Snuggly had bypassed them somehow and was now sitting right on the boundary between Fiji's lush and lovely yard and the bare weedy ground in front of the chapel. His tail was curled around his paws. He could have been a striped statue for sale in a home decor shop. This was a cat who had mastered the art of stillness.

The sight of the pet sparked a thought. "Do you ever have to go to the pet funerals?" Manfred asked. The discreet sign at the side of the church, along the narrow driveway that led to the back, had fascinated him since he'd first read it.

"Not too often. And I don't *have* to do anything, just so you know. Weddings, maybe seven, eight times a year. The pet funerals . . . the Rev will call to see if I'll come stand with the bereaved owner . . . just to be a shoulder to cry on . . . oh, not more than twice a year."

"So, does he pay you for this?" The second the words left Manfred's mouth, he knew he'd made a mistake.

Fiji's face went stiff. "No," she said. "I go because we're friends." She spun on her heel to walk away.

"Hold on a minute," Manfred said, making his voice an apology in itself. "I said that without thinking."

"Right." He could see he had not mollified Fiji. Manfred had no idea what to do to make it better between them.

She looked back at him, her eyes narrowed and her hands clenched. She huffed out a sound of exasperation. "Listen, Manfred, would it kill you to say the magic words? And sound like you mean them?"

Magic words? Manfred was totally at sea. "Ahhh . . ." he said. "Okay, if I knew what they were . . ."

"*I'm sorry*," she said. "Those are the magic words. And yet no one with a Y chromosome seems to understand that." And off Fiji stomped, the drops from the previous evening's shower blotching her skirt as she passed through the shrubs and flowers.

"Okay," Manfred said to the cat. "Did you get that, Mr. Snuggly?" He and the impassive cat gave each other level stares. "I bet your real name is Crusher," Manfred muttered. Shaking his head as he crossed the road, he was relieved to get back to his house and to resume answering queries for Bernardo.

But he stored a new fact in his mental file about women.

They liked it if you told them you were sorry.

6

On the same day that Manfred enlarged his knowledge of male-female relations—though hours afterward—Bobo had an entirely different sort of discussion. He'd had a genuinely busy day, as Saturdays sometimes were—especially toward the end of the month. Late in the afternoon, he'd gotten a lull for thirty minutes, and he'd sunk down into his chair for the first time since he'd opened.

Bobo had had enough work for the day—he really did need to hire a part-time assistant—so he was not pleased when two men who seemed vaguely familiar entered the pawnshop. He'd worked right past six o'clock, when he normally locked up until Lem took over at eight. It was at least seven, and dark outside.

"I'm just closing up," he called. "You need to come back in an hour, when we reopen." Then he recognized them as the two men who'd eaten at Home Cookin, and he was instantly sure they hadn't brought anything to pawn. He recognized the type. They were there to ask questions, the kind of questions Bobo had fled to Midnight to avoid.

They didn't waste any time.

"The night your grandfather got arrested," the shorter man said, "an informant told the police he had a secret cache of rifles and a couple of bigger pieces stashed away. The cops found a lot of stuff. But everyone in his group, including my dad's friend's cousin, knew he had more."

Bobo had a bitter moment. He'd been sitting in his own store, comfortable in his usual jeans and T-shirt, and he'd just set down a mug of instant hot chocolate. He'd been reading a Lee Child novel in the moments between customers. Jack Reacher was his hero. Bobo sadly wished Jack Reacher were there with him now.

Bobo was aware that he had relaxed into complacency, under the mistaken assumption that Aubrey's disappearance was his crisis for the year. He had been foolish to believe there was a term limit on bad-shit-happening-to-Bobo-Winthrop.

The import of the shorter man's words sank into him. If there was anything in the world Bobo disliked more than being interrupted on a pleasant day, it was hearing his own history told back to him. He understood that he was in for another hard time—probably a beating—and he sighed. He put his mug in a safer place, and he prepared himself for what was surely to come.

Bobo was a big man, and a fit one. He ran three times a week, and he did his martial arts warmups and katas every day. He didn't actually enjoy hitting people, but he figured he was going to have to this evening. "I don't know anything about my grandfather's secrets, and I don't believe in his racist, homophobic hogwash," he told his unwelcome visitors. "You might as well shove off." Bobo knew he was wasting his breath.

"No," said the shorter man. "I don't think we will."

Predictable, Bobo thought.

"We need those rifles, and we need those explosives. I think we're going to have to *talk* about this some more." The short man sounded certain he could make Bobo talk. He produced a knife. It looked very sharp. "You need to change your attitude, or we're going to have to change it for you."

"I don't think that's gonna happen," said a new voice, and the two strangers tensed visibly, their eyes searching the shadowy depths of the pawnshop, the deep interior where the sun didn't reach even during the day. From behind some shelves that held a memory lane of blenders, Olivia Charity appeared. Bobo's face relaxed in a smile. It was two on two, now.

When they saw a woman (a woman clad in a black bra and black bikini panties), the two men relaxed their vigilance, though Olivia was armed with a longbow, arrow nocked and ready. The taller man, the one with the trimmed mustache and beard, sneered, "You think you're Robin Hood's little girlfriend or something?" He pulled a gun with his right hand and seemed to feel that put him in charge of Bobo and Olivia.

Olivia shot him.

It was almost funny how surprised the taller man was when he saw the feathered shaft sticking out of his right shoulder. After a second of horrified astonishment, he screamed, and the gun clattered to the wooden floor from his useless right hand. His boss, the brown-haired man, dropped his own knife as insufficient. He pulled a pistol from under his jacket and fired at Olivia in a very smooth move.

But she wasn't there. Neither was Bobo, who'd moved into a shadow and crouched down the instant he'd heard the bow twang. The short man looked around, confused, trying to locate someone to shoot.

Instead, there was a quick motion and a noise from the floor to the short man's right, the motion and sound in such quick sequence they were almost simultaneous, and from a white blur that appeared by the short man's side two hands reached out, seized the shorter man's head, and twisted. There was a particularly nauseating meaty snap, and the short man folded onto the dusty floor. Bobo jumped up to see what had happened.

"Jesus, Lem," said Bobo, startled but not surprised. "That was pretty extreme." Olivia rose from the floor with a groan, shaking her head; Lem had knocked her down as he sped past, and she'd hit the floor hard.

The taller man, his sleeve soaked with blood, opened his mouth to scream again, but Lemuel was there before the sound could escape the man's lips. He did not break the man's neck. He clapped his hand over the man's mouth.

"Bobo," Lem said, in his deep, antique voice, "I'm taking this one downstairs so's I can ask him a few questions in the privacy of my room. Then I'll be up to work. Olivia?"

"Yes, Mr. Domination?" Olivia was scowling. She clearly felt she'd had the situation under control.

"Can you find a good spot for the dead gentleman? I can bury him tonight. There might be a customer here at any moment."

That was quite true. It was often the case that if one customer showed up late, the whole night was filled with a steady trickle of people bearing the oddest items. "Okay," Olivia said, though it was clear she wasn't appeased. "I can do that. The usual place, I guess."

"Should be fine," Lem said. He'd come up through the trapdoor in the floor, rather than take the conventional route of exiting his apartment door, going up the half flight of stairs to the common landing, and entering the store from the landing door. Only Lemuel and Olivia knew the trapdoor existed, it was so unobtrusive. "I know you can handle it." He began dragging the struggling man over to the trapdoor. Though his captive was several inches taller than Lemuel, and pounds heavier, the pale man handled him with ease.

"Thanks," Bobo called, reminded of his manners. "I should have said that right away. You two are the Speedy Rescue Team."

"Glad to help," Lem said. "Lucky you've got the foot alarm buzzer in here." Lem had installed it himself, with Bobo's help.

"Good thing Lem was awake," Olivia said. Bobo finally noted Olivia's state of undress and realized that Lemuel was absolutely naked. Since Bobo hadn't noticed those interesting facts until this moment, he'd been more upset than he'd realized.

"Yeah, I'm real lucky," Bobo said drily. "Sorry you two got interrupted."

"We don't speak of private things," Lemuel said reprovingly. "You might want to put the Closed sign up, Bobo." His voice floated up from the foot of the ladder. Bobo, at the top, could hear the sounds of Lem's feet as he went to his own door with the bleeding man tossed over his shoulder.

"Right," Bobo said. The door down below opened and closed. "Olivia, you need my help?"

"You better stay here and straighten up the mess," she said. "I can take care of this." "This" was the body of the short man.

Bobo knew better than to argue with her, especially since Lem had already rained on her parade by killing the short guy. Instead, he flipped the trapdoor shut, ignoring the subdued shriek he heard from Lem's apartment. He hoped Lem was getting some good information, and he hoped Lem was well fed afterward. If it had been up to him, he would have called the police . . . but with Lem, some things you just couldn't stop.

Luckily, the dead man had the keys to his truck in his pocket, so Olivia didn't have to interrupt Lemuel's interrogation/meal. Olivia ran down to her place to grab some jeans and a shirt, and while Bobo was cleaning up the evidence of the struggle, including blood, she drove the dead man's pickup to the back of the store and knocked on the rear door, which led onto a small loading platform. Bobo unlocked the door, and Olivia stepped through. She gave Bobo a fond smile and a pat on the shoulder as she went by, and when she came back, she had the body over her shoulder. There was a dreadful limpness to the corpse's arms and legs, which moved in rhythm with her walk. "I'm on my way," Olivia said. She wasn't even breathing heavily.

"How do you do that?" Bobo asked. "I guess I could pick him up, but I sure couldn't stroll around with him without getting short of breath."

She grinned. "Every now and then Lem gives me some blood."

"Does it taste awful?" Bobo made an effort not to look disgusted.

"Nah. Not in the heat of the moment. With all due respect to Lemuel's modesty."

"Thanks again, Olivia. I expected to take a beating." At the top of his bagful of emotions, he was relieved. A layer down, he felt a bit horrified that his attackers were dead and that they'd been made that way with such speed and efficiency. At the bottom, he was sad and angry that his grandfather, so many years gone, had screwed up his life again.

"No problem. See you in a bit." She moved quietly and quickly, even though she was lugging 185 pounds of dead weight.

After Olivia left to drive the pickup to "the usual place," Bobo scanned the floor and the items around the crucial area, looking for blood spots. Though he used a flashlight and wiped up what he could find, he soon realized that he'd have to complete the job in the daytime. He folded the old towel he'd used to wipe up and put it by his book so he couldn't forget to take it upstairs to his washing machine.

After he'd turned the store sign to "Closed," Bobo collected his hot chocolate (now tepid), his book, the towel, and his keys and went upstairs to his apartment. While he stood in front of his microwave (he was trying to salvage his drink), he thought the incident over. There was a lot to consider.

He led off with wondering where "the usual place" was and what Olivia would do with the dead man's pickup. Would she need a ride back? He'd be glad to do that for her. In fact, he texted her to that effect immediately. Then he began to worry about how the men had found him. They weren't the first ones to do so, but they were the first ones to find him since he'd moved to Midnight. The last ones had beat him up and left him in the store he'd run in Missouri, a souvenir stand outside Branson. He'd left the next day for . . . anywhere else. He'd landed in Alaska, and he'd stayed there working until he felt the cold and damp seeping into his joints. He'd saved his pay, and he'd sold the Missouri souvenir stand through an agent, and he'd still had some family money stashed away, so he was able to buy Midnight Pawn from the previous owner, Travis Bridger . . . who (though he was supposed to be Lemuel's great-grandson) had turned out to be Lemuel himself. Lemuel was not the original owner of Midnight Pawn, but he'd been in charge for over a hundred years, plus or minus.

That was a whole other train of thought, one whose tracks Bobo didn't want to follow, at least right now.

So how had they found him? Had they tracked him through some computer trail? Maybe he'd ask Manfred, because his new tenant seemed to know a lot about computers. But Bobo'd have to give Manfred something by way of explanation, and he didn't know how trustworthy Manfred was, yet. He'd ask Fiji's opinion. She seemed to "get" people pretty well. From Fiji, it was somehow a natural progression to thinking of Aubrey and how she'd left him.

Acting on an impulse, Bobo went back down the stairs to the store. At night, the store was even darker and more mysterious the farther you got from the front windows. The interior seemed impossibly deep—at least on this floor—and it held more goods than customers expected. At the very back, to the left of the rear door, was a large rectangular storage room. This was where the things that could still be redeemed were kept, the things not yet for sale and on display. He unlocked the padlock on the door and then the dead bolt, and he stepped inside. There were tiers of shelves to his right and left. They were crowded with flat-screen televisions. These were the items people pawned first these days, their televisions. Then came gold jewelry and guns. The guns were all together, the jewelry in a safe bolted to the lowest shelf. At the farthest point of the rectangular room, the west wall, there were no shelves, only a heat and air vent up high. That was where Bobo had stored the boxes of Aubrey's stuff. He'd envisioned some awkward and painful scenario in which she sent a new boyfriend to pick it up, a person he would not want to take upstairs to the apartment they'd shared. He'd managed to cram all her belongings into seven boxes, and three of those were full of clothes and shoes. Her grandmother's sewing machine was still upstairs in the apartment, because he couldn't box it. He'd intended to carry it down and put it in the closet, but somehow he never had.

And no one had ever come to claim her things, so there in the storage room the taped boxes remained. He was sure that someday she'd want her stuff, and she'd tell him where to send it.

It had been an awful long time, though. His faith that he'd hear from her was beginning to fade.

On his optimistic days, Bobo reverted to his first theory: Aubrey had had to rush away in response to a sudden message, and while she was on this mysterious errand, something happened to her, something that prevented her return. She would walk in the door tomorrow, perhaps with a bandage on her head, or in a wheelchair, and explain everything. Though Bobo knew it was foolish to cling to this fantasy, especially as time went by, he did so nonetheless.

On his worst days, Bobo was convinced that some trait of his own had deeply repulsed Aubrey, repulsed her to the point where she'd not even wanted to speak to him again, to the point where leaving all her clothes and jewelry and her grandmother's sewing machine had been preferable to dealing with him one more time.

He couldn't see a mirror while he was thinking about this, and that was a good thing. Bobo looked ten years older when he thought about Aubrey.

Bobo knew both his theories were bullshit.

Luckily, the shop bell rang, bringing him out of this valley of conjecture. He stepped out of the storage room, relocking it as he went, and hurried to the front of the pawnshop. A woman in her fifties was at the door, and ignoring the CLOSED sign. She was carrying a stuffed parrot.

Bobo let her in and gave her thirty dollars for the bird. He was fairly certain, from her haste to be rid of it, that the parrot was going to be his for keeps. It would join the others. To Olivia's amusement, Bobo had accumulated quite a menagerie of deceased creatures. He'd arranged them all tastefully in one corner of the pawnshop, so they had their own little area. Olivia had suggested he rig a tape recorder behind a raccoon, which had been posed rearing on its hind legs with a book in its hand (*The Wind in the Willows*). She'd had a number of suggestions for remarks the raccoon could make when shoppers were standing in front of it.

Bobo hadn't gotten that bored yet.

7

Manfred was hunched at his computer, telling a woman in Reno that her husband was uncertain about the location of a wristwatch she'd given him the year before he died—and why the hell was a bereaved widow fixated on finding a damn wristwatch?—when there was a knock on the door.

This was unusual, especially in the morning. Manfred assumed his caller would be Fiji, either bringing him something she'd baked or asking him to attend another wedding—though since the first time she'd visited, Fiji had been careful to call in advance. When he opened the door, he was looking at a woman he'd never seen before. She was in her forties, stout, wearing what Manfred characterized vaguely as an office pantsuit. She had a business card in her fingers.

"Yes?" Manfred said, in a none-too-friendly voice.

"Hi, I'm Shoshanna Whitlock," the woman said, smiling in a professional way. "Here's my card." She thrust it at Manfred, who took it and stared at it.

"A private detective?" he said. "What do you need from me?" *Nothing good*, he concluded.

"May I come in?" Her chin, which was definitely on the aggressive side, led the way forward, but Manfred didn't move. She stopped, thwarted in her progress.

"I don't think so," Manfred said. "I work at home, and I don't like to be interrupted."

"I'll only take a moment of your time," she said, her eyes crinkling at the corners with the force of her sincerity. "I just want to ask you a few questions on behalf of my clients. Would it help if I told you that they're Aubrey Hamilton's parents?"

"Not at all," Manfred said, and closed the door.

She hadn't expected that, either, and he could hear her say, "What the hell?" She didn't leave right away—no heel *thock!* against the rock of the porch—so he leaned against the door, half expecting the force of her exasperation to blow it open. After almost a minute, he heard her walking off. He stepped over to the window to watch Shoshanna Whitlock march across the road to Fiji's cottage.

Perhaps the detective didn't notice that Fiji's place was a business, since Fiji's yard sign was so modest. Ms. Whitlock knocked at the door. Fiji answered it very quickly and stepped out of the door with her purse on her shoulder. Manfred could see her headful of curls bob from side to side as she shook her head. Fiji was saying "no" to something, that was for sure.

The detective kept talking, trying to wear Fiji down, but Fiji was locking the door of her cottage behind her and marching over to her car, parked on the driveway. The older woman stepped briskly after her, her tailored pantsuit, sleek leather purse, and neat shoes a sharp contrast to the permanently disheveled Fiji.

Manfred wondered if he should pop out to run interference. Fiji seemed so flustered . . .

And then the detective got very close to Fiji, who was trying to get into her car. Though Manfred couldn't see his neighbor's expression clearly, he saw that her body went rigid with irritation. Fiji's hand reached out to Whitlock and gripped her shoulder.

The detective froze in place. Her mouth was open, one foot in front of the other to take a forward step. But Whitlock couldn't take that step; she couldn't move at all.

Manfred realized his mouth was hanging open, just like Shoshanna Whitlock's.

Fiji popped into her car and backed out of her driveway, leaving the detective standing in her awkward pose. Manfred was sure Fiji didn't even glance at the frozen woman again.

"Damn," said Manfred quietly.

He waited, checking his watch from time to time. For the next five minutes, pigeons could have landed on Shoshanna Whitlock's head and she would not have been able to do a thing about it. After the five minutes had passed, Whitlock whipped her head from side to side and staggered a little. Then for a while she stood still, obviously unsteady, patting herself as if to make sure all her parts were there and functional. She looked up and down Witch Light Road, clearly at a loss as to how her target had disappeared. Manfred almost smiled as he watched Mr. Snuggly stroll up to give the detective a long stare. Whitlock looked down at the cat and flinched.

Manfred would have given a lot to know what she was seeing.

Maybe Whitlock would be frightened enough to leave Midnight? But no, the detective was made of sterner (or more foolish) stuff. After a minute or two, she regrouped and resumed her march. This time she went to the chapel, which was open, as always. She went inside without knocking. By now nothing would have startled Manfred, so he merely nodded to himself when she ran from the chapel as if a tiger were on her trail.

That proved to be the end of Manfred's free entertainment. After Shoshanna Whitlock got into her car (parked in front of the pawnshop, Manfred noted), she drove away without looking back. And ten or fifteen minutes later, Fiji returned. She climbed out of her old car, looking around her—presumably to make sure Whitlock was gone—before she walked to the front door, where Mr. Snuggly was waiting for her. The witch and the cat went into the house together.

Though he sat in his office chair and prepared to work, Manfred sat for some time, lost in thought. Until Shoshanna Whitlock's visit, it had never occurred to him that there was any mystery about Aubrey's leaving Bobo. In Manfred's eyes, the only odd thing about it was why any woman would leave a handsome, affable guy like his landlord. He'd only picked up the bare bones of the story: Aubrey Hamilton, Bobo's live-in girlfriend, had left him. Chuy had promised to tell him about Aubrey someday, but that day hadn't come around so far.

Now a private detective was asking questions.

Had Shoshanna Whitlock really been who she said she was? Manfred looked down at her card. He'd just ordered his own business cards online. He knew from experience that he could have claimed to be a professional ice skater or John Wilkes Booth and had a card printed to "prove" it. Therefore, he didn't attach much weight to the printed words on her tastefully simple rectangle. There was a line with her name, then underneath, *Texas Investigation Service*, which sounded just quasi-official enough to impress a potential witness. *Probably the point*, Manfred figured. The two lines of type were followed by a phone number. No address.

Briefly, Manfred considered walking next door to Midnight Pawn and handing the card to Bobo. Maybe he ought to give his landlord a heads-up.

But he decided not to, for a cluster of reasons.

He wasn't sure that whatever the "detective" was after was any of his business. If he saw a good opportunity, he could tell Bobo tomorrow, the day of the picnic. And surely, Fiji would report Whitlock's mission to Bobo before that. The last thing Manfred wanted to do after this morning was to get in Fiji's way.

He didn't think he'd look good as a statue.

8

The next day, the Midnighters assembled behind Midnight Pawn in the residents' parking lot. When Manfred came out of his house, wearing a light jacket over his T-shirt and with a small backpack over his shoulders, he counted in his head: Olivia, Chuy, Joe, Creek, a boy he hadn't met, Bobo, Fiji, the Rev, and Teacher from the diner.

"All right, guys 'n' gals!" Bobo called. "It's the first Annual Picnic Day! Madonna's coming over with her truck, so if there's something you can't carry, we'll load it in. We got tables, and some people have already put stadium chairs in there. You can stow your food, too."

Rasta yipped and looked excited, and everyone laughed. Manfred went over to Creek to meet the kid, who had to be her younger brother. For a fourteen-year-old, he shook hands in a very adult way.

"I'm Connor," he said. He had dark hair like his sister's and a smooth oval face like hers. He was already as tall as Creek, and

Manfred figured that in the very near future he'd be taller than Manfred himself.

"Where's your dad?" Manfred asked. "Did he have to mind the store today?"

Creek smiled at him. She didn't seem to suspect he was prolonging the conversation just to look at her. "Someone had to," she said. "This is like a treat to us. No working the cash register or stocking shelves! And Connor got to come because there was a teacher in-service training day."

Looking at her light blue eyes, Manfred felt a decade older than Creek, rather than four years.

"We've got a great day for a picnic," he said, since he had to say something.

Creek raised an eyebrow, a skill Manfred envied.

"Okay," he admitted, "trite. But true."

"I love going up to the river," Connor said. The boy actually looked excited at this mild outing. Living in Midnight must be excruciatingly dull for a kid his age, Manfred thought.

It was a glowing day in the earliest part of fall. The sun was bright but mild, and the wind was brisk. The sky spread above them, dotted with only the occasional small cloud to better set off its brilliant blue.

"I think Bobo wants you," Creek said, nodding to indicate that Manfred should turn around. Bobo was waiting patiently, and when he saw he had Manfred's attention, he beckoned. Manfred went over to him, smiling. But he felt his face settle into serious lines when he saw how anxious his landlord was.

"Hey," Bobo said by way of greeting. His hands were tucked in his back pockets, and he rocked back and forth on his heels. "Manfred, let me ask you something personal. And no offense, for real. Are you truly psychic?"

"Sometimes," Manfred answered honestly. "Mostly it's guesswork or psychology, but I have times when I get true readings."

"Then I wonder if you'd come by someday, maybe check out some of Aubrey's stuff? Maybe you could get an idea of what happened to her?"

Manfred felt he'd stepped off a cliff. Finally he said, "Sure, Bobo. I'll try. I wish I could guarantee a result . . ."

"No, man, I understand. Just do your best. That's all I can ask. Ah, maybe I could knock something off next month's rent . . ."

"No. Absolutely not. I'll be glad to help," Manfred said, looking up into his landlord's face. He was a little surprised to find that he meant it—he actually wanted to help Bobo. "Though let me warn you, touch psychometry is not my strength." Bobo looked blank. "That's holding inanimate objects to get a reading on them," Manfred explained. "So, I'll come over tomorrow. Ah . . . by the way. There was a detective by yesterday."

"Teacher told me she came by his place, too. I didn't talk to her. She came to the shop door, but I figured since I didn't know her and it was my day off, I didn't have to answer the door."

Manfred was dying to ask Bobo if he'd seen what had happened to the detective, but he didn't think it would be right. Maybe Bobo had stayed at his window to watch Shoshanna's progress, maybe he hadn't. It seemed like tattling, to bring up what Fiji had done.

"Just call me when you're ready," Manfred said, after an awkward pause. "I'll do my best for you." That having been settled, the two men drifted apart as quickly as they could, as if something about the conversation had been embarrassing. Manfred figured it had probably made Bobo uneasy to reveal the depth of his sorrow at Aubrey's departure, and Manfred knew it had made *him* uneasy to recognize Bobo's grief and need.

Figuring it was time to get over his trepidation, Manfred had a casual conversation with Fiji, who seemed as artless and pleasant as ever. Manfred wondered if he'd had some kind of strange delusion the day before, but he decided it was impossible. Fiji had really frozen Shoshanna Whitlock. And Manfred couldn't forget the detective— the self-proclaimed detective—running from the wedding chapel as if the minions of hell were behind her. He glanced over at the Rev, who stood a little apart, dressed exactly as usual in a threadbare black suit and bolo tie. *There's kind of an invisible cocoon around the old man,* he thought. The only people who approached him were Connor and Creek, who talked to him with apparent ease. The Rev answered them with a few words, but to Manfred's eyes his affection for the two seemed obvious.

Madonna drove Teacher's truck into the little parking lot, and everyone cheered. She waved through the windshield. She didn't look particularly excited or enthusiastic, but Manfred was learning that was not the Madonna way. The only time she smiled with any predictability was when she looked at the baby. This morning Grady was in his car seat next to her, and the truck bed was loosely packed with picnic things. Manfred added a few boxes of cookies from the Davy Kroger. Some of the other walkers added their contributions.

Bobo called, "All right! Let's go! Next stop, the Cold Rock." He slapped the hood of the truck, made a "forward ho" motion, and off they set.

Manfred expected Madonna to go back out the parking lot to the left, to get on the Davy highway and go north. He assumed there was a track that ran parallel to the river, and she could access it off the highway. But Madonna simply drove out of the parking area, veered right past the abandoned building to the rear of the pawnshop, and then bumped across the landscape: mostly bare dirt, dotted with patches of grass, cactus, clumps of bushes and trees, with plenty of space between. Every now and then she had to navigate around an outcropping of rock bursting through the thin soil as though it were trying to break free.

The walkers left the parking lot heading due north, but almost immediately they began veering northeast to the Río Roca Fría.

"Where are we having the picnic?" Manfred asked Fiji.

"We're setting up by the Cold Rock itself," she said. "You'll be able to see it in just a few minutes."

Manfred, naturally quick on his feet, began to walk at a brisk pace, his light backpack slowing him down not at all. In a few seconds, he was walking right behind Bobo. After days spent at the computer, he realized that he was glad to get out in the brisk air, glad to stretch his legs.

Since the truck was acting as pack mule, no one had to carry much. A bottle of water apiece, some sunscreen. Joe Strong had strapped on a special carrier for Rasta, who was sure to get tired before they reached their destination. At the moment the little dog was dashing around on his retractable leash, full of excitement.

"You didn't bring Mr. Snuggly?" Joe called over his shoulder to Fiji.

"He told me he wanted to stay at home and guard the place," Fiji called back, and there was a smattering of laughter.

Soon Manfred was far ahead of them both.

9

Fiji enjoyed the first leg of the short hike to the river, but soon she began to fall behind. She was the slowest of the group. As she plodded along, she wished she'd elected to ride with Madonna (not that Madonna had invited her). It wasn't that Fiji was really fat or really unfit; she just wasn't as lean or as fit as the others, and she was by nature a slower-moving person.

That was what she told herself. Several times.

I'm lumbering, she brooded. *I'm a lumbering double-wide hippo.*

Though as a rule Fiji did not call herself names, today she was out of sorts. Not only had she had to use magical means to get away from the persistent Shoshanna Whatever-her-name-was, but she'd figured out that something had happened over at Bobo's store, something other people knew . . . but not her.

Two evenings before, she'd gone over to take Bobo a letter that the mailman had left in her box instead of his. In truth, it had been a piece of unimportant mail that she'd hoarded for just such an occasion—an occasion when she just wanted to talk to Bobo. It had been a hard day, and she was feeling lonely.

He was due to be off work, and she figured he'd go straight up to his apartment. And maybe she'd hoped he'd ask her to walk over to Home Cookin with him, since he hadn't gone out to dinner yet. She'd been dusting the items on the shelf closest to the front door, and she'd glanced through the window from time to time.

So she'd seen the two strangers go in at dusk.

But almost immediately, the business landline had started ringing, and she'd turned away to answer it. The caller had been her sister, which meant a long conversation. Twenty minutes later, when Fiji had looked out the window again, the strangers' truck was gone, so their business at Midnight Pawn had been brief. She'd headed over.

She'd found Bobo sitting in the store alone, not having gone up to his apartment yet, though it was time for the store to be shut prior to Lemuel's shift. Bobo had not greeted her in his usual relaxed way. He'd glanced down at the floor a few times, as if he'd seen something there he needed to take care of. And he'd been upset. Though Bobo was seldom anything less than warm and charming to Fiji, that night he'd been brief to the point of rudeness.

He hadn't even invited her to sit down with him for a spell. She hadn't had the nerve to mention going out to dinner.

She'd felt so unsettled she hadn't been able to concentrate on her garden the next day. Instead, she went to Davy to get her car's oil changed, to shop at Kroger for a week's worth of groceries, and to take her laundry to the Suds O Matic on the Davy highway. (Fiji's favorite fantasy, besides the ones featuring Bobo, was that a sweet motherly woman would reopen the defunct washateria in Midnight. This sweet woman would not only put customers' clothes through the washer and dryer, she would iron them and fold them.)

Fiji hadn't returned from her errands refreshed, though she had felt a mildly pleasant sense of accomplishment. But then, on her return, Shoshanna Whatever had come by. As she trudged along by herself, Fiji's face flushed with mixed pride and embarrassment. She'd showed off in public, but apparently she hadn't been observed. She almost wished someone would tell her they'd seen the detective standing there, because Fiji was really curious about how long the spell had lasted.

She raised her eyes from her plodding feet to look ahead. There was Bobo, striding out, with the smaller form of Manfred right beside him. Maybe Manfred? He was almost directly across the road from her.

She decided Bobo seemed lighter of heart today, though she hadn't approached him for any private conversation.

Maybe she could find out from Olivia what had made Bobo so odd and downcast. Olivia must know what had happened.

Olivia always knew.

Despite all Fiji had to occupy her thoughts, soon the walking became more difficult as the ground began to rise. This land had never been settled or farmed, and it had only been grazed by extremely hearty goats. She stumbled more than once as she made her way across the rocky terrain that gradually rose to end abruptly on the cliff overlooking the riverbed. Keeping her eyes on her feet was a pain, but necessary. There were rocks; there were snakes. You had to be alert here.

Fiji saw something slithering off into the shelter of a rock just at that moment, and she snarled at it. She was not a happy camper. She was not any kind of camper at all.

"You okay?" said Bobo, and she looked up. He'd walked back to check on her. Goddess bless him, he was a kind man.

"I'm fine," she lied, feeling the blush on her cheeks. "I'm not a great hiker. I'm kinda slow. But steady!" she added brightly. Briefly, she considered apologizing for intruding on him the other night, but she concluded that she had nothing to apologize for.

"You don't have to be fast," he said, falling into step with her. "You got nothing to prove."

"No, I don't," she agreed, glad to look at it that way. "Not a damn thing."

"Where are you from, originally?" Bobo asked. "I can't believe we've never talked about it. Shared our origin story, as they say." Sharing personal data was not a casual thing in Midnight. As if he feared his question might be too intrusive, he volunteered, "I'm from Arkansas."

"I grew up outside Houston," Fiji said. "But my mom's folks were originally from this general area. West of Fort Worth. My great-aunt, who was way older than my grandmother, married Wesley Loeffler, who had settled here. They met at a dance, Aunt Mildred told me." She smiled. Quite a few people had thought Mildred Loeffler was cross and crotchety, and a few more had feared her. But Fiji had loved the old woman.

"And what did Wesley do?"

"He ran the five-and-dime, the one that's boarded up just north of the filling station. Back then, they all thought that Midnight would grow, that it would outshine Davy."

"What happened to Wesley?" Bobo asked.

"He died pretty young; at least, what we would think of as young. I believe he had complications from a ruptured appendix. He and Great-Aunt Mildred never had any kids, and she never married again."

"Tough," Bobo said. "How'd she make a living?"

"She ran the five-and-dime herself until it wasn't making any money, and then she sold the building and the business to a Mr. Wilcox. He went under in two years. So she had that money and what she made as a—well, as a wise woman, I guess you'd call it. She sold potions and herbs. And she could cook and was willing to cater a bit, so she was hired for weddings and so on. Aunt Mildred always took care to go to church every single Sunday, though." Fiji grinned. "When I was a kid, we'd come to visit her about every other year. She took a shine to me. Since I'm the youngest, my sister was pretty mad when Mildred left me the house. If she'd had an idea the house was worth anything, I think she might have contested Great-Aunt Mildred's will. But since I wanted to live in it, not sell it, she's left me in peace." Mostly.

"Your folks ever come to see you?" Bobo was frowning. "I don't remember meeting them."

"They haven't come yet," she said briefly. She'd been in Great-Aunt Mildred's house for over three years. "What about you?"

She realized they were covering ground literally, as well as figuratively. This walking business went so much better when she had someone to talk to, a point she made a note to remember.

"I'm the oldest of three. I have a brother and sister," he said.

From his unhappy expression, Fiji knew there was a story behind that.

"And now they're . . . ?" she prompted.

"Oh. Amber Jean graduated from the University of Arkansas in Fayetteville. She's a registered nurse, and she's married to a pharmaceutical supplier. Howell Three, my brother, he got out of college and got a job with Walmart."

"With Walmart?" She tried not to sound surprised. "Stocking shelves and so on?" She remembered meeting Howell Three briefly, and he hadn't seemed the manual labor kind of guy.

Bobo laughed. "No, he works at the headquarters. In Bentonville. He's engaged to another guy." His smile lingered, as if that had been a good joke on someone else. "Amber Jean has two kids, both girls."

"Has she come here?"

He laughed. "Touché. No, and I don't expect her to. And Howell Three only came the once, when you met him. Wasn't that about seven months ago? I wanted him to meet Aubrey. He thought I was living in the ass end of nowhere."

"What did you tell him?"

"That I liked it here. Which I do."

"What do you like about it?" She hadn't meant to sound coquettish, but she was afraid her words had come out that way. She risked a glance up. Bobo was looking ahead without a hint of self-consciousness, and she breathed a sigh of relief.

"I like being my own boss," he said. "I like the old building and all the pawned stuff that's been there forever. I like the random way people come in, bringing me strange things they're sure are worth big bucks."

"What do you do if you can't tell them one way or another?"

"Look the item up online. Call another dealer. Check some of my reference books." There was a laden shelf right by the cash register, and Fiji felt ashamed she'd never asked what the thick volumes were for.

"How about you?" he asked in return. "Do you like selling charms and candles to women? Though," he added hastily, "I know you make a lot of them happier."

Fiji smiled, though it made her face hurt a little. "Bobo, that sounds like you believe I'm all bells and chimes and New Age spirituality," she said.

Apparently that was exactly what Bobo believed. For a long moment, he didn't say a thing.

Taking pity on him, Fiji said, "I'm showing them that going to church and praying on your knees to a male deity isn't all there is.

There's another path, one that will put women in tune with their own spirit and truth."

"And I'm sure that helps a lot of the ladies," he said quickly. "Hey, look, we're almost there." He strode forward.

The edge of the cliff was thick with stubborn growth: yucca, small live oaks, firs, cactus, a huge variety of grasses . . . interspersed with rocks ranging in size from babies' fists to giants' feet. A haze of tiny yellow blooms lent the scene an almost fairy-tale effect, though the weed that bore them was about a foot tall. The wind tossed the blooms about cheerfully, and the leaves on the trees shivered, some of them loose enough to fly off and flutter through the air.

Fiji thought, *Coming here was a good idea. This is really pretty, and healing.* Then she went over to the truck to help Madonna, who'd arrived first and started unloading the truck in an area that wasn't too rocky. After getting the baby and his infant seat ensconced on the lowered tailgate, Madonna was pulling the coolers down to the ground. Teacher jumped up to push the coolers and the food forward, and Fiji began putting it on the white plastic folding table that Bobo and Manfred had already arranged. Joe set up the wildly assorted stadium chairs after handing Rasta over to Chuy, who took the little dog on a frantic exploration of the cliff's edge. Rasta found an exciting assortment of new smells, so much to sniff and pee on. After an exhausting five minutes, Rasta drank a bowl of water, ate three treats, and curled up for a nap on his special blanket, laid down under the tailgate so the Peke would be in the shade.

Fiji thought the curling-up-and-napping part looked like a good idea, but she hadn't brought a special blanket. With an inner sigh and an outward smile, she helped to unpack the food and set it out on the table. She weighted down the napkins and paper plates with rocks, because the wind was making everything dance.

They were perched above the section of the Río Roca Fría that ran east–west, more or less, before it turned north to Davy. Looking to her left, Fiji could see the lazy bend where it recovered its northern goal. Not even a hint of Davy was visible because of a slight rise and fall in the terrain.

In fact, the Midnighters had set up their picnic at the steepest point of the slope; twenty yards in either direction, the ground descended. Scrambling down to the water was much easier there, but the best view was up here, right by the Cold Rock itself. The Roca Fría was a huge white boulder, about the size of a La-Z-Boy recliner. Sadly, there were scrawled messages all over it, some dating from the nineteen sixties.

"I can see for miles," Olivia said to Fiji. "That is, if it weren't for my hair!" Olivia gathered up a smooth auburn handful with her right hand and pulled out an elastic band to secure it with her left. (Fiji hoped there was a similar band in the pocket of her jacket, but she hadn't even thought about it that morning.) Having slicked her hair back into a neat ponytail, Olivia said, "I can't believe I've never hiked out here before. Great idea!"

"Not mine," Bobo said. "Fiji's."

Fiji took a bow as a ragged round of applause went up.

"Who wants a beer?" Teacher called, and there was a general movement over to the ice chest. "We got cold water, too, for the wusses."

Fiji liked her wine, but she was not a beer drinker. "I'm a wuss," she said with a smile, pulling a bottle of water out of the chest. Suppressing her yearning to sink into her dark green stadium chair, she took a big swallow of water before she strolled eastward, away from the Roca Fría. Fiji picked up a stick as she went, and she began thwacking at weeds in an idle way. A large cricket leaped up, startling her.

Some adventurer I am. I might as well have stayed at home if I'm going to walk around sulking and hitting things with a stick, Fiji reflected, half smiling at her own foolishness. Fiji had looked forward to the picnic, but now she wasn't enjoying it as much as she'd hoped. She had the uneasy feeling that things were happening in Midnight that were outside her understanding: the abrupt desertion of Bobo by Aubrey, Bobo's out-of-character behavior two nights ago, Shoshanna Whitlock's questions. But those events should not bother her. They didn't have to be different facets of the same incident.

Trying to think positive thoughts, Fiji stopped at a large clump of yucca. She wondered if she could transplant some to her front yard. She crouched to figure out if the plant could be divided. Fiji never liked to leave a hole in a natural landscape. But now that the air currents were gusting down the riverbed and apparently floating up to hit her nose, she was aware, abruptly, that something had died. That something lay very close to where she knelt.

Fiji pushed awkwardly to her feet and stepped closer to the edge. At this point, the undergrowth was significantly thinner than at any other spot. She noted a broken bush, long dead. She looked down. There was only a slight impression of a tire in the dirt; some rain, some wind, had altered it but left its memory intact. So she was fairly sure the bush had been run over.

She held on to a stunted oak while she leaned out to look down the slope to the partially exposed round rocks of the riverbed. At the moment, the river was more of a small stream that burbled its way across the submerged stones, making them even smoother. After a heavy rain, the water speed would be almost frightening, but right now the sight and sound of the river was playful and delightful.

The thing lying close to the streambed was not. Though she was not a fan of CSI shows or detective novels, Fiji knew a decayed corpse when she saw one. And she knew the corpse was human.

Fiji didn't know whose name to call first. For a fraction of a second, she was tempted to say nothing at all to anyone, but her sizable conscience would not permit it. Though she'd never predicted the future and she'd never been interested in any of the methods used to do so, for this one moment Fiji could see the futures of all the people present changing at this moment, their lives altering as this body toppled all their pursuits in a domino effect, and she was profoundly sorry that hers was the finger pushing the first tile.

"Olivia!" she called. She could not have said why she'd chosen Olivia, but Fiji was confident she'd called the person most competent to deal with death. *Instinct at work,* she thought.

Olivia had a tortilla chip topped with guacamole in her hand, and she popped it into her mouth as she walked. She looked good-naturedly resigned, as if she were assuming that Fiji would not have anything very interesting to show her or tell her. She stopped by Fiji and looked down the slope at what Fiji had discovered.

There was a long moment of breathless silence. The wind wreaked havoc with Fiji's curls, while Olivia's ponytail danced around.

"Fucking hell," Olivia said. Then, after another moment's contemplation of the pathetic and grisly sight, she said, "*Very* fucking hell."

"Right."

"I better go down and look closer," Olivia said.

"Why?"

"Sheer curiosity." Olivia went effortlessly down the slope, then bent over the body for a few long moments. She straightened, shook her head in a dissatisfied way, and came back up to Fiji in a rush, as if she were getting her cardio in.

"There's a hole in her sternum," Olivia said. "I don't know if it's a bullet hole or not."

Fiji had fished her cell phone from her jacket pocket, and for the first time in her life she punched in 911.

"What's your emergency?" asked a brisk voice.

"I guess this isn't really an emergency, since it's clearly been dead quite a while, but we just found a body," Fiji said steadily.

"Where are you? Have you checked for signs of life?"

"Well, we're at the big boulder on the Río Roca Fría, having a picnic," Fiji said. "Though one of us did go down to check, this body has been here for a while. It's"—*a nightmare, a woman, a pile of bone and gristle*—"decomposed."

"You're sure it was a human being? Not a deer or horse?" The dispatcher sounded skeptical. It was like she didn't *want* there to be any problem.

"Not unless deer and horses have started wearing clothes," Fiji said. "We'll wait here until someone comes." She hung up.

"Something wrong, Feej?" Bobo was walking toward her.

That put some starch in her legs. She pulled away from Olivia and stood between Bobo and the cliff. "No," she said. "No, you don't come over here." She picked out the nearest person. "Joe, don't let anyone come over here," she called.

Simultaneously, Olivia said, "There's a body."

Joe, looking bewildered, nonetheless heaved himself out of his stadium chair and went over to Bobo. He said, "Hey, man, let's just stay here," as he took Bobo's arm. Bobo didn't struggle, and he didn't protest. His eyes met Fiji's, and she knew he was reading the pity in her face. Bobo yanked free of Joe's grip and inexplicably threw his beer bottle as hard as he could. Fiji watched the arc of white foam marking its trajectory. The bottle hit the ground and broke, and Bobo covered his face with his hands.

After all, there was only one person missing from the county: Aubrey Hamilton.

10

"You knew her, I guess," Manfred said. He'd come to stand by Fiji when Olivia had walked away to explain to everyone what they'd just discovered. "I've only heard her name mentioned."

Together, he and Fiji looked down the gentle slope at the wizened, almost skeletonized, body. It was not white and clean like a laboratory skeleton; far from it. There were disgusting wads of hair around the skull, and tendons stretched like dead vines around the bigger bones. The smaller ones were scattered, some right around the corpse. Flying, walking, all the little predators of the area had come to visit Aubrey Hamilton's remains. Her shoes were still there, which seemed pathetic. They were—had been—bright Zoot Sports running shoes. When Aubrey had told Fiji how much they cost, Fiji (who bought her shoes at Payless) had almost choked.

"I did know her." Fiji sighed heavily. "She started dating Bobo . . . maybe a little over a year ago, and she moved in about five months after that. More or less. Two months ago, she just vanished. Bobo came back from an overnight trip to Dallas, and she was gone." Fiji looked around for Bobo. He was sitting in the cab of Teacher's truck, leaning forward, his head resting on the dashboard. He was not crying. But what was he thinking? She could not guess.

"She just left?" Manfred said. "Clothes and all?"

"No 'and all,'" Fiji said. "She'd left some stuff in the washing machine. She only took the clothes on her back . . ." She looked down the slope and she shuddered. "And the shoes on her feet."

"Did Bobo report it?"

"Report what? That his girlfriend had left him? They would have laughed. But he did call after a week, because it was just weird that her stuff was there. She didn't have a car, as far as we knew, but all her clothes and her hair straightener and her razor and even her toothbrush . . . who leaves stuff like that behind? The sheriff sent a deputy over to ask a few questions. He got her phone number and her parents' information. But with no signs of a struggle and no phone calls or any communication, I guess there really wasn't anything to go on."

"I see what you mean. Did Bobo *ever* hear from her?"

Fiji said, "I have to sit down," and they dragged a couple of the chairs to a spot in the shade. When she was slumped back into the chair, grateful to be off her feet, Fiji said, "To answer your question, no. Bobo never heard from her. At the time, I assumed she was being a bitch, putting Bobo through the most hell she could. But I see now how weird that was. You'd think she'd call to say, 'Box up my stuff, send it to wherever. I just couldn't stand the way you snore or grind your teeth or whatever.' But she didn't. She didn't call any of us. Or send a letter. Or a text. At least, not that I've heard."

"Did she have any friends here? Or friends from before she moved in with Bobo?"

Fiji looked at Manfred, a bit startled. "Now that you mention it, no. Isn't that something? None of us liked her much. Even the Rev." They both glanced over to the older man, who was hunkered down in the scant shade of a small oak. Fiji was sure he was praying. She nodded approvingly. That was just what a minister should be doing under these circumstances.

"How did you figure out the Rev didn't like Aubrey? I can't believe he'd talk about it. It doesn't seem to me that he talks about anything."

"I deduced it," Fiji said, with dignity. "When the Rev would talk to her, his face would get all tight. Like he was suppressing something." Fiji tried hard to imitate the expression. She saw that Manfred was trying to suppress a smile.

"I saw you freeze that woman," he said. "I take you seriously."

"That's good," she said. "I like to be taken seriously. I know I look . . . silly. I know everyone thinks I'm either a fraud or deluded. So be it."

"I don't think you are," said a voice behind them, and Chuy sank down on his heels. "I have faith in you." He looked at Fiji. "Course, that's probably my gullible Mexican background."

"Right," Fiji said. "'Cause you're so superstitious."

She and Chuy smiled at each other.

"I wish the police would come." Manfred said. He smiled, too, but not happily. "I never thought I'd hear myself saying that."

The Midnighters set themselves to wait. Grady began to cry, and Madonna gave him the only bottle she'd brought with her. Teacher burped and changed him, and Grady fell asleep, to everyone's relief.

Creek and Connor sat together, hunched in the shade of the truck with Rasta panting beside them. Connor looked excited and frightened, all at the same time. Creek, who had a talent for looking inscrutable, was doing an especially fine job. Chuy took Joe a beer, which he drank in four gulps. While the Rev continued his solitary prayer, Olivia crouched by Bobo, who had gotten out of the truck to squat out in the open, staring into the distance. Every now and then a tear would roll down his cheek.

Each tear made Fiji more miserable. She fell into silence. Manfred got up to roam around. He went over to the big white boulder to read all the graffiti; he climbed down the steep slope upstream to look at the dinosaur footprints clearly visible below the running water. Since he'd never known Aubrey, he had the right to fidget.

After a few minutes, Olivia seemed to tire of the role of grief counselor. She gave Bobo a small package of tissues from her backpack, and she stood effortlessly to walk over to Fiji.

"I don't know what cracked her chest bone, but she didn't just have a heart attack."

"I don't think so, either," Fiji replied. "But she did walk and run. She did like to exercise. Maybe she came out here and fell? Broke her ankle?"

"Then what was to stop her crawling up the slope? It's not that steep. And why didn't she use her cell phone? You can't tell me she took a step without that phone in her pocket."

"That's true." Fiji pressed her lips together. "Well, maybe she got snakebit."

"And crawled down the slope, rather than back toward Midnight?" Olivia said. She didn't pooh-pooh the idea that Aubrey had been bitten; this was a place where you had to be aware or take the consequences.

"That is weird," Fiji conceded. "But I hope they can find some clear reason." There was a lot unspoken in that hope.

"You saw her after Bobo left, right? Didn't you tell the sheriff's deputy that?"

Fiji turned her head so that her eyes met Olivia's. "Of course I saw her after Bobo left," she said. "Didn't you?"

"Sure," Olivia said, after a moment. "Sure, I saw her."

Fiji nodded. "Well, then."

"The law's here."

From the west came two white cars, driving carefully. They both had lightbars on the top.

Fiji had not met the sheriff, but she recognized him from his campaign posters. Arthur Smith, with his thick chest and shoulders and large eyes, reminded Fiji of a bull. His short curly hair, though mostly still a pale blond, had a heavy sprinkling of silver. She'd voted for him, last election; more accurately, she'd voted against his opponent, a known bully. It was a measure of the previous sheriff's unpopularity that Smith, not a native Texan, had won the contest.

Sheriff Smith was calm, businesslike, and in charge; there were no two ways about that.

"Fiji Cavanaugh?" he asked, when he emerged from his car. Fiji raised her hand like a schoolgirl.

"Where's the body?" When Fiji pointed down from the right point at the cliff edge, he sent two deputies scrambling down, laden with cameras and other paraphernalia.

After that, having looked over the people at the site, one by one, he began by talking to Fiji. She pegged him for about forty-five and automatically noted that his wedding ring finger was bare. He didn't have any obvious signs that screamed "bachelor," though; he was absolutely trimmed, pressed, shaven, and starched.

"I remember reading your name in the report when Mr. Winthrop first said his girlfriend was missing. You found the body, Ms. Cavanaugh?" he said. His accent was softer than the local one, from much farther east, though still south of the Mason-Dixon.

"Yes, we all came out here for a picnic, and I was just walking along the cliff."

"And what drew it to your attention?"

"The smell," she said bluntly.

"And who do you think this is, here on the slope?"

Fiji stared at him. "The shoes are Aubrey Hamilton's," she said finally. "And what's left of the hair is the right color to be Aubrey's."

"So," he said, "Ms. Hamilton vanished after Mr. Winthrop spent the night in Dallas?"

"During the time he spent in Dallas," she corrected him.

"And did you see Ms. Hamilton after he left? For this business trip?"

"He'd gone to meet with some friends of his in the pawn business. They'd talked online and they wanted to meet face to face. So he drove over to Dallas."

"Did you see her after the time he'd left?"

"Yes. Yes, I did."

"Did you see her in the pawnshop?"

"No," she said, without even thinking about it. She'd never dropped into Midnight Pawn after Aubrey was in residence. Never. She could feel her face become tighter, as all her muscles hummed with tension.

"Then where?"

"I saw her come out of the door," she said. "She came out of the side door—not the pawnshop door, the door to the landing, where the stairs lead up to Bobo's apartment and down to Olivia's." She did not mention Lemuel.

"To get to the apartments, you don't have to go through the store."

"There's a door into the store from that landing, too. But it's usually locked."

Arthur Smith was trying very hard not to look impatient. "Okay. She came out of the side door."

"I saw her come out that door and turn—well, it would have been her left. To walk between the pawnshop and the rental house. On her way back to the parking area. I just thought she was going to run an errand . . . but that can't be right, because Bobo had the truck." Would Olivia have lent Aubrey her car? Without thinking, Fiji turned to look at Olivia, who was in conference with Chuy and Joe.

"Did you talk to her, or do you know what she planned to do while Mr. Winthrop was out of town?"

"No." She shrugged. "We weren't close friends." *We weren't friends at all.*

"And who has Mr. Winthrop been seeing since Miss Hamilton vanished?"

"You mean . . . like dating? No one," she said. "He's been really depressed."

For once, she'd surprised the lawman. They both looked over at Bobo Winthrop. He had scrambled to his feet with the arrival of the police cars. The wind was blowing his golden hair. He looked like a slightly aged catalog model—maybe for casual clothing or for a rugged lifestyle involving trucks and mountain climbing.

"*He* was depressed?" Sheriff Smith asked, clearly having a hard time imagining that. Then his cell phone rang, and he got it out of his pocket.

"Yes?" he said impatiently. He listened to whatever the caller was saying. Then Smith said, "That's really interesting. Thanks." He hung up.

"Bobo was depressed," Fiji told him again, determined to make her point. "He was really devoted to Aubrey."

"That's interesting," Smith said. "Since she didn't exist."

11

B obo looked over to see that Fiji was staring at Sheriff Smith as though he'd informed her the earth was made of pie crust. He could just hear her speak. "How can you say that?" she asked, and Olivia joined her. The sheriff looked at Olivia, like every man did, but Olivia stood in front of him with her arms crossed over her middle, her face intent. "Let's hear about this," Olivia said.

"Mr. Winthrop," the sheriff called, and Bobo walked over, his feet reluctant to go in the direction he had to. He could tell this was going to be a bad conversation, as if anything could make this day worse.

"Fiji?" he said, when he'd gotten to her. "What's the matter?" Fiji didn't speak, but she didn't leave, and neither did Olivia. Bobo thought the sheriff looked as though he'd like to ask them to.

"I just heard from one of my deputies," Smith said, looking directly at Bobo. "What did Aubrey Hamilton tell you about her background?"

Whatever Bobo had expected, it wasn't this. "What do you mean?" he said, floundering around in his thoughts to make sense of Smith's question. His head felt thick as cotton wool, his grief making him slow and stupid. "She was working in Davy when I met her. She was a waitress at the Lone Star Steakhouse."

"What did she tell you about her background?"

That was definitely an ominous turn of phrase, but Bobo said, "She told me her parents were dead and that her sister had thrown Aubrey out of the house when she'd turned eighteen . . . and she'd been fending for herself since then."

"That's what she had told her coworkers at the steakhouse, too. We talked to them briefly when you reported her missing. However, one of my deputies looked a little deeper after we got the call to come out here, since she's the only missing person on our books. None of that is true."

Bobo felt the shock clear down to his bones. "What are you saying?" Bobo asked. He looked at Fiji, whose face was locked down tight, for some enlightenment.

Fiji said, "Sheriff, are you saying that Aubrey kind of made herself up?"

"That's right. Her name was Aubrey Hamilton, right enough," Arthur Smith said. "But she's got living parents. She's got no sister. She does have a brother. And she's been married before."

"But I *knew* her," Bobo said, feeling that if he said it often enough, it would erase what the sheriff was saying. "I saw her driver's license. I met her by chance . . ." And then he remembered the two men who'd come into the pawnshop. He began to let a new idea sink into his brain. "I thought I knew her."

"How did you make her acquaintance?" the sheriff asked.

"I love the Lone Star Steakhouse," Bobo said. "I go there at least once every two, three weeks to have steak. I met her there."

Olivia's face flushed red with anger. "Son of a *fucking* bitch," she snarled, and stomped away.

Bobo watched as the other townspeople gathered around her, and Olivia began to talk, her hands flying upward from time to time in outrage.

"Olivia has no problem at all believing that Aubrey was a liar," Bobo murmured, the enormity of this revelation about the woman he'd loved beginning to sink in.

"I don't, either," said Fiji, almost in a whisper. She put her arm around him, awkwardly, and he could see the unhappiness in her, the unhappiness she felt on his behalf.

The rest of the Midnighters had clustered around Olivia. Even Madonna, who'd been glowering at the crowd while she sat in the pickup with the door open, came closer with Grady in her arms.

Smith gave a loud, exasperated sigh. Bobo figured he hadn't planned on telling the whole community at once, or this early. But the sheriff must have decided to make the best of the situation, since he raised his voice to a public announcement level. "I might as well tell all of you at the same time. Aubrey Hamilton was not the woman she said she was. More accurately, she was Aubrey Hamilton Lowry."

The people of Midnight moved closer to Smith, Bobo, and Fiji. Bobo saw that they were all tense and angry, and if he'd had room for any other emotion, he would have felt touched.

"Married?" The Rev looked as though the word had been torn from his throat. He looked even sterner than usual.

"Formerly married," the sheriff said. "Though she told them at the steakhouse that she'd gotten divorced and was in the process of changing all her legal papers back over to her maiden name. In fact, her husband, Chad Lowry, was shot and killed by police officers in Phoenix, Arizona."

"Shot? Doing what?" Teacher asked.

"Robbing a bank."

"He was a career criminal?" Bobo said. He almost hoped that would be the case.

"Not exactly," the sheriff said. "He was a member of a white supremacist group, Men of Liberty. MOL is based in Arizona, but it has branches in all the southwestern states, including Texas."

"No," said Bobo. He turned to face Olivia Charity. "It's all part of the same thing," he said.

"What is?" Olivia said. But she narrowed her eyes at Bobo, who caught that warning a second later.

"It's all part of her pattern of deceiving me," Bobo said, making a good recovery. "I was a fool to think she loved me."

That made everyone acutely uncomfortable, and they all looked away. All but Fiji. He looked down into her eyes and saw nothing but steadfastness. "I was a fool," he repeated softly.

"Never," Fiji replied. "She was the fool."

There was a shout from down the slope, and they all turned to look in that direction. A deputy came up, a woman, her black hair pulled back into a tight bun. She was carrying a plastic bag. In it was an old gun. Smith went over to her and held it up to have a good look.

They all stood silent. Bobo didn't know what anyone else was thinking, but he was back in that land where unpleasant revelations were the norm. He hadn't lived there in a while, and he hadn't wanted to return, ever.

Olivia was standing right behind him, he could see from the corner of his eye. She was looking at the gun. "I know that piece," she said, making sure her voice was low, but of course, Fiji heard her.

"From where?" she asked, equally quietly.

Bobo wanted to tell the truth, if only to Fiji. "It was in the shop," he said. "It's been there for years."

The sheriff told them they could go home. "We'll come to talk to you individually later," he said. "Don't leave town until one of us has interviewed you."

The trek back to Midnight seemed twice as long as the hike to the river. In silence, they straggled back to town, not talking, lost in their own thoughts. Bobo walked alone, not able to bear the company of anyone else, not even his closest friend, Fiji. When they got to the pawnshop, Bobo had already gotten the keys from his pocket, and he went in the side door and up to his apartment without a word.

12

Creek and Connor went directly to Gas N Go. Creek had begun crying on the way back to Midnight, and her brother had put his arm around her. He had looked almost proud, Fiji thought, at being the one who was standing up to adversity. She hadn't known Creek had ever talked to Aubrey, but maybe it was the sudden face-to-face encounter with death that had shaken the normally serene Creek.

"The rest of you, come to the diner," Madonna said from the window of her truck. "We got to eat this food, might as well do it there." Fiji went over to Home Cookin with the rest of them, since she couldn't think of anything better to do. She wasn't ready to be alone yet. The sight of the horrible remains of Aubrey Hamilton—Aubrey Lowry—were still too much in the forefront of her mind.

Functioning on autopilot, Fiji helped unload the truck and spread out the food on the diner counter as it had been on the table at the riverside. Everyone filled a plate and found a place at the round table, including the Rev. The need to huddle together for comfort affected even the minister. He hadn't spoken since Fiji had made her discovery, but now, as the last person sat down, he raised his right hand. They all fell silent.

"In the name of the God who made all of us, man and beast, bless this food and those who prepared it. Bless the soul of our departed sister, Aubrey. Despite her shortcomings, may she rest in peace. May we see her at the last rising and greet her with joy. Amen."

"Amen." The response was ragged, but it seemed to satisfy the Rev.

For all of half a minute, Fiji felt ashamed of her earlier rage against the dead woman. But when she recalled the look on Bobo's face as he'd discovered Aubrey's true identity, the rage surged back. She looked down at her plate, suddenly realizing she was hungry. Everyone at the table seemed to experience the same appetite. There wasn't much conversation, but there was some serious food consumption.

After all of them had finished, they divided the remaining food. Fiji, walking home with a take-out container, found her thoughts scurrying around in her head like hamsters in a cage. She wondered if she could use witchcraft to help Bobo. She wondered how long Aubrey's body had lain down by the river. She wondered who had killed her and how it had been done. She imagined, somewhat vaguely, a séance conducted by Manfred, the ghost of Aubrey appearing in the darkened room. What would Aubrey say from beyond the grave? Fiji tried to remember a single memorable thing Aubrey had said when she was alive . . . and couldn't come up with an instance. And the gun . . . how had it found its way to the river from Midnight Pawn? Fiji knew that if Bobo had used it to kill Aubrey, he would not have left it for anyone to find. Bobo was dumb about people, but he was smart about things.

Mr. Snuggly was waiting for her, curled up picturesquely at the foot of the birdbath. He rose and stretched in the sunlight as she approached.

"Oh, for goodness' sake," she snapped. "Stop being so damn cute."

The cat looked up at her with golden eyes, his brushy tail adorably wrapped around his pristine paws.

"Yeah, right, it's your second nature," she said, and the cat walked beside her to the front door. As she unlocked it, she said, "Wait till you find out what you missed today, Mr. Snuggly. And Rasta was there for it." Mr. Snuggly gave her a contemptuous cat look and went to sit in front of his food bowl.

Fiji got some kibble and dumped it in.

13

M ost of the Midnighters were wakeful during the dark hours that night.

Bobo sat in his apartment over the pawnshop, all the lights off, looking north out the rear windows at the moon glowing over the land leading to the Río Roca Fría, where Aubrey had lain decomposing for two months. He hadn't eaten anything, though Manfred had dropped off some food. He hadn't had anything to drink, either, though he'd thought about having a traditional drinking bout.

Bobo was alternating between feeling some kind of comfort and a lot of grief. At least Aubrey hadn't left him voluntarily. That knowledge relieved some ache deep inside him. However, he was sure that Aubrey had met with a fate more lurid than a snakebite or an accidental fall, especially since he'd seen the gun. Whether or not she'd been shot, something terrible had happened to Aubrey, and someone else had had a hand in that terrible something.

When Bobo could think of anything besides his horror that a

woman he'd loved had died by violence and lain in the open for weeks, and his grief over her permanent loss, he brooded over the revelation that Aubrey had ties to Men of Liberty. He wondered if Aubrey had truly cared for him. Ever.

After a while, he moved to look out the front window, looking over the crossroads that had established Midnight. He saw lights come off and on all night as the residents of the town got up, sat for a while, returned to their beds.

Bobo felt lonelier than he'd ever been in his life. He hadn't talked to his parents in a year, maybe longer, but he thought of calling his sister or his brother. In the end, he didn't pick up his phone.

14

The next day everything in Midnight should have resumed its pace.

Granted, that wasn't a very brisk pace, but everyone's business should have been open. Fiji opened the Inquiring Mind right on time, but she watched out her front window anxiously to see if the Midnight Pawn CLOSED sign would flip over to OPEN.

The pawnshop never opened that Tuesday, though. The CLOSED sign stayed up all day.

When she walked down to Gas N Go to get some milk, Fiji discovered Shawn Lovell was having a banner day. Some of the law enforcement officers were stopping in to top up their vehicles with gas and to get cold water and snacks. When Fiji went to the counter with her purchase, Creek was working the cash register while Shawn ran the credit cards and stocked the shelves.

"Connor at school?" Fiji asked Creek.

"Yeah, he needs to be busy, and he doesn't need to miss any classes," the girl said. "For once, we could use him here."

"Hey, Fiji," called Shawn. "You doing okay after yesterday?"

"Yeah. At least you're doing good, huh?"

Shawn shrugged as he tucked some more bags of peanuts into a clip-type dispenser. "I guess so." He didn't seem happy about this rush of business. He seemed exhausted and worried. "Be better when Connor gets here. It's almost time for the bus."

Fiji glanced over at the desk in the corner that Shawn had put there. It was a place for Connor to do his homework. Shawn didn't even trust the fourteen-year-old to do his homework in his own home, a small house to the north of the gas station, on the Davy highway. Shawn Lovell was not a man long on trust, Fiji thought, not for the first time. The Lovells kept their history to themselves, and everyone in Midnight respected that.

Carrying her bag of milk, Fiji decided to walk a little farther, down to the Antique Gallery and Nail Salon. It was open. To her surprise, there was a woman she didn't know sitting in Chuy's special chair getting a mani-pedi.

Fiji had planned to have an idle conversation with Joe, whom she knew a little better than Chuy, who was more reserved. But just as she came in and Chuy told her where Joe was, another customer came in, a rancher's wife from Marthasville way, and she was there to buy a picture frame she'd admired the previous week.

Next, Fiji crossed the road to Home Cookin. Madonna was sitting at the counter working a crossword puzzle while Grady napped.

"Hey," said Madonna, without much enthusiasm. "Too late for lunch, but I got some leftovers I can sell you."

"I just wanted to see how you all were doing," Fiji said, knowing as she said it that she sounded weak. She had never dropped into Home Cookin between mealtimes before, and she'd never set foot in the double-wide trailer set up behind the restaurant. "Teacher working today?"

"Yeah, he's working about six miles east. Helping a retired postal worker rebuild his front steps. That means Teacher's doing it while the old man sits watching and talking." Madonna looked longingly at her crossword, and Fiji took the hint and left.

The Rev was not in the chapel. Fiji found him behind the fence in the pet cemetery. It was a place that fascinated her, partly because it was one of the few concealed places in Midnight. The wooden fence, the planks pointed at the top, was at least six and a half feet tall and painted an immaculate white.

The Rev had left the trees in place, so it was peaceful inside. Fiji didn't know how long it had been since the Rev had established the cemetery, but she estimated it was about half full of graves.

Some were marked with crosses, some with Stars of David, others with pentagrams. There was a cat statue on one little rectangle, a dog's leash mounted on a forked stick on another, and an actual small headstone carved with "Tonks." There were pictures on frames sticking up out of the dirt marking some graves. Some were marked only by mounds.

"What are you doing today?" she asked. The old man was standing at an especially large monument in the middle of the "occupied" area.

"It's bless the graves day," he said.

"Oh . . . appropriate," she said. "I'll leave you to it."

But she watched for a few minutes, the plastic bag with the milk hanging from her hand, while the Rev moved slowly from grave to grave, praying for each departed soul. This ritual, which he performed monthly, often took him two days. Seeing he was absorbed in his task, she eased out of the gate without further comment.

She looked across the street at Midnight Pawn. She glimpsed

Bobo's face at the window of his apartment. But he did not raise his hand or acknowledge her in any way, so she trudged back to her house, the milk banging against her leg.

After dark that night, Fiji saw that the pawnshop lights were on, and she walked over to the store. She needed some company. She was too wired up to read or to watch television.

Lemuel was at his post. Fiji was not at all surprised to find that Olivia had come up from her apartment to keep him company. There was a customer, too. Lemuel appeared to be striking a bargain with a strange, hunched man.

The most interesting people come in at night, Fiji thought. She stepped past the men to sit by Olivia in the two chairs that matched a breakfast table.

"I could kick myself now that I know about Aubrey," Olivia muttered to Fiji, as Lemuel and the hunched man agreed on terms. "I should have investigated her, when it became obvious that she didn't fit in."

Fiji didn't ask any questions about what qualified Olivia to investigate or how she would have gone about such a thing. If you were going to live in Midnight, there were some subjects you didn't delve into. "When were you sure you didn't like her?" she asked, trying not to sound too eager to know the answer.

"After she'd been here a couple of weeks," Olivia replied without hesitation.

Fiji suppressed a triumphant smile. Her spell had been effective, maybe! Though if it had *really* worked, if Olivia had understood Aubrey's true nature as Fiji had hoped everyone would do, Aubrey's true nature hadn't seemed quite as repulsive to Olivia (or anyone else) as Fiji had hoped. For a moment, Fiji didn't think well of herself. If it required a spell for Aubrey's true nature to become apparent . . . didn't that mean her false one was pretty damn good? In fact, close to being true? Was Fiji's spell-casting only an exhibition of sour grapes? What if her *own* true character was open to everyone's interpretation? Thinking of her many failings and weaknesses, Fiji shrank from the idea.

"What can we do to help Bobo?" she said.

"Aside from saying we saw her after he left? I didn't know you could lie so convincingly," Olivia said. "I think that's a pretty damn good thing, that we did that."

"If he did it, I don't care," Fiji said. "Especially in view of what we've learned about Aubrey."

"I wouldn't have cared even if she'd been a saint," Olivia said calmly. "I'm sure our focus should be on who *else* could have killed Aubrey, and if we find another viable suspect . . ."

The hunched man had left, and now Lemuel spun around on the stool behind the counter. "Yes," he said. "That's what we must do. The gun is worrying me. From Olivia's description, I remember it. It was here in the shop for years." Lemuel's icy eyes glinted with excitement.

Fiji wasn't surprised at Lemuel's being on topic. He'd always had amazing hearing and the equally interesting ability to listen to two conversations at one time. She respected Lemuel, and she wasn't afraid of him . . . much. Once, when Olivia's return from one of her mysterious trips had been delayed, Fiji had offered Lemuel some blood. She'd been glad when he'd taken some energy instead, standing silently in her kitchen holding her hand for five minutes that felt like an eternity. Afterward, he'd thanked her briskly and then left with as much haste as if they'd done something much more intimate and embarrassing.

Olivia had come over to thank her, perhaps a bit cautiously, a bit warily, when she'd returned. But after a sharp look at Fiji's face, she'd given her a hug, and they'd been almost-friends ever since.

Now Olivia said, "Not only was the gun from here, Bobo took it out to shoot targets a couple of times."

Fiji's heart sank at this piece of information. Surely the sheriff would consider that damning evidence. "I can think of twenty explanations for the gun being out there," she said, though that wasn't literally true. Two or three, maybe, and none of those particularly convincing.

"Sure, so can I. I'm leaving on a short trip tomorrow, but I'll be back soon, and we'll talk about how to get this done." Olivia nodded to them both. "I'll be thinking on the plane."

"Where you going this time?" Fiji asked. She didn't know if she'd like to travel as much as Olivia did, but it would be nice to find out someday.

"San Francisco," Olivia said, and from the corner of her eye, Fiji saw Lemuel's head jerk. Obviously, this was new information to him. He began to speak but snapped his pale lips shut on his comment.

Olivia looked at him directly. "I'll be fine," she said. "Don't worry. Quick in and out."

What the hell is this about? Fiji asked herself.

"All right." There was no expression on Lemuel's face whatsoever. "I'll be fine," Olivia repeated.

Lemuel nodded reluctantly, and silence fell. The three sat in an uneasy companionship (Fiji trying to think of a graceful way to leave without being obvious) until a ragged woman came in to pawn a very old gold wedding ring.

The ragged woman reeked. There was no other word for it. Fiji had never smelled anything like the odor that surrounded the woman like a cloud. She held her breath as long as she could, which wasn't long enough.

Quickly and wordlessly, Lemuel gave the woman forty dollars and took the ring. The ragged woman, whose sticklike figure and huge dark eyes made her look like something out of a cartoon, hurried out into the night, her movements both furtive and jerky.

Lemuel turned the ring in his fingers, holding it close to the desk lamp. "N.E.S. to his Leticia," he read. "It's engraved on the inside of the ring."

"Where'd she get that, I wonder?" Fiji asked.

"I suspect she dug up a grave and stole it off a corpse's finger," Lemuel said.

"Oh, my God," Olivia said, her nose puckering with disgust.

"That's just rank," Fiji agreed.

"Has the sheriff come by to talk to you?" Lemuel said suddenly.

"No. He spent this morning with Bobo, though," Fiji said. "I saw his car." She didn't try to sound disinterested. They'd know it was a lie.

"He didn't talk to me," Olivia volunteered. "But I did notice he drove over to the Reeds' place."

"From the most involved to the least involved," Lemuel said thoughtfully. "I must think on that some."

And maybe there's something about the Reeds we don't know, Fiji thought.

15

On Wednesday morning, Manfred woke up thinking about the people of Midnight, starting with the mysterious Olivia. When Manfred imagined her with Lemuel, it gave him a frisson of something he didn't care to examine. (He called it distaste.) Based on Manfred's own experience, he couldn't deny that Lemuel had a powerful presence—though if Lemuel had been human, he'd hardly have been an attention-grabber by virtue of his looks alone.

As Manfred ate whole-wheat toast at the little Formica table his grandmother had had in her own kitchen, his mind next wandered to his happiest thought target, Creek Lovell. He wondered how she'd feel today. He'd noticed the discovery of Bobo's girlfriend's body had been both shocking for Creek and exciting for Connor. Manfred figured neither of the kids had encountered as much death as the older Midnighters. Creek had locked down emotionally after a few tears, while Connor had looked from one person to another, soaking it all in.

Manfred had worked the day before, as usual, but he'd paused often to think over the disastrous picnic. And the lack of grief over the death of a young woman they'd all known. None of them had looked shattered besides Bobo and the flash of sadness from Creek.

And that brought Manfred full circle back to the girl at Gas N Go. Reaching a sudden decision, he downed the last of his Coca-Cola (his morning beverage of choice) and left the house to saunter past Midnight Pawn, navigate the Davy highway (three cars!) before crossing the apron to the belled front door of the convenience store. Inside, everything was bright and shiny and fluorescent. All the walls were freshly painted and the linoleum was clean.

A dark-haired man in his early forties was behind the high counter. He was loading cigarette packs into the display, and as Manfred entered he locked the clear plastic door and turned to face him. "Hi!" he said, leaning over the counter to extend his hand. "You're the new guy, right? Manfred? I'm Shawn Lovell."

"Nice to meet you, Shawn. Yeah, I'm the newbie. I came in to pick up some stuff."

"Sure. What you see is what we got." Shawn swept his hand through the air to indicate the shelves of junk food and small necessities, like batteries and tissue and cooking oil. Shawn Lovell looked like Everyman. About five foot ten, short dark hair with a little gray, not thin or fat, clean-shaven, no scars or birthmarks or moles. If a movie role had called for a generic guy, Shawn Lovell would have been up for the part. But while he was smiling, he was wary; that was the interesting thing. Shawn was an easy read.

Manfred bought a Coca-Cola, a box of graham crackers, and some Slim Jims. He placed them on the counter and hauled out his wallet. He could hardly ask exactly where Creek was. He'd been sure he'd see her. "How are Connor and Creek? I mean, after what happened?" he asked, hoping to come at his goal sideways.

Shawn said, "They were pretty shaken up." Though he almost sounded neutral, Manfred could feel the tension and anxiety in the man. He supposed that was natural in a father with teenagers who'd been exposed to the nastier side of life.

"I'm glad they didn't see the body," Manfred said.

"Me, too—especially Connor." Immediately, Shawn looked as if he wished he hadn't spoken.

Manfred was so tempted to say, "Why not Creek?" But he knew that any singular mention of Creek would be a mistake. "Glad they're okay," he said, his voice as neutral as Shawn's had been. He took his bag of unnecessary purchases and turned to leave. "Good to meet you," he added over his shoulder. "I think now I know everyone in town."

"See you, man," Shawn said. But he looked as if he hoped he wouldn't see Manfred any time soon. The bell over the door rang as a patrol officer came in, and this time Shawn turned away as if he were glad this conversation was over.

Manfred nodded and left. As he walked back to his house, he thought, *Shawn Lovell is one tense guy. I guess like everyone else here, he's got a secret.* Manfred was almost tempted to try to forget about Creek Lovell and her smooth skin and her intelligent eyes. Getting past her dad was going to be a piece of work. *I should locate the nearest honky-tonk and meet a woman my own age,* he thought, but the idea was kind of ridiculous. He was not much of a bar person. He liked parties well enough, but he didn't know anyone in this area who'd invite him. He was not a churchgoer, he was not political, and he knew all too well the perils of meeting someone online.

Especially since Creek was so wonderful.

He shook himself. This was a circular train of thought and he had work to do. Manfred put the Coca-Cola in the refrigerator, the graham crackers on the shelf that served as his pantry, and the Slim Jims he slid into the drawer of his desk as emergency rations.

His phone rang, and he picked it up. "Bernardo the psychic," he said. "Yes, Anita Lynn, tell me what's troubling you today." He settled in to listen. He noticed absently that the tree outside his east window was moving in the wind.

Across the street, that brisk wind was causing Fiji trouble. Her curly hair blew around her head like a light brown nimbus, and she couldn't see a thing. She was kneeling next to the rose bed that ran around the low back porch, snipping the deadheads off the bushes. This was the last time she'd have to perform the task this year. Before long, the first frost would fall, and she'd prune the roses down for the winter and cover the soil with pine straw or hay.

Soon, very soon, she had to start putting out her elaborate Halloween decorations. What costume should she wear this year?

She was trying to think about anything besides Aubrey Hamilton Lowry.

"Fiji," called a voice, and she was surprised, when she swiveled around and looked up, to see Bobo standing to her left. He'd come around the side of the house. His blond hair was blowing in the wind like hers, but his eyes were surrounded by dark circles and his clothes hung as though he'd lost ten pounds in the past two days. He looked like hell warmed over.

"Come have a seat on the back porch," she said, trying to sound easy and natural. "I just got a little more to go." Self-consciously, she bent again to finish her task, all too aware she was presenting her posterior to his view.

"Go get a Coke out of the refrigerator if you want one," she called. "Or put on some coffee, if you'd rather." He was out of his apartment. He'd come to her house. She tried not to feel an ignoble blast of jubilation.

Bobo went inside and returned with a cold drink. He didn't speak, so neither did Fiji, and it seemed oddly companionable, her working while he watched. The sun on her back made her feel relaxed and a little drowsy. The pile of deadheads in the bucket mounded up in a satisfying way. She kept at her task until she could not find another single one to lop off.

"I'm scared to ask how you're doing," she said, heaving herself to her feet and stripping off the thick gloves. It was time for her to open her shop, but this was more important.

"I loved her, so I miss her. She died, and I'm sad. She lied to me, so I'm hurt. I have enemies, so I'm worried."

Fiji couldn't think of anything to say in the face of such honesty. She dusted off her hands before placing her clippers in the bucket along with her gloves. Setting the bucket aside to deal with later, she went in to pour some iced tea and came out to sit beside Bobo. She felt ridiculous, suddenly, that when she'd seen the gun, she'd had a split second where she'd believed it was possible Bobo had killed Aubrey.

But he had not told her everything. She wasn't in doubt about that.

"You better tell me about the enemies part," she said. She'd brought some Keebler chocolate chip cookies, and she put them on the little table between their chairs. She didn't care if it was nine in the morning, they were Bobo's favorites. Absently, Bobo took one and ate it in two bites. Then another. She wondered how long it had been since he had something to eat.

"My grandfather owned a lot of businesses," he said. He stared across Fiji's well-planted backyard. Mr. Snuggly stared back, but Bobo's gaze didn't see anything closer than a thousand yards away. "Best of all, when I was a kid, was the sporting goods store. Before the big box stores opened in Little Rock, people would drive for miles to see it. It was really big." A ghost of a smile passed across Bobo's face. "He also had a lumberyard and a construction company. He was silent partner in some other stuff. I was in and out of his and Gram's house my whole life. My dad worked for him. This was in Shakespeare, Arkansas." He smiled at her. "Big fish, small pond."

Fiji's family had never been big in any size pond.

"So I thought I was hot stuff, all the way through high school and into college. But I also came to realize—it took me long enough, I was so *dumb*—that my grandfather's political and social views were right up there with Hitler's."

Whatever she'd expected, that hadn't been it. "Really that extreme?"

He nodded. "Really. He would have joined something like Men of Liberty if none of his old golf buddies would have found out. I loved the old guy; since I was the oldest grandchild, oldest grandson, he made a lot of me. When he was still physically able, he took me out shooting and hunting, introduced me to lots of his cronies, encouraged me to make friends with their grandkids . . ."

"What did you think of that?"

"I never questioned it." Bobo laughed, but not happily. "It just seemed natural to me. He would tell me why we shouldn't let black people—of course, that wasn't what he called them—live in the same buildings with us, date us, intermarry with us. He never got over integration, for God's sake. He was still pissed that black people could eat in the same restaurant as him and Gram, go to school with me and my brother and my sisters. He practically screamed at Mom and Dad to get them to send us to some private school in Little Rock or even farther, maybe Memphis, but to give my parents the credit they're due, they wanted us in town with them."

"Good for your mom and dad. You didn't buy what your grand-father was selling?" Fiji asked. She was painfully conscious that she must not cross any number of lines. "How did you keep from being totally messed up?"

"I'll tell you something weird. Football and karate saved me. Football, because we were all one team and we were all colors."

"Karate?" Fiji said. "Really?"

Bobo actually laughed. "It was great. My sensei was this amazing Asian guy who could kick major butt before breakfast, and one of my favorite class buddies was a black guy named Raphael Roundtree. And a white woman named Lily Bard. She could knock me down with her little finger. My grandfather revered women—as long as they were dependent and decorative."

"So your class was a revelation to you." She used the extravagant word with some hesitation. But Bobo hopped on it with glee.

"Yeah. No one in the class thought about what color or sex they were. Gaining the knowledge was the thing. So I knew from karate and football and my own common sense that there were just as many nice black people or Jews or gay people or whatever as the white people my grandfather thought were all so wonderful." Revisited resentment made Bobo's face look curiously young again.

"I'm assuming your grandfather didn't have a good end."

Bobo sighed. "When he was well into his eighties, he began using the like-minded employees who worked in his sporting goods store to start stockpiling guns illegally. He was siphoning them from the stock. But my dad . . ." And here, for the first time, Bobo faltered.

Fiji waited patiently.

"My father suspected his dad was up to no good. He hired a private detective to work in the sporting goods store, keeping watch and digging stuff up. The guy's name was Jack Leeds. Jack couldn't stop them from bombing a black church. People died. A child. Other people." Bobo took a deep breath, almost a sob. "One night—I can't remember how—the men working for my grandfather found out that Jack was working undercover, but they didn't know who he worked for. They thought it might be the government, and as you might expect, they went a little nuts. They really hurt him." Another deep breath. "They tortured him. Right in front of me. My grandfather made me go with him. I was too young to say no and call the cops. I was too scared and weak." Bobo's voice was full of scorn for his younger self. "I was looking for a way out when Jack's girlfriend came to rescue him. She was the great fighter from my karate class."

That was a lot to figure out, and Fiji wasn't totally sure she had the story straight, but she put that behind her to puzzle over later. "So she rescued Jack?" Fiji liked that part.

"Yeah. I'm simplifying, but she did. And I just carried my grandfather out of there. He was cursing up a storm, but I couldn't let him stay there and keep on . . . being evil."

"What happened?"

"All the men involved got arrested, including my grandfather."

"That's *terrible*." While Fiji's family had never been rich or influential, none of them had been arrested. *Oh my gosh, I pick jail terms to be snobbish about?* she thought. She said, "What happened after that?"

"While my grandfather was out on bail, he had a stroke. He never had to go to jail. But he never spoke again, and he died within three months. All the other men who were charged got prison sentences; the ones who set off the bomb in the church got life with no parole."

"Which was right," Fiji said. "Those sentences." She stared at Bobo's face. She couldn't discern how he felt about these events.

"Which was right," Bobo agreed. "Which was what Grandfather deserved, too. But he dodged that, like he dodged all the responsibility for what he'd done, by having the stroke."

Fiji found it easy to decipher her friend's emotion now; he was bitter.

"The point of this story is that after the stroke, supremacist groups began to circulate the rumor that Grandfather had a huge secret cache of all kinds of wonderful weapons. And the rumor turned into a legend, which then became accepted as fact. I've visited some of the websites, from organizations like Men of Liberty to After the Apocalypse, and it's just horrible, the way the story gathered bulk and momentum on its way downhill."

"So why do they—the nutcases—think you know about the location of this fabulous treasure trove of weapons? I suppose this was why Aubrey was here?"

Bobo looked as though he'd swallowed something bitter. "Since it was my dad who blew the whistle on his father, the nutcases cast him as the villain. They figure my grandfather would have been too smart to tell his evil son where the arms were stowed, they say. Instead, since I was with Grandfather the evening everything fell apart, obviously I was the chosen successor. So I must know where the cache of guns is. Only now it's not just guns, it's rocket launchers, grenades, mines . . . whatever can kill lots of people at once, that's what I'm concealing. That's the story."

"And why would you be concealing all of these weapons of destruction? Rather than putting them to good use against minorities?"

"That's a good question. I'm not sure I know why I'm doing that." Bobo smiled wryly.

"Is this the first time? I mean, with Aubrey . . . is this the first time you've been approached?" She didn't know how else to put it.

"No. There were some guys in the pawnshop a few days ago."

"So what happened?"

Bobo looked at her, obviously torn.

She came very close to leaning over to put her hand on his, but in the end she said, "I'll keep it to my grave."

Bobo said, "Lemuel and Olivia happened."

Fiji's mouth opened to ask a question, but then the implication had had time to sink in and explain itself. "Good for them," she said faintly. Mr. Snuggly butted her leg, and she reached down to scratch his head. The cat's golden eyes looked up at her. If cats had expressions, Mr. Snuggly's would be saying, "Buck up! Hang tough!"

She smiled down at the cat. "I'm glad they were there for you," she said.

He smiled, too, but his was not nearly as certain. "I was ready to take a beating," he admitted. "But I was mighty relieved I didn't have to."

"Olivia recognized the gun."

Bobo knew what she meant the minute the words left her mouth. "Feej, I don't have any idea how that old Colt got out there. I did take it out target shooting, because I'd never fired a gun like that, but I brought it back to the shop. Maybe I didn't lock it back into the case? Maybe I left it in the truck? But I know you know I didn't kill Aubrey."

"I do know that," Fiji said steadily. She suppressed the awful split second of doubt she'd experienced. "And Olivia knows that, too."

"Even if Lemuel thought I'd killed her, he'd back me," said Bobo, not as if he exactly approved of that.

Fiji now had had time to think of a hundred questions about Olivia and Lemuel and their landlord protection program, but she kept them to herself. It was not the time; just as it wasn't the time for her strongest impulse, leading Bobo to her bedroom so she could distract him from all these worries. It was too soon, he was still struggling with his conflicting feelings about Aubrey . . . that was what she told herself.

But really, she didn't do it because she feared he would say no.

16

In the days that followed the first and only Annual Picnic, the residents of Midnight resumed trundling along their accustomed paths and pursuits, though they all (except Grady, Rasta, and possibly Mr. Snuggly) felt they were operating under a cloud. Manfred certainly felt that way, and when he looked at the faces of the other townspeople, he could read that in their faces, too.

Bobo opened Midnight Pawn on Thursday morning. It was garbage pickup day, and he wheeled his garbage can to the curb along with Olivia's, which Lemuel shared. Bobo took the time to gather all the newspapers that had collected in his driveway. Manfred watched through his front window as his landlord resumed his life, and he was glad.

Manfred saw the other denizens of Midnight at Home Cookin, which had a few more customers than usual, thanks to reporters, law enforcement, and the idly curious. Sometimes the residents could not sit at their accustomed table.

Teacher told Manfred he'd made some extra money changing tires that had gotten punctured on the rocks over by the riverbed.

Both Fiji and Chuy made grocery runs to Davy. Fiji got the items on the Rev's short list and delivered them to his little bare house, and in her own kitchen she cooked between helping store customers, so she could take Bobo chicken and dumplings and some seasoned green beans. Another night, Chuy cooked Tex-Mex with Joe's assistance, and they invited Manfred and Bobo to come to dinner.

Manfred accepted when Joe called him, for several reasons. Manfred loved meals he didn't have to cook, he liked Joe and Chuy, and he understood that their main goal was to get Bobo out of his own place and encourage him to eat some hot food.

Manfred and his landlord walked west to the Antique Gallery and Nail Salon together, not talking much along the way, and Bobo showed Manfred the outside flight of stairs that led up to Joe and Chuy's apartment. The building itself had been constructed long after Midnight Pawn, and as a result the ceilings weren't as high, so the whole structure was shorter.

"I'm glad they can't see in my windows," Bobo said, and he almost laughed.

"Can you see down into theirs?"

"I can see a sliver of their kitchen, but that's all," Bobo said, knocking on the weathered wooden door.

"Come in, and welcome!" Joe said, standing aside. "I'll take those jackets." Manfred looked around him with some amazement. The apartment wasn't large, but it looked amazing. The colors were attractive and harmonious, there were "window treatments," and the furniture had *not* been picked up at a curb before the garbage men could toss it.

Manfred had to admit to himself that he had had no idea that men could make their surroundings look anything more than utilitarian. He was genuinely impressed, and at the same time he called himself an idiot for not realizing that two people who between them could price antiques and style hair and nails would know something about putting together a good-looking home. He did feel a little strange when the tour included their bedroom, where Rasta was curled in the middle of a paprika and turquoise bedspread.

After five minutes, Manfred forgot that Joe and Chuy were men who had sex with each other. Instead, he was able to revel in the happy discovery that Chuy was a very good cook and that Joe kept a stock of excellent beer in his refrigerator.

Even Bobo became more cheerful as the evening passed. He talked sports with Joe and raising peppers with Chuy. They talked about the Westminster Dog Show, the difficulties of getting into vet school (Chuy hadn't managed it), and the pleasures and frustrations of buying on eBay. Chuy told them about his cousin Rose's fling with the Home Shopping Network and how he'd brought Rose's minister in to pray with her over her addiction.

The way Chuy talked about Rose made Manfred regret his lack of family.

After dinner ended with a wonderful pecan pie, Manfred offered to do the dishes. Joe gratefully accepted his help. "If Chuy does the cooking, it seems only fair I clean up," he said, "but it's always nice to have another pair of hands." Most of the supper dishes went into the dishwasher, but Manfred scrubbed the pots and pans while Joe dried them. Afterward, Chuy showed them some snapshots of his and Joe's vacation in Amsterdam, one of the many places Manfred had not been.

As Manfred and Bobo walked home around ten o'clock, conversation was sparse. "Nice dinner," Manfred said, and after Bobo replied, "Man, those chicken enchiladas . . ." they were both done with talk, but in a content way. Manfred thought the evening had accomplished part of its goal, in getting Bobo out of his shell. Manfred himself had enjoyed the company because it was not one of his "sensitive" nights, when he learned more than he wanted to know about his companions.

But he was the one who noticed the car parked across Witch Light Road between the empty two-story building (its ghost of a sign read RÍO ROCA FRÍA HOTEL 1920) and the Home Cookin Restaurant. The car was deep in a shadow. Even as he recognized the shape of an automobile roof, Manfred was reluctant to emerge from the haze of well-being, but he couldn't ignore the alarm bells going off in his head. He grabbed Bobo's jacket sleeve and yanked him into the alley behind Gas N Go.

"What the hell?" Bobo protested, but mildly.

"Someone's parked over there in the shadows," Manfred whispered. Bobo appeared to hear that silent alarm signal, too, because he instantly moved farther back into the shadows. "Do you see any people?" he asked. He didn't whisper, but his voice was very quiet.

"No, and that worries me even more," Manfred said.

"'Cause we're right behind you," a man's voice said from the shadows.

Manfred wasn't ashamed to tell Fiji the next day that he screamed like a teenage girl in a horror movie.

But even as he screamed, he jumped toward danger, not away from it. So did Bobo. Manfred hadn't been in many fistfights—or fights of any sort—but he figured if he kept punching he'd hit something, and he swung away like a wiry windmill. Bobo gave a more practiced exhibit of self-defense.

"Help!" yelled Manfred, which was probably the most useful thing he could have done. He had no idea who might hear him in

Midnight, but he had to try. To his astonishment, a light came on as the back door of Gas N Go flew open, and Creek Lovell charged out swinging a baseball bat.

It took her a second to identify the combatants, but when she did, she got behind the man Manfred was fighting and laid into the middle of his back with a formidable swing. He screamed and staggered, and Manfred actually got in a good hit on the man's jaw. Down he went, in a most gratifying way, leaving Manfred shaking his bruised and battered hand.

By then Shawn Lovell had pelted from the store to join in the fight, and he grabbed Bobo's assailant around the arms in a bear hug. Bobo socked the pinned man in the stomach, and the air left the man's lungs in a whoosh. He sagged.

By that time, Lemuel was there.

Manfred, bending over with his hands on his knees and panting for all he was worth, took a second to marvel that Lemuel had heard him call for help from the pawnshop.

"Uncle Lem, they were trying to beat up Manfred and Bobo!" Creek yelled. She didn't seem to notice her voice was raised. Her eyes were wide, and she was still gripping the bat. "Dad! They were hiding behind *our store!*" She was all over the place, her gaze skittering from one man to the other, her body tense and ready to swing the bat again.

"Deep breaths, little lady," Lemuel said. "You have done a good thing tonight, and I'm sure Manfred and Bobo are most grateful."

"I am *so* grateful," Manfred gasped, and when Creek looked at him sharply, thinking he was teasing her, he said, "Believe me, Creek." After a couple of more wheezes, he was able to straighten up and look more manly; or at least he hoped so.

"Pretty funny," Bobo said. He leaned against the back wall of Gas

N Go. "That we were trying to get away from them and instead we hid where they were hiding."

"Hilarious," Manfred agreed.

"I've called the police," Shawn said. He didn't sound pleased at all; he sounded very angry. "Creek, please go in the store and put the bat back where we keep it. Tell Connor everything's okay. I don't want you to have to talk to the cops."

"But . . . Dad! I did so good!" Creek was half indignant woman, half floored child.

"You sure did, honey, but I don't want our name anywhere in a police report." Shawn's voice was even, but you could tell he meant every word.

As soon as Manfred's brain began working again, he absorbed the idea that the Lovell family had a complicated back history.

That didn't surprise him at all.

The two attackers were conscious, and the one Creek had swung on was groaning. "That bitch broke my back," he said. Manfred knelt by him and made sure the man was looking into his eyes. "You say that again, I'll jump on you with both feet," Manfred told him.

There was a rusty sawing noise, and Manfred looked up to discover that that was what Lemuel sounded like when he laughed. The other prisoner, firmly caught by Lemuel's cold grip, was looking feebler by the moment. *The Lemuel effect*, Manfred thought, and almost smiled.

"I don't know what you said on the phone, Shawn, but I can hear the lawmen coming from Davy already," Lemuel said, his head cocked to the right side.

After a few more seconds, they all heard the sirens, but the first car to get there was a private car with a blue light stuck on top. It was Arthur Smith's car, and he was out of it and among them with a speed the much younger Manfred envied. Oddly, Manfred didn't realize his opponent had landed some good blows until he saw the sheriff. When Smith's eyes met his, Manfred became sharply aware that his jaw hurt, and his ribs, too.

"These two men jumped us," Bobo said, paring the story down. "It was lucky our friends came when we called."

"Yelled like a banshee," Manfred muttered.

By then a patrol officer was moving in right behind the sheriff, and Smith said, "Cuff this one and that one," pointing to the two assailants. He looked from Bobo to Manfred. "I'm taking your word for it because you live here and I've never seen these men, so it doesn't make sense that you attacked them."

The one on the ground said, "Ask them where Curtis and Seth are, you think they're so innocent."

"Who?" Manfred said blankly.

"I don't know a Curtis or Seth," Shawn said. "You, Bobo?"

Bobo spread his hands, and Manfred saw that the knuckles were bleeding. "Not me."

Lemuel said, "I don't know them."

"They came here," the man insisted. "And they never came back."

"We need to think about you, rather than your invisible friends," Arthur Smith said, squatting beside the downed man. "You want to start with telling me your name and why you were waiting in a dark alley for these guys?"

"I don't want to tell you shit," the man said, trying to sneer, but not managing very convincingly. "Hey, help me up. I can stand now."

"Oh, so your back isn't broken?" Manfred said. He stepped back as Smith hauled the man to his feet with apparent ease. The man gasped, and Manfred saw he was in genuine pain, but as Manfred tenderly touched his own ribs, he felt no sympathy at all.

"I am a citizen of the free country of Stronghold," the newly upright man said suddenly. "I'm not obliged to give you my slave name. My true name is Buffalo. I'm a soldier of the army of the Men of Liberty. You must treat me as a prisoner of war according to the Geneva Convention."

That speech stopped all movement. Everyone gaped at him. The second man, who seemed exhausted now that Lemuel had been holding his arm for almost ten minutes, said, "I am a citizen of the free country of Stronghold, and I am not obliged to give you my slave name. My true name is Eagle. I'm a . . . I'm a soldier in the army of the Men of Liberty. You must treat me as a prisoner of war according to the Geneva Convention."

"Damn," said the uniformed officer, who happened to be black. "That's pretty big talk, coming from you two. Buffalo and Eagle, huh? Those the names on your drivers' licenses? And I'd like to know who enslaved you."

"The false government of the United States."

Lemuel let go of the second man, who almost collapsed. The patrolman took advantage of the moment to cuff him.

Arthur Smith dipped into the pocket of "Buffalo," and his hand was clutching a wallet when he pulled it out. "This man's slave name is Jeremy Spratt," he said. "No wonder he likes 'Buffalo' better. Tom?"

The patrol officer extracted his prisoner's wallet. "This here's Zane Green," he said. "Otherwise known as Eagle. He lives in Marthasville, it says here."

Smith reexamined Jeremy Spratt's license. "He's from Marthasville, too." He looked at Jeremy Spratt quizzically. "Now, where did your missing buddies live, Buffalo?"

"Lubbock," Buffalo said, and immediately looked as though he'd bitten into a lemon. "Damn," he muttered. Bobo started laughing, which made Buffalo (aka Jeremy) even angrier.

"And why did you drive thirty miles from home to hang around in an alley in Midnight? Is there something wonderful about Midnight that I don't know?"

Both prisoners clamped their mouths shut, and that was the end of their answering questions. They were hauled off to jail in Tom's patrol car, with Arthur Smith following behind in his own vehicle.

Lemuel vanished as quickly as he'd appeared, and Manfred wondered why his buddy Olivia hadn't shown. Maybe she was out of town. No one else seemed to have heard the ruckus.

Manfred and Bobo thanked Creek and Shawn profusely. Creek was still twitchy with excitement, while Shawn just as clearly wanted to get rid of them.

"Time to go home," Bobo said, and began to walk toward the pawnshop. "You coming, Manfred?" As they crossed the Davy highway, he added, "Thanks for giving me a heads-up, even if we ended up walking into the lion's den."

"Sure. I was real helpful," Manfred said ruefully.

Bobo laughed. He sounded more like himself than he had since the body had been found. To Bobo, the fracas had been stimulating, apparently. Manfred was deflating like a balloon with each step he took, though.

He unlocked his front door in a daze and barely made it to the bedroom before he crumpled. He toed off his shoes, pulled off his blue jeans, and crawled under the blanket.

And he was out. He didn't think he'd changed positions all night when he opened his eyes to find sun streaming around the edges of the bedroom curtains.

Getting up was an unexpectedly painful process. Since Manfred had never been in a serious fight before, he was not prepared for how sore he'd be. He hadn't realized he should take some pain reliever, or at least soak in a hot tub, before he slept. *This is what it must feel like to be old,* Manfred thought, as he hobbled into the bathroom. After a hot, hot shower, two Advil, and a multivitamin, plus some toast and Coca-Cola, Manfred could walk without looking weird. But as he went to his desk, he still felt tender and achy in many places.

He gripped the back of the chair, telling himself to sit, but he stood in the middle of the floor indecisively. He felt that he should *do* something . . . go see Bobo, drive to the jail in Davy, call someone. But if Bobo was as uncomfortable as he was, he wouldn't want to be bothered by Manfred's dropping in, and what would he do at the jail? Yell at the men who'd attacked him? And who should he call? His mother would just freak out.

He'd finally resigned himself to sitting down at his computer (with a definite feeling of anticlimax), when there was a knock at the door. He hobbled over to open it. He was astonished to see that his caller was the Rev. He was just beginning to say, "Please come . . ." when the Rev began speaking himself, in his rusty voice. He put his thin mummy hand on Manfred's head.

"Lord, thank you for saving this thy servant Manfred from serious harm. Thank you for his courage in defending our brother Bobo. Bless him in his endeavors and keep him in the councils of the wise." The Rev walked away.

Bemused, Manfred watched the older man stride over to Midnight Pawn, presumably to bless Bobo in the same manner. He wasn't surprised that his cell phone began to ring, or that the caller was Fiji.

"The Rev gave you a blessing," she said. "I saw it out the front window. What happened last night? Because I'm really, really tired of being left out."

"You didn't hear me scream like a stuck pig?"

"No! What time was that?"

"A little after ten," he said. "Bobo and I got jumped on our way home from Joe and Chuy's."

"Is Bobo all right?" He couldn't miss the alarm in her voice.

"Sure, though I have a broken leg and a concussion," he said, and then had to listen to Fiji apologize for several seconds before he could break in to tell her he had exaggerated.

"I do have an herbal remedy that would make you feel better," she said tentatively. "It's nothing crazy. I mean, it's all natural."

So was pig shit, but Manfred refrained from saying that. "I'll give it a try," he said bravely. "I've never been in a real fight before, and it didn't agree with me."

"Not a good part of a balanced lifestyle," she said, a hint of laughter in her voice, and after a few minutes she was carrying a mug across the road, its contents steaming.

"Drink all of this," she said. "And if it works for you, I don't mind making you some more."

Manfred supposed you would call it tea, because it was made from steeped vegetation. The hot drink didn't taste good, but it wasn't disgusting, either. Since he didn't want to offend Fiji and she was standing right in his living room with her eyes on him, he sipped until it was gone. He handed Fiji the mug. Instead of thanking her and making it clear he needed to get right back to work (his original plan), he found himself sitting on the couch in the former dining room with Fiji, telling her all about the evening before. She listened with wide eyes.

"So they said they lived in the free state of Stronghold and they actually mentioned the Men of Liberty," she said when he was finished. "And that their two buddies had come here and never returned to this fabulous free state, which I suspect is nowhere but in their little minds?"

"That sums it up," Manfred agreed. Fiji's face did not adapt to "grim" and "serious" very well, but that was how she looked. "Do you know anything about the two vanishing friends?" he asked.

"No, I do not," she said very firmly. "I never saw them and I don't know where they are now." Manfred thought she was being at least partially truthful. "But I think it's very suspicious that they say they belong to the same organization of wackos that Aubrey's deceased husband belonged to."

Another knock caught them both by surprise. Manfred glanced out the peephole before he opened the door. Arthur Smith had been able to hear him walk across the creaking wooden floor, so Manfred figured he had to let him in. "Sheriff," he said, "What can we do for you today? My neighbor is here, so maybe you can kill two birds with one stone."

"Ms. Cavanaugh," the sheriff said, ducking his head and removing his hat. "You doing okay today?"

"Yes, fine, thank you," Fiji said. "I brought Manfred one of my herbal remedies for soreness. Manfred, are you feeling better?"

"I am," he said, trying not to sound surprised. He shifted his shoulders experimentally and bent to touch his toes. Yes, he was actually almost pain-free.

"The two men who attacked Mr. Bernardo and Mr. Winthrop have gotten a public defender," Arthur Smith said. "And on the advice of their counsel, they're not talking to me anymore. They've abandoned their Men of Liberty spiel, since I think the lawyer told them it made them sound crazier and more dangerous than just saying they jumped some guys in the alley because they thought they were being jumped themselves."

"What were they doing in the alley behind the gas station, anyway? I'm sure you asked them that."

"They don't seem to feel they have to explain their presence," Arthur Smith said dryly. "That's what the lawyer told them to say."

"So . . . are they going to get out of jail?" Fiji looked as though Smith had told her the truth about Santa Claus.

"They may," Smith admitted. He ran a hand over his close-cropped hair. He'd settled on a straight-backed chair opposite the couch, and he turned his hat in his hands as he sat there. "Of the two, only one of them has any kind of arrest record, Zane Green, and that was one incident, a bar fight. The guy he beat up didn't press charges."

"A bar close to here?" Manfred asked.

"Yeah, the Cartoon Saloon."

Manfred started to ask where that was, but Fiji shot him a narrow-eyed look that said, *Don't draw attention to this by asking about it.*

Instead, he said, "So the whole incident's over for now is what you're telling us. And you're not getting anywhere on Aubrey Hamilton's death?"

"I wouldn't say that. The coroner confirmed the body is that of Aubrey Hamilton Lowry, and her parents are claiming the body for burial when we release it."

Fiji looked startled, as if the concept of Aubrey's parents taking charge was a surprise to her. "Of course there's no reason why her parents wouldn't grieve, though Aubrey was . . ." she murmured, and then stopped abruptly. In a more public voice, Fiji said, "I hope they'll keep Bobo in the loop about the funeral plans. That would mean a lot to him."

The sheriff, who had gotten up to leave, looked at Fiji as if she'd grown another head or begun talking in Urdu. "That's hardly likely," Smith said. "They think he killed her."

Manfred, who had turned to Fiji, saw all the color drain from her face and then flood back. He thought she might faint, and he was glad she hadn't stood up.

"He loved her," Fiji faltered. "They can't think that."

Arthur Smith looked at her with a lot more interest. "Think about it, Ms. Cavanaugh. She comes here to live with him, she vanishes, her body turns up in a riverbed close by. He didn't report her missing right away. We might think his reasons are understandable, but the Hamiltons don't. He admits he didn't search for her. She's the widow of a white supremacist. You know those men Mr. Bernardo's attackers claim are missing? They're white supremacists, too. Though Green and Spratt call themselves 'patriots,' it's clear they're in the same boat politically."

"But he thought she'd gone all on her own," Fiji said stubbornly. "Why would he look for someone who'd kicked him to the curb?"

"On the other hand, who else had reason to want her dead?" His eyes were intent on her face.

"Given the company she kept . . . the, ah, associates of her husband . . ." But she couldn't say anything else without revealing information she wanted to keep quiet—more importantly, information that Bobo wanted to keep quiet. She found herself on her feet, feeling a little wobbly but practically bursting with things she wished she could say.

Smith said, "Just because she hung out with a crowd we consider over the political edge doesn't mean her death was anything but personal. Or even accidental. The medical examiner's still looking at her."

Manfred said, "Fiji, don't worry, they'll find out who did it, and that person won't be Bobo. Sheriff, thanks for coming by to let me know about those guys. If you need me again, you know where I am." He was all smiles and geniality as he walked Sheriff Smith to the door, but when the door closed behind him, Manfred turned to give Fiji a very grim face.

"From the way you're looking at me, I screwed up," she said.

"Of course you did," Manfred said. "You acted like you were defending your kid from a bully. Bobo's a grown man. He can look out for himself. The more you go on the defensive, the more Smith's going to think there's a great reason you're protecting Bobo."

Fiji muttered, "Aside from the fact that I'm an idiot?"

"I know you're not. I know you're his good friend." Out of mercy, Manfred did not say, *Because you're clearly nuts about him.* Also, he had no desire to be frozen into a statue for an indeterminate length of time.

"So, you're going to the Cartoon Saloon with me, right?" Fiji said.

"Wait, are we police? No, we're not going there."

"But we have to find out more. Why didn't the other guy in the fight press charges?"

"Why? Maybe because he didn't want to spend time in court, or because he decided he'd been in the wrong, too? Or maybe he just wants to wait until he can catch this Zane guy alone in an alley and get his own revenge."

Fiji was practically tapping her foot, waiting for him to finish speaking. "We have to try to find him," she said, and Manfred threw up his hands.

"Okay! Okay! But we're not going by ourselves."

"Olivia," Fiji said, and the proposed expedition suddenly became a little more interesting to Manfred.

"You think she'd go with us?"

"I think if I ask her the right way, she will," Fiji said. She looked at her watch. "She's not going to be up for a while, so I'll try her this afternoon."

"What about Lemuel? He's pretty, uh, capable," Manfred offered.

"He doesn't go out much," Fiji said. "I mean, he only goes out at night, and most nights he's working in the pawnshop. Besides, he's too scary and no one would talk to us."

Manfred did not want to think about this too closely, or at all. "So why do you want to take Olivia?"

Fiji's eyes went wide. "She's very good at finding out things," she replied. "That's kind of her business. And we've got to get a name."

"Really? What does she do?" Manfred didn't realize he'd gotten into forbidden territory until he saw Fiji give him a very direct look. "Okay, okay, I overstepped. You ask her. Let me know what she says."

"I'll do that." Fiji went to the door. "I hope the tea helped."

"Yes, thanks," he said, rotating his shoulders. "I'm lots better."

"Great!" Her smile was radiant. "That was Aunt Mildred's recipe."

Manfred was almost curious enough to ask what had been in it, but he was afraid to find out. He said, "She must have been a great witch."

Fiji said, "You have no idea." She was all cheer when she left. He saw Mr. Snuggly sitting at the edge of her yard, obviously waiting for her. As Manfred watched her cross the road, he saw the sheriff coming down the steps of the pawnshop. Manfred thought of going over to see Bobo to check out what the sheriff had told him, but then he thought twice. As he'd just pointed out to Fiji, Bobo was a grown-up, and he could handle himself.

17

Arthur Smith had found Bobo sitting in his favorite chair, but Bobo was sitting forward with his elbows on his knees, his hands covering his eyes. When he lowered them, he looked exhausted.

"The gun we found down by the river," the sheriff had said.

Bobo had nodded.

"Came from this pawnshop, according to our records."

Every gun coming into the shop was entered on the computer and law enforcement had access to all such reports.

Bobo had nodded again.

The sheriff waited for more explanation, more reaction, more anything. But Bobo had only said, "I didn't kill her."

"There aren't any prints on the gun," Smith told him, with no inflection in his voice. "We're waiting for the medical examiner's final report on the cause of death. I'll be back. But you know, Mr. Winthrop, it doesn't look good for you if the medical examiner's report shows Mrs. Lowry died of a gunshot."

"Yeah," Bobo said. "My ass will be toast."

"I've checked into Buffalo and Eagle's allegations." Smith took a step closer. "At least five members of this group have told me that two Men of Liberty, Seth Mecklinberg and Curtis Logan, came over here to talk to you. They were very vague about what these two gentlemen had to say to you, or why they came from Lubbock instead of the Marthasville branch of MOL. My guess would be so you couldn't recognize them, as you might recognize someone from Marthasville."

"I did not do anything to those men, and I don't know why they'd think I did," Bobo said. "I have no idea what happened to them."

"Since no one has filed a missing-person report on them, they're not part of our investigation at the moment," Smith said. "But if they really are missing and we find someone to say they saw those two men in this area, you know this is going to get much worse for you."

"I understand," said Bobo. He stood up. He was several inches taller than the sheriff, but at the moment he felt that Arthur Smith was the larger man.

18

Olivia had had some mysterious business to take care of, and she had to uncover the name of the man who'd been beaten by Zane Green. According to Fiji, Olivia had great computer skills and a lot of knowledge and connections in the lawyer community. Evidently Olivia was able to exercise one of her talents, since Fiji called Manfred after a day to tell him that they'd go on their "field trip" (as Manfred privately called it) to the Cartoon Saloon that night.

Olivia, the only one who'd already been there, said that the saloon lay between Midnight and Marthasville, but much closer to the larger town. "I promise you a sight worth seeing," she promised them as they piled into Manfred's car.

"Wow," said Manfred, when he parked by a huge cutout of Yosemite Sam. "Cool sign. But weird."

"Hmmm," said Fiji. "Interesting."

Olivia just smiled broadly. "You ain't seen nothing yet," she said. "By the way, we're looking for a guy named Deck Powell."

Manfred walked into the bar with an unaccustomed feeling of pride. He was accompanied by two attractive women, both older than himself. Fiji had made an attempt to style her hair, which had resulted in a headful of brown curls in a sort of Shirley Temple effect. She'd worn a flirty black skirt, a black and green patterned shirt that emphasized her bosom (and there was plenty to emphasize), and some black heels, which she managed with more grace than Manfred had expected. Olivia had worn designer jeans, a halter top beneath a kind of mesh sweater (since, after all, it was early October), and boots that boosted her up way above Manfred. Olivia led the way and paid their cover charge, and while they were being shown to their table, Olivia's eyes were everywhere.

Manfred realized that Olivia was armed. He didn't know what kind of weapon she was carrying or where it might be—her purse? Strapped to her leg?—but he could read her well enough to know she was ready for trouble.

Manfred thought, *I'm more worried, and yet I feel safer.*

Actually, he felt pretty badass. One of the ladies with him could freeze you, and one could defend him with weapons.

The waitress appeared at their table in a pleasantly short time. She correctly identified Olivia as the group alpha and turned to her first.

"Mezcal, straight up. Extra añejo, if you got it," Olivia said.

"Reposado okay?"

"That'll do."

Fiji looked blank during this exchange, and she ordered a glass of chardonnay. Manfred thought he might look wussy if he ordered wine, too, but his talent sometimes acted up if he drank too much. He settled on a Michelob.

He had time to look at the walls while they waited for the drinks. "Damn," he said.

"I agree," said Fiji, staring. The walls were decorated like a crazy day care center, with three-foot-tall cartoon characters in a frieze that circled the room. Manfred couldn't figure out how they'd been made, but they were expertly drawn and mounted. SpongeBob SquarePants and Foghorn Leghorn, Mickey Mouse and Bugs Bunny, Porky Pig and Marge Simpson, Jessica Rabbit and Meg Griffin, Wile E. Coyote and WALL-E.

They were all drinking alcoholic beverages.

"I'm sure the Disney lawyers would like to know about this," Manfred murmured. "And that's just the first company on the list."

"I didn't expect to find something this bold and bizarre in Marthasville," Fiji said.

Marthasville, about thirty-five miles west of Midnight, had pretensions to artiness. With a population of fifty thousand, it was a sizable town compared to Midnight, and it was in another county. There was a whole row of bars in Marthasville, and they were all decorated and themed. The presence of a college may have accounted for the bar boom, but the age range of patrons went from lean dried-up men in their seventies (wearing cowboy hats as part of their normal attire) to young people who were just barely legal, like Manfred.

When their costumed waitress returned with their drinks, Manfred noticed that she was dressed and styled as Wilma Flintstone. Another waitress was Betty Boop. The bartender was a superhero— maybe Aquaman?

He laughed out loud. "This," Manfred said, "is a *great* bar."

"It'll be a greater one if we can find out what we need to know," Olivia said.

"How do we do that?" he asked, confident she had a plan.

Olivia shook her head, as if she despaired for him. She looked from him to Fiji, making mental calculations. "You and Feej make a more credible couple than you and me," she said. Manfred didn't know whether to be flattered or insulted, so he just nodded. "Okay, here's our scenario," Olivia said, and they bent their heads together like experienced conspirators.

The next time their waitress approached the table (and since Olivia had tipped big, that was pretty soon), Manfred said, "Wilma, maybe you can help us out, here? My friend Livvy has a blind date with a guy, but we don't see anyone who looks like the picture she got, and we're afraid he's standing her up."

"Wilma" looked from Manfred to Olivia. She seemed to be trying to decide if he was joking. "Anybody who'd skip out on a date with her has to be out of his mind," Wilma said frankly. She seemed relieved to be standing still for a moment.

"True, but maybe he doesn't know that," Manfred said. "Guy name of Deck Powell?"

"Deck? Deck has a date with *you*?" Wilma looked at "Livvy" with flattering disbelief. "He must have been praying hard, or your brother owes him money, or something. He's usually in by now. I'll come over and tell you when I see him."

"Oh, thanks," Manfred said. Olivia did her best to look embarrassed by the whole situation. Manfred ordered another round of drinks because he figured it was his turn, and he tipped Wilma as liberally as Olivia had. Wilma gave him a surreptitious wink.

None of them had quite finished the first round, so their table began to look a little crowded when the fresh drinks came. Fiji took care of her original glass of wine and lifted her second. She said, "I'd take pictures of the walls with my phone, but I'm afraid the bouncer would step on it and crush it. Not that I would mind if he came over."

Manfred glanced over at the door. The bouncer was a hard,

handsome man with some miles on him. "Fiji, I'm betting you don't drink a lot," he said, trying to suppress a smile.

"I don't," she confessed. "How did you know?"

"Just a lucky guess."

"You think he'd like my phone number?"

"Feej, that guy is tough as nails, and he's not only been around the block, he's run a marathon. He could eat you for breakfast," Olivia said, half smiling.

"And wouldn't that be a great way to wake up?" Fiji said, with a broad wink. Manfred laughed; he couldn't help it.

"Wilma" caught Manfred's eye. She tilted her head toward the bar. A newcomer stood there waiting for his drink, and he wasn't looking around at the walls like a first-time visitor. He was looking at the people. He had a receding chin with a sort of billygoat beard, a nose that had been broken more than once, and prominent blue eyes.

Manfred nudged Olivia. "Sic him," he said. "There's your blind date."

Olivia narrowed her eyes. "Well, damn, no wonder the waitress was surprised." She got to her feet with a smooth economy of movement.

As she made her way to the bar, Manfred turned to Fiji. To his surprise, she was watching him with sharp eyes. "You're not as drunk as you sounded," he said.

"I do think the bouncer's cute," she said. "And I'm a *little* tipsy. But I'm not likely to get drunk. It's too dangerous."

"For you?"

"For other people."

Manfred remembered the frozen woman in Fiji's yard. He had to agree with her policy. He glanced over to see what progress Olivia was making with Deck. Deck was clearly startled but delighted. He didn't seem to be questioning his good luck.

"Such fools," Fiji muttered, and Manfred said, "Hey, I'm a man, remember?"

"Sorry," she said. "You're a better man than most."

"Thanks," he said, though he didn't feel truly mollified. Olivia worked her way through the crowd to arrive back at their table. Along the way, she commandeered another chair for her new acquaintance.

Olivia introduced them all, first names only, and then began a convoluted conversational path designed to discover more about Zane Green, the Man of Liberty who'd punched Deck out at this very bar. If Manfred hadn't known her strategy, he never would have guessed her goal. He helped as much as he could by telling an utterly fictitious story of a bar fight he'd been in. Fiji, who'd been mostly silent, said, "Manfred here got knocked clean out, and he pressed charges against that asshole." That proved to be the clincher.

"Wow, you did? My hat's off to you, man," Deck said. "When I got knocked out here at the saloon, the guy who beat me up was such a badass I thought I'd be worse off taking him to court. As a matter of fact, the next night his posse, along with the head honcho, showed up at my house and told me I better not, or they'd burn me out. And I believed them."

"That's awful," Olivia said. "Who was this . . . head honcho?"

Deck leaned in to indicate this was very confidential news he was telling his friends of ten minutes. "Price," he said, and waited for them to react with shock and horror. When they didn't react at all, he said, "Price *Eggleston*. The rich guy. He belongs to one of them militia-type groups, and he's one mean sumbitch, 'scuse me, ladies."

"You mean, this group isn't just all e-mails and threats . . . ?"

"No, they are the real deal," Deck said solemnly. "You do *not* cross them."

Fiji said, "Sounds pretty hard-core. And they're based here?"

Deck nodded, after a swig of beer. "Two miles out of town. But enough about those bastards," he said, "let's have some fun! Livvy, you want to dance?"

"Sure," Olivia said, and off they went, two-stepping around the floor.

"It's not fair that she can dance, too," Fiji said. "But I'll forgive her, since that was a masterly interrogation."

"I can't dance at all," Manfred confessed.

"I can dance a *little*," Fiji said. "I can cook. I can cast spells. Dancing? Not so much."

"You're a good friend," Manfred said. "You can do friendship well."

"Thanks," she said. "That's a fine compliment. And you know what, I'm going to give that bouncer my phone number on my way out."

"Bold move." Manfred was confused, because he was sure Fiji was nuts about Bobo, but he wasn't about to bring it up, not with her mood being so peculiar.

"Do you think he'll call me?"

That was a trick question if Manfred had ever heard one. "He'd be a fool not to," he said, and Fiji laughed.

It took Olivia an hour to extricate herself from Deck, an hour in which Manfred and Fiji had a third drink apiece, though they sipped them as slowly as they could.

On their way out, Fiji handed a piece of paper to the bouncer and introduced herself. He did not seem startled by this, but he nodded at her politely and introduced himself right back. "Travis McNamara," he said. "You have a good night, you hear?"

"You, too," Fiji said, with a sideways smile full of fun.

Manfred had never seen her look so—flirty.

"Could have gone worse," Fiji told them, as she walked carefully across the gravel to Olivia's car. She was talking about the bouncer, but Olivia answered about Deck.

"Yes," Olivia agreed. "He looked like a guppy with a beard, but he could really dance. Plus, eventually he gave me all the information I needed to know."

"Which was?" Manfred said, buckling his seat belt.

"That Price Eggleston and his buddies have a house about two miles east of Marthasville. Which you heard. But he narrowed down the location. It's on the way home. It's the MOL Big Secret Club-house. I bet they only let girls *in* if they put *out* for the membership." Olivia looked calm, but it was an angry, tight-jawed sort of calm.

Sure enough, a couple of minutes' drive out of the Marthasville city limits, there was a driveway on the right. As a ranch had to be, it was fenced, and the driveway was crossed by a gate that had to be opened and closed every time a car drove through. Also, like many ranches, the name of the place was on an iron sign arching over the gateway. MOL, it read.

"Nothing like being up front about it." Manfred was leaning down in the front seat to look up at the sign. "And I see the gate is locked."

"So what do we do with that information?" Fiji asked. "It's good to know where the evil hatemongers hang out, I see that. But how are we going to stop them from coming after Bobo again?"

There was a moment of silence. Manfred couldn't think of any procedure on earth that could be done openly and legally. And it was out of the question to kill the MOL members. At least, it was to Manfred. Maybe Fiji was thinking of freezing them all permanently.

"We'll think of a way," Olivia said. She was smiling, and it wasn't a pleasant smile. Maybe Olivia had something else in mind.

To Manfred's bemusement, Fiji looked at Olivia with a sort of exasperation, and said, "You can't do that to all of them."

Manfred, sleepy and puzzled, waited to hear some explanation. But Olivia didn't say a word.

19

Since he'd played his part in the "help Bobo" movement, Manfred felt free to think about himself and his own concerns the next day. He worked late, not turning off his computer until after dark. When he finally got up, he realized he'd been sitting in the same position for far too long. Walking off the stiffness, he strolled over to the window. The light over the storefront of Midnight Pawn was humming with bugs, and the two cars parked there looked forlorn in the bleak glare. Manfred had known that Lemuel kept the shop open at night, but he'd never particularly noticed any customer traffic. Now he saw a strange, hunched shape come down the six steps to the street level. It paused to stuff something in its left coat pocket (it was just cool enough this night to make a sweater feasible but not a coat). Then, left foot dragging, the creature made its way to the driver's side of a Ford Fusion. Manfred found it impossible to tell if he was looking at a male or female; whatever this individual was, he was fairly sure it wasn't human.

He wondered what it had pawned. But he thought it would be indiscreet to actually go in the shop to ask Lemuel.

Plus, Lemuel might want to hold his hand again.

Manfred had tried not to brood about that little incident in the diner, but it had shaken him . . . Lemuel's intensely cold hand, the hard grip, the creeping weariness that had gradually sapped Manfred's strength. There had been something eerily pleasant about it, but the incident had also been really, really terrifying. And why had Lemuel picked him, Manfred, to feed from? Manfred had never doubted his own sexual identity was hetero, but the connection had not been completely without intimacy.

Okay, he asked himself, trying to face and conquer this inconvenient uneasiness, *how do you feel about the idea of kissing Lemuel?*

He felt an instantaneous *Yuck.* Somewhat relieved by this response, he was not as tentative about exploring the question further. *Do I seriously believe Lemuel thinks of me as a potential sex partner?* was the next question. *Probably not,* he thought. After all, though he didn't have any direct evidence, he'd gotten the definite impression that Olivia and Lemuel were a couple, or at least were having sex. Since this internal conversation was relieving an anxiety he hadn't realized he harbored, he thought he'd carry it one step further. He'd face Lemuel; he'd erase this lingering uneasiness.

Manfred slipped out his front door and went up the steps into the pawnshop. The chilly night was silent, except for the tiny noises of the bugs overhead and the hum of the light. If there were this many insects in October, he hated to think of what it would be like in July. As the car outside had indicated, there was still a customer in the pawnshop, a woman. She was talking to Lemuel, who was sitting on the stool behind the counter. Manfred began browsing the shelves; there were so many to browse. The inside of the pawnshop was far larger than the outside might indicate.

The shelves and display cases were full of interesting things, dusty things, ancient things, deadly things—and many things that were out-and-out weird. There were freestanding shelving units and built-in cabinets, and there were antique pieces of cabinetry that were stuffed with other pawned items. There were wooden shelves and metal ones, and the wooden ones ranged from weathered and silvery to smelling of pine.

There was a section for old electric appliances; there was a section for weapons; there was a section for jewelry, for old clothes, for pots and pans, for "collectibles"; and there was one section for items so strange Manfred could not imagine how they'd be used. Manfred was instantly intrigued by that area. There was a very old book bound in wooden plates; there was a sort of sculpture—structure?—made of twigs bound together at odd angles with purple ribbon; there was a cloudy crystal ball; there was a Ouija board with an endlessly gliding planchette. Manfred felt the hair stand up on his arms. These objects were magic and eerie and subtly dangerous, and yet he felt he could examine them forever. The cases of guns were much less interesting in Manfred's view, though Bobo had told him what a draw they were to other shoppers.

He was vaguely aware that the customer was concluding her transaction with Lemuel. Then, suddenly, she was by Manfred's side. It was no woman, but it was a female creature. She was thin and angular, with eyes black as pitch. Her short hair was just as ebon, and it looked as though it had been cut in the dark with a dull knife. She leaned over to smell Manfred, her tongue flicking out in a most disconcerting manner, and she hissed at him.

Manfred held as still as a mouse hoping a cat will not sense its presence. But she seized his arm.

"Tassssty," she said.

"Glinda," said Lemuel quietly. "No. He's a friend."

The black eyes blinked more than once. Did she have two eye-lids? Manfred did not twitch, much less speak.

"Sssssssshit," she said, and released his arm. The next instant, she was gone.

"Buddy of yours?" Manfred asked, when he was sure his voice would be even.

"I don't think snake shifters have buddies," Lemuel said. "They just know people they haven't tried to eat yet."

"She doesn't try to eat you?"

"They only eat living things," Lemuel said, turning to walk back to the counter. "Did you want to pawn something, buy something, or were you just stretching your legs?"

"A little of taking a work break, a little of wondering about your energy drainage thing," Manfred said, thinking if he didn't say it out loud now he might chicken out.

To his relief, Lemuel smiled. "I should have explained," the cold man said. "As I'm sure you've puzzled out, I'm a sort of vampire. I'm not what has become known in popular literature as a traditional vampire. I can feed on energy or blood or both simultaneously. That's the best meal, but I don't get it often."

"Because the feed-ee dies if you do that?"

"Yes, the one I'm feeding on dies." Lemuel smiled.

"And that night at the diner?"

"The strangers caused me concern. I estimated I might need to be as strong as possible in the near future. I tapped you."

"Why me?" To Manfred, this was the most important question. Not that he wouldn't have to think hard, later, about Lemuel's diet and the fact that Lemuel hadn't given him a choice, but this was the question that had worried him.

"I could tell you were an open-minded person," Lemuel said, pale eyes on some small repair he was making to a piece of jewelry under a magnifying lamp. "Not likely to jump up and scream, 'Oh sweet Jesus, another man is holding my hand!'"

Manfred laughed weakly.

"And I also believed that you would stay here, that you were not passing through, and that it was, therefore, the quickest way to let you know what I was."

Manfred wanted to ask Lemuel if Olivia was his girlfriend, but in Lemuel's presence he could see how silly that would sound. How intrusive.

"You are interested in Creek," Lemuel said unexpectedly.

"She's very attractive," Manfred said cautiously. "I realize she's younger than me, and I'm not going to, ah, initiate anything improper. But I would like to get to know her better."

Lemuel's eyes were almost white, now, when he glanced up. "She is a lovely child," Lemuel said. "But I realize she is on the cusp of becoming a woman. If she decides to become a woman with you, you had better be damned sure she is fully aware and agreeable to every step of the process."

Manfred replied with complete honesty, "I would never do otherwise."

"Then we are not enemies," Lemuel said. "And we may become friends, as I told the snake woman we were."

"When were you born, Lemuel, if I can ask?"

"I was born in 1837," Lemuel said. "My name was not Lemuel then."

"A big adjustment, from then to now," Manfred said, since it was all he could think of to say that wasn't fatuous. But that was fatuous enough.

Lemuel discarded one tool and selected another. "That is true," he agreed. "Good night, psychic."

"Good night, vampire," Manfred said. Since he'd clearly been dismissed, he went home.

20

Bobo was by himself the next morning when Sheriff Smith came in. Normally, he'd have taken Monday off and let Teacher work in his place, but he'd missed enough work, he figured. And he didn't have anything better to do. He'd perched on the stool behind the high counter with a large mug of coffee. He was looking at a piece of jewelry that had been mended, apparently the night before, by Lemuel. The clasp had not worked on the brooch since it had been pawned twenty years before (Bobo had looked it up once in the ancient ledger), but now it did, and the brooch was in the display case that formed the counter, with a new tag on it in Lemuel's curious handwriting. It read, "Twenty dollars. Will be called for."

Bobo held it out, and the sheriff bent over the counter to look at it.

"If you have a lady in your life, she might enjoy something like this, Sheriff," Bobo said. "If she's old-fashioned." The brooch was hand-painted with a picture of yellow flowers in a pale green vase, set against a gray-blue background. The frame was gold, set with tiny pearls.

Bobo wondered if he was about to be arrested. His heart pounded furiously, but he did his best to sound calm.

"I have a wife, my third," Smith answered. "But she doesn't like anything but modern stuff."

"Not a traditional woman, then," Bobo said.

"Not in the best sense of traditional," Smith said. "But traditional in the way that means she expects me to provide everything for her while she sits at home on her butt."

"Children?"

"No, she doesn't even have children to look after," Smith said. "I have a child by another marriage, but she lives in Georgia with her mom."

"I guess you don't get to see her often," Bobo said. "That's sad. What can I do for you today?"

Bobo found himself on the receiving end of one of Arthur Smith's concentrated looks. Sheriff Smith didn't blink much, so the stare was pretty effective.

"You can tell me more about your history with Aubrey Hamilton," the sheriff said. The sheriff turned Bobo's favorite chair to face the counter and settled himself in it. He looked quite at ease. "And by the way, she wasn't shot. Someone wanted us to think she was, or someone was trying to put the blame on you. But we hired a specialist to look at the remains. The hole in her chest was not from a bullet."

Bobo let out a long, unsteady breath.

"You don't seem to be regarding me as a prime suspect in her death any longer," Bobo said, manfully accepting the fact that the sheriff was sitting in his favorite chair. After all, the guy wasn't arresting him for murder. He could have the damn chair. "And since

I've already been into the police station once, you've searched my place, you've told me she wasn't shot so I'm in the clear on the gun, and I have a lawyer on speed dial, I'm wondering what my status is now."

"For the time period in which Ms. Hamilton—well, Mrs. Lowry—must have died . . . if we accept the testimony of Fiji Cavanaugh and your tenant . . . your presence in Dallas has been confirmed," Smith said, sounding neither pleased nor displeased. "We could drum up a charge based on the fact that that gun was supposed to be here and secure, not laying on the ground by a river, but of course we can't prove you were negligent enough to leave it there. It could have been stolen from here, though in that case your security needs some tending. Or your employees Lemuel Bridger or Teacher Reed could have taken it out. Unless more evidence turns up, you're in the clear."

"Wow," said Bobo, as he absorbed this information. "Well, I feel relieved, of course." He shifted around on the stool, not sure where to look.

"You don't sound as happy as I expected."

"I'm not happy," Bobo said. "I loved Aubrey, and she's dead. Not only did I lose her, but I've found out our whole relationship was a lie."

"You believed everything she told you?"

Probably the sheriff was trying to sound neutral, but Bobo caught a hint of incredulity. "You seem to be a skeptical kind of man," he said. "I guess in your line of work, that's inevitable. I have a sister and a mother. They aren't really pleasant women, or very smart . . . but they do tell the truth, as they see it. I know a lot of truthful women. And I guess I'm not conceited enough to imagine women making up elaborate schemes to meet me, like you say Aubrey did. My family's had trouble enough in the past. I don't need any more."

Both men turned to the front door as it flew open.

Fiji came in, skidding to an abrupt stop when she realized both men were sitting calmly. "Oh!" she said. "Ummm, I saw your car outside, Sheriff . . . and I wondered if everything was okay over here."

"As far as I'm concerned," Smith said mildly. "How do you feel, Mr. Winthrop?"

"Call me Bobo. I'm feeling okay, the way things are now," Bobo agreed. He smiled at Fiji, who'd been all wound up to attack and now was floundering to deal with the rush of adrenaline. "You're so great to come to my rescue, Feej. I have the best neighbors."

"We feel the same way about you," she said, almost at random. She'd caught her breath, and now she drew herself up with some dignity. "Okay, you obviously don't need me, so I'll get back to work."

"Hey, let's go to the diner tonight," Bobo suggested out of an obscure sense of obligation. He was relieved when Fiji nodded and spun around to leave, her long skirt swirling around her legs as she pushed out the front door. A gust of wind turned her curly hair into a tornado around her head. *She's a woman full of movement,* he thought.

"Monday. It's not open," she said over her shoulder.

"Then we'll go to the Barbecue Shanty in Davy."

"Okay, come by when you're ready to eat," she called over her shoulder. She obviously wanted to say more, but she bit down on the words.

"Thanks," Bobo called, loud enough for her to hear as the door swung closed behind her. "And that's why I live here," he told the sheriff.

"Because everyone loves you?"

"Oh, I don't think that's true at all," Bobo said. "But we do help each other out."

"To the extent that one of your buddies might kill Aubrey Lowry if they discovered that she was exploiting you?"

Bobo looked stunned. "No, of course not! That's so drastic. Besides, no one knew Aubrey's background until you told us."

Smith looked skeptical, but he didn't press his question. "What was Aubrey like? Did she ever express any extreme political views to you?"

Bobo resigned himself to a painful conversation. "Aubrey was . . . she loved the outdoors. She loved shopping on the Internet. She liked cowboy boots and blue jeans, and she was a barrel rider in her teens. She grew up on a ranch. At least that was what she told me. Was that true?"

Smith nodded. "True."

Bobo looked away for a moment. "Okay, good. Of course, she also talked about her dead parents, and you tell me they're alive. She told me a lot about her nonexistent sister, not a word about the brother you said she actually has. Had. But she never discussed politics. Never said anything extremely right-wing. That would have been a red flag, for sure."

Bobo climbed off the stool and opened a little refrigerator on the floor behind the counter. He asked Arthur Smith if he wanted a Coca-Cola, and Smith said, "No, thanks."

After Bobo got back on his stool and popped the tab on his drink, he said, "I'm assuming you know all about my grandfather."

Sheriff Smith didn't answer. He'd taken off his hat and was twirling it slowly, his fingers working their way around the brim.

"So you do," Bobo said, nodding gently. "Well, I've definitely swung the other way. I'm pro–gay marriage, pro-choice, pro-environment, pro-whales and tuna and wolves and every damn thing you can think of." He put the mended brooch back in the case in front of him and regarded the other man very seriously. "If there's anything in my life I wish I could erase, that time I spent listening to my grandfather spitting out hate would be what I'd pick."

The sheriff looked down at his hat as he said, "You know it's all over the Internet hate groups that you have some fabulous cache of guns and grenades and rocket launchers hidden away somewhere. That you can't get rid of 'em and you can't destroy 'em, so you've hidden them. And all those hate groups feel that you owe them that cache, because of your grandfather's martyr status."

"His legend is bigger than he was," Bobo said, with a kind of sad anger. "I can't show you any such treasure cave." He sighed. "I can't imagine why they think I'd hold on to such a stockpile."

Arthur Smith stood. He was not a tall man, but he was a serious man, and his presence was large. "All right, Bobo. You take care. I'm sorry we had to search your place."

Bobo shrugged, in an unhappy way. "That's okay. I know you had to do it. Her parents have all her stuff?" Two days ago, two deputies had shown up with a warrant to remove Aubrey's belongings. Since they'd all been boxed up and in the pawnshop storage closet, that had been quick enough; but they'd had to comb Bobo's apartment in case he'd forgotten anything.

"Yeah, they've filled out the paperwork. There wasn't anything you wanted?"

"Nah. I've got pictures and memories, and none of her stuff ever belonged to me in any sense. She didn't bring any furniture or appliances, other than the toaster and the air filter and her grandmother's sewing machine. I made sure that went with the other stuff."

"Okay, then. I'll be in touch."

"Thanks. Do you know when the funeral will be?"

"Her parents don't really want you to know, and they don't want you there. I don't know any nice way to tell you that."

Bobo felt like he was shrinking moment by moment. Everything of hers was gone. They'd take her memories from him if they could. He wasn't a person who'd cared about Aubrey, not to them. He was the person who'd ended her life. He shook his head to dispel the sensation. "Well, I won't try to go since they don't want me," he said. "But . . . they know I've got an alibi that held up, right?"

"I made sure they knew," the sheriff said. He seemed sympathetic. "Their good sense hasn't caught up with their grief and anger."

Bobo nodded. He could understand that. "Okay, then. I hope you find out who did this." He didn't think he'd really breathe deeply again until Aubrey's murderer was caught and imprisoned.

Arthur Smith concentrated on his hat brim. "For what it's worth, I believe you. But I have to investigate, and I have to be impartial, and I have to evaluate the evidence on its own. So far, the evidence says you're telling the truth. But if anything I find contradicts that, I'm going to come down on you like a ton of bricks."

"And I'd expect that. Hey, we're bonding." Bobo smiled.

The sheriff smiled back, albeit reluctantly. "You people who live in Midnight. You're all marching to the beat of a different drummer." Hat back on his head and tugged into position, he half turned, ready to leave.

Bobo smiled more broadly. "You hit the nail on the head. We are different, Arthur Smith. I'm the most average person you'll meet here." The smile faded.

The sheriff thought of another question. "And now I've got to go bother some of your neighbors. Is Olivia Charity around? I understand she has an apartment below the store?"

Bobo said, "Yeah. You can see if she's awake, but please knock softly on the door marked B. The guy who rents A works nights, so he sleeps days. That's why he wasn't on the picnic."

"Lemuel Bridger? I haven't met him yet. I definitely need to talk to him. I'm interviewing everyone who knew her. I guess that would naturally include him since he lived in the same building."

"Yes, he knew Aubrey, though I don't think he knew her well.

But you'll have to wait until it's dark. He really can't wake up when he's deep asleep."

Sheriff Smith looked at Bobo, a little skeptically. "Even if I pound on his door, he won't wake up?"

"You really don't want to do that," said Olivia, and the sheriff jumped.

She'd come into the pawnshop from the door that led onto the landing. Her feet were bare, and the rest of her was swathed in a pair of blue fuzzy pajamas decorated with sheep. "I'd be glad to talk to you right now, Sheriff. Did you want to come down to my place? I'm sure Bobo's got things to do."

"That'd be fine." The sheriff followed her to the door to the stairs. He turned before he went through it. "Oh, Bobo? One more thing you ought to know. Aubrey's brother, Macon. He's pretty upset about Aubrey. If you meet him, watch out."

After the door had closed, Bobo said, "Thanks, Sheriff. 'Hey, Bobo, there's this guy who wants to kill you because he thinks you killed his sister. So you watch your step, now!'"

Bobo got off the stool. The sheriff had left the velvet chair facing the counter, so Bobo turned it to face the street door, its proper position. He retrieved a Craig Johnson novel from a nearby piecrust table and settled down to read, the Coca-Cola on a coaster on the table beside him. Somehow, his conversation with Arthur Smith had cleared his mind. He was officially not a suspect. He was not going to be arrested for murder. On the other hand, the publicity about Aubrey's death had resurrected all the gossip about his grandfather, and Aubrey's family hated him, including Aubrey's unknown brother.

"Two steps forward, one step back," Bobo muttered out loud. He glanced up just as a car paused at the stoplight outside, and he smiled as he remembered Fiji dashing to his rescue. It would be nice to go to dinner with her tonight, resume his normal life.

Not his old normal in which the woman he loved had left him because he'd done something awful that he couldn't fathom, the old normal in which he waited to hear from her every day.

It would be the new normal; the world in which Aubrey had never loved him, had told him many lies, and had vanished through violence.

21

The next night, at the diner, the Rev preached after his dinner. He finished his food, patted his lips with his paper napkin, and stood up, turning to face the round table.

In a surprisingly deep, sonorous voice, he began to give them the Word as he interpreted it. Bobo put down his fork and folded his arms across his chest, prepared to listen. Olivia looked down at her plate regretfully and followed suit. On her left, Manfred was just beginning to cut his meat, but Olivia laid a hand on his arm. "Nope," she whispered, not turning her gaze away from the Rev. "Respect."

Another mysterious Midnight rule. Manfred resigned himself to waiting until the Rev was through, but he was peeved. He'd come in late, and he'd just gotten served—sadly, not by Creek, but by Madonna. His food was hot and smelled delicious, but here he sat, still and hungry.

As he listened, Manfred became interested despite himself. This was not the fire-and-brimstone message he'd been expecting, but an elaborate explanation that began with the Garden of Eden, detailing how God had created creatures that combined the features of animals and man, the were-creatures so feared today. The Rev believed that key verses had been deleted from the Bible so that bad men could repress the were-creatures, so that they would be humbled away from their pride in their superiority. The Rev believed that men only had power over the two-natured because of their vast numbers and their willingness to kill what they didn't understand.

It was confusing but fascinating, even though Manfred's mouth was still watering over the baked chicken and green beans with new potatoes that were cooling on his plate. The Rev certainly knew his Bible, and he knew a lot of extra scripture besides, verses that had been "left out." Manfred now heard a few of those verses. "I'm amazed at how convincing that sounds," he whispered to Joe on his left. To Manfred's embarrassment and surprise, Joe seemed offended at his skepticism. Again, Manfred was at a loss.

For five more minutes the Rev rambled, and even Madonna stood behind the counter at attention during the impromptu sermon. Abruptly, the small man came to the end of what he had to say, and he concluded with "Amen!" His congregation echoed the word with varying degrees of enthusiasm. The Rev gave a decided nod, as if he were satisfied with the response. Then he stalked from the diner, his hat firmly planted on his head, his back straight as a ramrod.

"How often does he do that?" Manfred asked, hoping it was okay to inquire.

"Not often. Usually means he's worried about something," Joe said. "I didn't mean to go all righteous on you, but the Rev believes what he says, and we go along with him. You don't want to upset him."

Manfred said, "Of course I don't want to be rude to him . . . but you sound almost scared."

"You would be, too, if you ever saw him angry," Joe said, and then firmly turned the conversation in another direction. "Bobo, I saw the sheriff's car at your place yesterday. Everything okay?"

"The sheriff said they're satisfied with my alibi. Apparently, I'm in the clear." Bobo didn't look particularly happy, though. "And here's another thing," he said. "The gun, the one they found? It was from the shop, which I knew when they held it up. That day we found her."

Everyone around the table froze for a moment. But Manfred got the distinct impression this was not news to several of the people at the table.

"But Smith said she wasn't shot," Bobo added.

Manfred said, "Great, man. Congratulations." Then he realized that this was not the happiest wording, and he ate another bite of chicken. *This is one of those nights I wish I'd stayed at home and opened a can of soup,* he thought.

"What happened to her?" Joe asked Bobo. "Did the sheriff say?"

Manfred glanced up in time to see Bobo shake his head.

"So, you're in the clear. Why are you so grim?" Olivia asked bluntly.

"Her family doesn't want me at the funeral." Bobo looked down at his plate. He mauled a potato with his fork.

Olivia went steely. "They can't stop you if you want to go," she said. "We'll all go."

Joe leaned forward, looked at each person at the table in turn. His eyes were very serious. "Do we want to make a terrible day worse for them? If Chuy were here, that's what he'd be saying."

There was an awkward silence. "No, we don't want to do that," Olivia said. "But if Bobo's been cleared . . ."

"Smith told me he had let them know I didn't kill her, but that they were still bitter," Bobo said.

No one had a response to that. Manfred was able to finish his meal in peace.

Lemuel had not come in to sit with them that night. Fiji had taken home enough leftovers from her barbecue meal the night before that she was having her dinner at home. Chuy was visiting his brother in Fort Worth, so Joe had brought Rasta with him to the diner. The dog sat quietly in a compact circle by Joe's chair. Joe was rigid about no one feeding him from the table.

Shawn Lovell had come in to get three to-go meals, and he'd given everyone a casual wave before carrying the bag of take-out containers back to the service station. Only Manfred, Bobo, Olivia, and Joe were left after the preacher exited.

As he finished his meal, Manfred wondered how Madonna managed to keep the diner doors open. But he was sure glad she did.

"I'm going to Fiji's class on Thursday night," he said. "I couldn't say no. Anyone else want to try it out?"

"Sorry, I'm just not in the mood for strangers," Bobo said, and Manfred felt a stab of envy that he had a good excuse.

"I have to pack," Olivia said. "I have an early flight Friday."

"Chuy is coming back on Thursday," Joe said. "Sorry, buddy, seems like you're flying solo."

"Great," Manfred said. He had already been kicking himself for agreeing to go to Fiji's class, which would undoubtedly be all mystical kumbaya and talk of every woman's inner goddess.

On Thursday evening, Manfred was kicking himself even harder. The women gathered in Fiji's store ranged in age from twenty-one to sixty. A couple of the younger women had made an effort to look "witchy" in black dresses or leggings, heavy black eyeliner, and dyed black hair—Goth with pentagrams, he told himself. The older women tended to the scarves-and-skirts style of witchiness, though one lady in her early forties was cinched into a black leather bustier and a black lace skirt, with huge silver earrings swaying from her multiply pierced ears. Manfred felt like he'd come to a bad costume party, especially when the women stood to form a circle and held hands to begin their meditation. "The full moon will make tonight an especially favorable one for self-enlightenment," Fiji told the group before she began the invocation.

Manfred had never linked his psychic ability to witchcraft, and he had no particular religious beliefs. Fiji's directions to implore Hecate to help those present develop their powers left him just a bit bored and faintly contemptuous. He had no idea who Hecate was. Only his certainty that Fiji herself possessed real power kept him in the store and holding the right hand of the forty-something would-be hottie and the left hand of a white-haired grandmother in a sweeping skirt.

While Fiji implored and invoked, Manfred did the mental math about what he'd clear that month, and then abruptly his brain took a left turn down a dead-end road. He found himself catching a glimpse of the awful corpse of Aubrey Hamilton. As Fiji's singsong voice went on and on, Aubrey's skull, with its hanks of ragged hair, rotated toward him. The darkened teeth moved under their remnants of flesh and muscle. Horribly dead Aubrey said, "I truly loved him. Tell him."

Manfred's eyes flew open and he looked up to meet Fiji's. She was looking at him steadily, as if she knew he'd had a true and direct communication. She smiled. And then her eyes shut and her head dropped again, and Manfred was left to compose a grocery list for his next trip to Davy to stave off any other unwanted revelations. As long as he told himself over and over again that he needed orange juice, bread, and peanut butter, plus lightbulbs, he could keep the dreadful vision at bay.

After those few seconds of freezing fear, he was bored silly. Two of the gray-haired women employed the Ouija board, which told them they were never too old for love. After that, there was a round of dream interpretation, though Manfred figured cynically that most of the dreams had been constructed well after the sleep session. If there was anyone approaching Fiji's talent there that night, Manfred could not detect it. Since he always watched the money flow, he'd noticed right away that Fiji kept a pretty blue bowl on the counter, and he also noticed all the women dropped twenty dollars in it discreetly before they paraded out the door, chattering excitedly about astral projections and ley lines.

Fiji stood on her porch smiling after them, pleased with the evening and with herself, as far as Manfred could tell.

"Was that a typical class?" Manfred asked, making sure his tone was polite and respectful.

Possibly he hadn't succeeded, because Fiji looked a bit taken aback.

"I would say so," she said. "You got a true reading, didn't you?"

"I had a vision," he said, reluctantly. "At least, I guess it was a vision."

"Tell me about it, if it wasn't too personal."

"It wasn't personal at all. It was a message for someone else." He described the brief scene. When Fiji heard about Aubrey's corpse talking, she shuddered.

"Do you think I should tell him?" Manfred asked.

"Of course," Fiji said immediately. But she looked anything but happy. "If you have a true vision, you should tell the person involved. He'll be glad to hear that . . . if he believes you."

"People mostly believe what they want to," Manfred observed. "My whole business is based on that principle. How do you square this class with that piece of truth?"

Fiji's round face was sad, and Manfred felt at once as though he'd kicked a puppy. After a moment, she returned to the easy chair she'd occupied during the "class." She crossed her legs, and her boot-clad foot swung back and forth. "It's like teaching ballet," she said. "Or piano." She looked very serious.

Manfred laughed. "You mean, ninety-nine percent of the students have no aptitude at all, but you keep doing it for the one student who has talent?"

"Exactly," she said. She thought that over and nodded some more. "Plus, it gives them something to do, something to think about besides the here and now. That's not a bad thing, either."

"You sound like they were all fuzzy kittens," Manfred said. "Don't you ever worry about them doing harm with what you're teaching them?"

"Meditation? Planchette work? Dream interpretation?"

"Witchcraft? Spells? Blood magic?"

"I don't teach them that," Fiji said indignantly.

"But it's the next step. They'll look at your books, ask you questions about your own spells, your own beliefs, and next thing you know . . ."

He could tell from the way she hunched her shoulders that this had already happened. "The next thing I know, *what*?" she snapped.

"You'll have a dead husband or an enslaved boyfriend," Manfred said, speaking what he knew to be the unpleasant truth. From the corner of his eye, he saw the marmalade cat with the stupid name leap up from its cushion to stare at him. "I like you, Fiji, and I hope we're getting to be friends . . . but if you don't think about the next step, you're being irresponsible." He shrugged and opened the front door. "Thanks for inviting me. See you later." He couldn't think of anything else to say, and Fiji didn't open her mouth. After a moment of standing there feeling like a fool, and a jerk, Manfred left.

As he crossed the road, which was shockingly visible under the full moon, he chewed over his last pronouncement to Fiji. Though he was sorry they were at cross purposes, he still believed he'd spoken the truth. He gave a mental shrug, shoving the problem to the back burner. He noticed that Olivia's car was gone from the rear of the pawnshop, and he was surprised she wasn't home packing for her trip. Then he noticed that the pawnshop was closed. Lemuel ought to be in there. Well, that was strange but none of his business. As he was unlocking his front door, he glanced back to see Mr. Snuggly sitting at the edge of the yard, watching him.

22

Fiji stood on her porch for a minute in the chilly night air, admiring the moonlight and the peace of the night. It felt good after the stuffiness of the store with all the witch-wannabes crowded inside, all their chatter and busyness.

She was a little disappointed in Manfred's negative reaction. He'd definitely had a real vision there tonight, no matter how superior he tried to act. "Self-righteous idiot," Fiji muttered as she locked her front door, but she was not truly angry. She hadn't really expected an enthusiastic participation. Nonetheless, she admitted to herself that she would have been happy to have an older witch around, someone she could talk to about how Manfred's opinion made her feel.

She decided she would think about it the next day, when she was rested . . . and calm. As she turned off lights in the big front room, her thoughts moved from one troubling topic to another. When she'd been down at the Antique Gallery and Nail Salon to look at a small round table Joe had thought might interest her, Joe had told her that the Rev had preached at Home Cookin on Tuesday night. The Rev preached when he was worried. When the Rev was worried, there was cause for concern.

Mr. Snuggly came in the cat flap in the back door after Fiji had put on her nightgown and brushed her teeth. He ran into the room as she pulled down the sheets.

"He got home okay?" she asked the cat. Mr. Snuggly stared up at her without expression . . . naturally. "Of course he did," Fiji answered herself. "Or you'd have come in a lot quicker. Well, let's turn in, Snug. It's been a long day." The room was furnished with her great-aunt's bedroom set, though Fiji had stripped the wood of its chipped varnish and painted it sky blue. The walls were painted white, and the throw rugs on the floor were bright and colorful. It was a cheerful room, and Fiji was always glad when the time came for her to sleep in it. She went through her usual nighttime routine before climbing onto the high bed, pulling up the covers to relax with a clean face and a fairly clear conscience. Mr. Snuggly jumped up to curl at her side. Fiji fell asleep with her fingers in the cat's fur.

She remained asleep two hours later when something big brushed up against the outside of the house. Mr. Snuggly was awake, though, his golden eyes wide and unblinking as they followed the progress of the creature on the other side of the wall. When it paused outside Fiji's window, Mr. Snuggly hissed, his ears flattened back on his head. But after a few seconds, the cat heard huge feet padding away. Mr. Snuggly lay awake for a few minutes, staring into the darkness, to see if the creature would return. When it did not, he put his head down on his paws and slid back into sleep.

The same creature visited every inhabited house in Midnight, sniffing at the air, inspecting the doors and windows. It spent the longest time giving its attention to the trailer in which Madonna and Teacher lived with their baby. There, it rumbled, deep in its throat. But no one woke.

23

The next morning, Bobo turned on the local radio station while he was making toast for breakfast. The big area news was about a fire outside Marthasville, and Bobo found himself standing, knife poised over the butter tub, while he listened.

"Arson investigators for Pioneer County are at the site of a blaze at a ranch house owned by Price Eggleston, thirty-two, of Marthasville. Eggleston said he and his friends used the house as a hunting lodge and that no one should have been in the building at the time of the blaze. Chief arson investigator Sally Kilpatrick said she'd turn in her findings to the sheriff as soon as her investigation is complete. In other news, rancher Cruz Vasquez, in the Cactus Flats community south of Midnight, reported that one of his cows was killed by a wild animal . . ."

Price Eggleston. He'd heard that name before, hadn't he?

As usual, by the time Bobo went downstairs, Lemuel had been asleep in his apartment for over an hour. Bobo reopened the shop, turned on the lights, and sat down to read the customer register that Lemuel insisted they keep, though everything was entered on the computer as it ought to be. Lemuel had had two customers during the later part of the night, but that wasn't what Bobo was checking for.

Yes, Price Eggleston had been in the store a few weeks ago. Bobo had a good memory (one better than he wanted, actually), and he recalled the man clearly once he saw his register. Eggleston had come in with an antique gun he'd wanted to pawn. The whole time he was in the shop, Eggleston had looked around constantly, as if he expected to see someone in the corners. Then he'd haggled over the money he could get for the weapon, but with a suspicious lack of fire. The gun was worth something, though it was no fine family heirloom. In fact, it needed some work to be usable. Eggleston had suggested Bobo restore the gun.

"I don't know anything about working on guns," Bobo had replied, surprised. "You'll have to get someone else to do the work. You'd get a lot more money for it if you have it cleaned up and in working order."

Eggleston had looked at him sharply and with some contempt. "All right, then," he'd said, clearly angry, and he'd accepted the low price Bobo had offered. The more Bobo thought of the conversation, the more clearly he could recall Eggleston. The man had been tall and tan, his face broad across the cheeks and narrow at the chin. Cowboy boots, jeans, western shirt. He'd been wearing a ball cap, not a western hat.

Bobo felt as though he should tell someone about Eggleston's visit, but he couldn't think why, when he got right down to it. Since he was alone in the shop, he sat at the computer and Googled "Price Eggleston."

After five minutes of reading, Bobo was pretty happy that the man's "hunting lodge" had burned down. He was only theoretically sorry that Eggleston hadn't burned along with it.

A couple came in to see if there were any old wedding rings that might work for them, and for half an hour Bobo was busy taking out the cases of rings (some of them had been sitting in the worn velvet slots for longer than he'd been alive) and showing them to the middle-aged couple, who seemed charmed by the assortment. They actually bought silver bands, and he entered the sale carefully. He was glad to see them smile at each other as they left the pawnshop.

Bobo had plenty to think about when he was alone once more. He reviewed his memory of Price Eggleston's visit to the shop. In hindsight, Bobo became convinced that the man had wanted a look at him. He was sure that Eggleston had deliberately tried to provoke a discussion about firearms, perhaps to see if Bobo actually liked guns, was adept in their care and maintenance.

Or maybe, to have a legitimate reason to meet Bobo, Eggleston had grabbed the nearest object someone might be likely to take to a pawnshop.

Bobo had to abandon this rearview reassessment when the bell over the door rang. An old, old woman came in. She moved oddly, and something about her made the hairs on Bobo's arms tingle, and not in a pleasant way. This was surely one of Lemuel's customers. She sidled through the shelves and the furniture as if she wasn't able to walk in a straight line, and her stringy long hair, which was as many shades of gray as a cloudy sky, slid around her face.

"Are you the current proprietor of this establishment?" she asked, rolling the words around in her mouth as if she were pleased to be saying them, glad to exhibit a skill she didn't often exercise.

"I am," Bobo said. Perhaps Olivia might come up? She knew more about the night customers than Bobo did. But then he recalled he'd seen her getting into her car from his apartment window, right after he'd gotten out of bed, and he realized she'd been leaving for the airport.

Well . . . okay. He could handle one old woman, even if she did give him the creeps. Wasn't he tired of being rescued all the time? *No*, he decided as she grew closer and he could see her more clearly. *No, I'm not. I'd love it if someone else came in right now. Fiji, Manfred, Chuy, Connor, anybody.*

"I'm sure you are wondering who I am and why I've come to patronize your store," she crooned.

"Yes," he said. That was all he could manage.

"I mean you no harm," she said unconvincingly. "I understand that you are a friend of Lemuel's and of Emilio's."

Emilio. Bobo was stumped for a second. "The Rev," he said. "The Reverend Sheehan."

"Yes, of course." She was right up in his face by that time, and he could see a lot of detail. The view was not encouraging. The lines in her cheeks were deep enough to look etched, and she smelled like dirt and rain. "I could not wait until tonight to pick up the brooch Lemuel repaired for me."

Bobo felt a certain measure of relief. She was a legitimate customer. She wanted something tangible. She wasn't going to rip his throat out and feed him to the dogs. (Where had *that* image come from?) "Yes," he said, hoping that this was the right customer. "I think the brooch you're talking about is right here in the case." The pretty one he'd been showing Arthur Smith, it had to be. Bobo found he was incredibly pleased to be behind a counter, which provided a handy bulwark between him and . . . "I'm sorry, I don't know your name," he said.

The thick gray brows rose. "And so you don't," she said. "You may call me Maggie."

"Nice to make your acquaintance, Miss Maggie," he said, and she actually cackled with laughter. He'd never heard anyone cackle before. It was as unpleasant as he'd always imagined. Bobo's hands weren't completely steady, but he managed to reach under the glass counter to extricate the brooch. He looked at the little tag Lemuel had attached to double-check his memory. "That'll be twenty dollars, Miss Maggie."

"Oh, that's dear," the hag moaned, shaking her head. (He thought she might say "Tut, tut," but she didn't.) "Oh, that's such a price!" She cast a sly glance at Bobo to see if he was going to negotiate. He gave her a level stare. "However, Lemuel does wonderful work, and he's such a sweet boy," she said, seeing that Bobo wasn't going to cave.

Lemuel had been a boy well over a century and a half ago, by Bobo's quick estimation. The odds were good that Lemuel had been sweet to someone, at some point. "He's repaired it," Bobo said agreeably. "Worth every penny."

She groped around inside her clothes for the money, a sight Bobo could have lived without. Eventually, she handed him twenty one-dollar bills, incredibly rumpled and soiled. She grasped the brooch as soon as he accepted the money, and she pinned it to her chest with fingers shaking with eagerness.

Suddenly, in front of him was a lovely, straight-backed woman in her forties, a woman wearing a dress with a tight bodice and full skirt. She was wearing heels, too, instead of the cracked flats Maggie had worn into the store. Her glossy brown hair was put up in a French thing—he couldn't remember what his sister had called it—on the back of her head. There was a mirror propped against one of the columns in the store, and she sprang over to eye her reflection.

"I look lovely," she said, and at least her voice was the same.

"Yes, ma'am," he agreed. "You look great."

She gave him a gleaming sideways look. "Oh, you're just the cutest thing! If you weren't off-limits, I would just *eat you up*."

"Sorry, I'm off those limits," he responded with as much of a smile as he could manage, spreading his hands in deprecation. "Thanks for your patronage, come again." He didn't mean that, but the words rolled out of his mouth from long habit. He picked up his cell phone, punched speed dial at random, and when Fiji answered, he said, "Lemuel! I just wanted you to know that Maggie came in today to pick up her brooch. She's pleased with your repair. I know you'll get this the second you wake up." He disconnected instantly before Fiji could start talking, since he had no idea how acute Maggie's hearing was.

Maggie was looking a bit hangdog. "Well, if you're going to be like that," she said pettishly, "I'll say good-bye."

"Good-bye, Miss Maggie." He put as much finality into his voice as he could and still be on the side of courtesy. He didn't think Maggie would react well if he were rude.

The door tinkled as she left, and he heaved a huge sigh of relief. He waited for Fiji to show up, as she did a minute later.

"Sorry I had to do that," Bobo said instantly. "I had a hinky customer in here. I figured if she was sure someone else knew she'd been here, she'd leave me alone."

"She must have been pretty quick on her feet!" Fiji looked around in confusion. "I didn't see anyone come out."

"She did, though. She was scary as hell. Lemuel had told her to come back to pick up her jewelry at night—I don't know how, because that brooch had been here at least twenty years, from the tag it had the last time I looked at it—but she didn't do that."

"Are you gonna tell him?"

"Absolutely. Though it does seem like I'd be tattling to Daddy, doesn't it?" Bobo shook his head. "On the other hand, Lemuel will see that the brooch is gone." He was relieved to have a valid (uncowardly) reason to tell the vampire about Maggie's visit. Lemuel's customers should come at night, as he bid them, in Bobo's view.

"I'm going to work on a circle of protection for you," Fiji said, her mouth compressed in a tight line. She was staring off into the distance, but when she focused on Bobo, her expression softened. "I know you don't believe that'll really protect you," she said. "But it can't hurt, can it?"

"Any help gladly accepted," Bobo said hastily. He didn't want to hurt Fiji's feelings. She was a generous woman, and (though he'd never said this to her) she always smelled good—like laundry hung out on the line, a smell he remembered from childhood—and she looked soft and warm, like a comforter you really wanted to draw on top of you on a cold night.

The front door had not closed completely when Fiji entered, and Mr. Snuggly glided in. He went right to the spot where Maggie had stood holding the brooch, and he sniffed very thoroughly. Then he yowled.

"That's one smart cat," Bobo said respectfully. He liked all mammals; dividing the world into cat lovers and dog lovers had always seemed weird to him.

"You have no idea," Fiji muttered. Mr. Snuggly looked up at Fiji with a bland expression and yawned, having told them how he felt about Maggie. He began to pad around the store, looking and sniffing with great curiosity.

Bobo hoped Mr. Snuggly wouldn't try to sharpen his claws on any of the furniture. But the cat seemed pleased to do an inspection tour without testing any of the upholstery. Finally, he stopped in front of a shelf of new items—well, items new to the store—and meowed. Fiji had been watching the cat's progress, too, and she went to his side.

"What is it?" she asked the cat. He looked up at her, then at something on the shelves. Bobo was at a right angle to the cat and couldn't decide what Mr. Snuggly was eyeing so intently. Fiji, however, picked the cat up and said, "Are you showing me the old camera?"

For a moment, Bobo expected the cat would reply. Instead, Mr. Snuggly reached out a golden paw and touched the back of the camera. To Bobo's surprise, Fiji put the cat down and turned the camera around, opening its interior.

"Come look," she called, and Bobo went over. He looked inside. Though the overhead lights were none too bright, he could see something small and electronic with a green light.

"What is it?"

"It's some kind of surveillance equipment, I assume. When did this item come in?"

"The camera's been here for years. A girl was fiddling with it a couple of days ago, I think. She just came in to look around. Said she needed some furniture." He scrambled to remember more about her. "She was real young, and she told me she was a newlywed, said she got married at the Rev's chapel. She finally bought a drying rack. She used a debit card."

"Really." Fiji's eyes narrowed. "Huh. Did she have brown hair and bad teeth?"

"Yeah," Bobo said, with undisguised surprise.

"Okay," Fiji said. "I guess I need to have a talk with her. You got an address?"

Bobo went back behind the counter and looked on the computer. "Here," he said. "Here it is."

The girl's name was Lisa Gray and she lived in Marthasville.

"What a surprise," Fiji said.

Bobo said, "Do you know you're snarling? You know this girl?"

"Yes. I was at her wedding."

"What should I do with this thing?" Bobo regarded the electronic item dubiously. "Smash it? Sell it? Put it in the bathtub?"

"I already took care of that," Fiji told him. "It's still broadcasting, but it can't hear our voices."

She sounded very sure. "But if it can, it knows where we're going," he said.

"We?"

"Yeah. We're going to talk to this girl. We're going to find out why she did this. She sure didn't look like any spy to me."

"I know you feel like you need to go do this. But . . . well, I guess I can't talk you out of it."

"No," Bobo said. "I'll see you at six."

He walked with her to the door. She picked up Mr. Snuggly as she crossed the road, and put him down when they'd reached her yard. The woman and the cat went up the walkway together side by side, and she looked down at the cat. He saw her lips move. Bobo smiled. She was talking to it.

"You deserve a whole can of tuna," Fiji was telling Mr. Snuggly as she opened her front door. "Let's get you one."

"About damn time," said Mr. Snuggly.

24

At six o'clock, Bobo picked up Fiji and they set out to the address Lisa Gray had given when she'd bought the drying rack. Bobo had already entered it into his GPS.

He didn't feel much like talking on the way to Marthasville. He was bracing himself for an unpleasant confrontation. When he rang the doorbell of the dilapidated rental house, in the middle of a row of identical dilapidated rentals, the girl he remembered from the pawnshop answered the door.

He glanced over at Fiji, and she nodded. This was the girl whose wedding she'd witnessed. From the way her tight T-shirt fit, Bobo was as sure as shooting that Lisa was expecting a baby.

Lisa's reaction to seeing them was a dead giveaway. She was scared; more than that, she clearly felt guilty when she looked at him.

"I'm sorry," she said in a rush. "Mister, I'm really sorry." She stepped back to let them in.

Feeling old and sad, Bobo stepped in after Fiji. It was no surprise that the rent house was small, or that it was in ill repair, or that Lisa and her new husband didn't have much. It was a surprise that the living room was not only neat, but clean. The only sign of activity was a huge basket half full of laundry.

There was an ancient green Naugahyde couch in front of the big (and new) television, which was tuned to a game show. An old cushioned armchair was at one end of the newly polished coffee table. Lisa instantly switched off the TV and gestured to them to sit down on the couch.

The already-folded clothes from the basket were on the chipped coffee table, along with magazines, a romance novel, and a box of tissues.

Lisa sat in the flowered armchair. After her guests were settled, she muttered, "Okay, I did a bad thing. I don't know how else to say it."

Bobo felt his store of righteous anger seeping away. He said, more gently than he had intended, "Lisa, I know you remember Fiji from your wedding. And maybe you remember me; you put a spy camera in my shop without telling me. Fiji tells me your husband's name is Cole. Did he know what you were doing?"

"No, sir. And he's at work now. Today is my day off."

"Then I'm glad we caught you at home," Bobo said. He paused, tried to think of how to phrase what he wanted to say. "You seem like a nice young woman. I don't know why you'd cooperate with a man who wanted to do something illegal." It was illegal, wasn't it, to tape someone's activities in their own place of business, without their consent?

Lisa looked miserable. She pulled some T-shirts from the basket and began to fold them, as if she had to be busy.

"Here's what happened," she said, not looking at either of them, concentrating on the garments she was folding with speed and precision. "One of Cole's daddy's friends came by, said he'd heard Cole and I had gotten married in Midnight. He'd also heard we have a baby on the way." She glanced up, as if to see their reaction. Fiji and Bobo both nodded. "So he said he figured we needed money, and I said, 'Sure.' Cole's got a job at Western Auto, and I got a job at Dairy Queen, and we're doing . . . okay."

"Okay" must be the new "barely scraping by," Bobo thought.

Lisa put aside the stack of folded T-shirts and started on the underwear with no self-consciousness at all. "But we got a baby due in five months. Babies need a lot of stuff. Our folks are just barely paying their bills, and my sister's still using all her baby clothes and furniture. So when he told me he'd give me two hundred dollars if I just put a little transmitter thing inside an old camera in your store, I said I would. He said he was trying to catch you selling drugs, that he owned the pawnshop."

"You knew he was lying," Fiji said sternly.

"Yes, ma'am, I did figure he . . ." And tears started to roll down her face. "I apologize, I really do. Please don't send me to jail."

Fiji looked startled. *She has a soft heart,* thought Bobo. *She never even thought about that.*

"Lisa, I won't send a pregnant woman to jail if I can help it," Bobo said. "But I can't say that I'm happy with you, either. You did a bad thing, the kind of thing that can get you hurt, or locked up, and you did it knowing you were wrong." He shook his head, and Lisa's tears accelerated.

"I did," she said, with the air of one facing a firing squad. "The Devil tempted me, and I gave in." She grabbed up a clean T-shirt and blotted her face with it.

"What's the name of this man who came by here, Cole's daddy's friend?" Bobo said. And there wasn't any sympathy in his voice at all. He knew giving her sympathy would just make the girl weep again.

"I shouldn't tell you," she said.

"You owe Bobo that, at the very least," Fiji said. "Also, you can keep your mouth shut about our visit. You kept your mouth shut about what you put in the pawnshop, after all."

Lisa looked as though she were at the end of her tether. She made a helpless gesture with her hands. "It was Mr. Eggleston, him that owns the real estate agency and the lawn service company," Lisa said. She used another tissue to blow her nose.

Bobo said, "We'll leave now, but I'm counting on you to keep this to yourself. It's for your own good. You don't want to get drawn into this any deeper."

"I will," Lisa said. "I ain't gonna say a word to Mr. Eggleston." She rose, and they rose with her. "Like I said, I never want to get mixed up in anything like this again." Her nose reddened as if she were about to cry again.

Bobo gave Lisa a steady look. He'd come loaded for bear, but all he could summon up now was pity. From the dilapidated rental house to the visible pregnancy to the low-paying jobs, it seemed that life had stacked the chips against Lisa Gray Denton. At the same time . . .

"You really don't want to be involved in this, Lisa," he said, and the girl looked at him with wide eyes. For a moment they gave each other a very direct look. Lisa turned to go to the door. She opened it for them, standing aside to let them pass. As they left, she wiped her cheeks again with her sleeve.

"I'm glad I came with you," Bobo said, as he backed out of the graveled area in front of the little house.

"Why?" Fiji asked, surprised and a bit indignant. "I could have done this by myself. She came clean right away, she was hardly threatening . . . she's just a baby expecting a baby."

"Feej, she was *lying*," he said. "I don't know if it was her being poor or her being pregnant or her crying that threw you off, but nothing she told us was the truth."

Fiji felt like someone had let the air out of her tires. "Seriously?"

He paid more attention to the road ahead than it probably needed. "Yeah, seriously."

"Why are you so sure?" She tried to keep the incredulity out of her voice.

"I don't always know when women are lying," he said painfully. "Like Aubrey. But this girl was just like my sister when she was trying to put one over on my mom and dad. She played the 'pitiful' card, she left out a lot of information, and any newlywed would surely have told this 'Mr. Eggleston picked on me' story to her husband."

"Unless her husband worked for Mr. Eggleston," Fiji said defensively.

"Could be," Bobo said, shrugging.

"But you believe she planted the bug because . . ."

"Because she's as right-wing as he is? Because he gave her a lot of money and she didn't think she'd get caught? Because her husband belongs to Eggleston's group? Take your pick." Bobo almost shrugged again. "Any or all."

Fiji looked straight ahead. "I'm just mad at myself now for being so gullible. I thought she was so young and remorseful," she said.

"I'm sure she is. But she's other stuff, too."

Fiji was silent for a while. When they were well east of Marthasville, she said, "I don't know you as well as I thought I did, Bobo."

He found himself smiling. "Maybe that's a good thing," he said. "Have you heard any more about the fire that took out Eggleston's alleged hunting lodge?"

"Are we going to stop there? I know where it is. It'll be coming up here on the right; the iron sign over the gate says 'MOL.'"

She'd surprised him again. "How do you know that?" he asked.

"Well . . . Olivia and Manfred and I spent a night over at the Cartoon Saloon," she said. "We needed some background."

Bobo gave her a long look.

She said hastily, "Yesterday, a customer of mine from Marthasville e-mailed me to see if her order had come in. She'd been working overtime on an arson investigation and hadn't had time to come to the store. I asked her how the investigation was going, because I knew whose place had burned, I heard it on the news. She told me it was Price Eggleston's 'hunting lodge.' She put that in quotes. Anyway, she said they'd found evidence that two people had set the fire." She looked at Bobo expectantly.

Bobo wasn't sure what he was supposed to conclude. "I wonder how the arson investigator figured that out? That the fire was set by two people?"

"Footprints, I think. Though how you could say, 'These are the footprints of the arsonists,' I don't know. But they found a cell phone, some other stuff, that belonged to Curtis Logan and Seth Mecklinberg, the two guys from Lubbock who went missing. Allegedly."

"You're telling me that Olivia and Lemuel . . ."

She nodded. "It's like having evil superhero friends, huh?"

He shook his head helplessly. "I can't even figure out how I feel about that," he said. "I didn't want to be beaten up. I didn't kill them. But on the other hand . . ."

"I understand," Fiji said. "Hey, there's the gate." Today it stood open. In the daylight, it was easy to see the crudely paved driveway running over a hill. They followed it. Down in a gentle dip stood an old ranch house, surrounded by yet another fence, a suspiciously high palisade fence.

"That's pretty unusual," Bobo said. "You just see wire fences around ranch houses, to keep the livestock out of the yard."

But the fence wasn't an obstacle, since this gate, too, was open. It was also scorched and sagging from its post.

Bobo said, "I'm going in." Fiji nodded.

It was especially rocky out here, and sparse vegetation told Bobo that there was almost no topsoil. The house had been an average-size ranch-style house with a stone chimney and foundation, and the lower part of the walls had been stone. Those were still standing. The wood in between had been consumed, and the roof was mostly gone, too.

There was a mute violence about the burned house.

A certain awareness of what had happened here crept over Bobo.

"There was a fingerprint on a gasoline can," Fiji said. "Curtis Logan's fingerprint. And a receipt from a gas station, turned out to be Seth Mecklinberg's debit card was the one used."

"She told you all that? She must be one indiscreet arson investigator."

Fiji said, "She's lonely, and I acted interested. Also, it wasn't an act."

"Wonder what would have happened if there'd been people in there," Bobo said. "Would they have gone through with it?"

They didn't talk much all the way back to Midnight.

25

Manfred was busy with the woes of an eighty-year-old man from Arizona when his cell phone buzzed. He ignored it, of course, but after he'd told the man he'd find companionship at a church (fairly safe advice), he checked the listing. He whooped out loud. Then he sat for a moment, composing himself, before he hit "Call."

"Manfred," Creek said, sounding almost shy. "Thanks for calling me back. I got your phone number from Fiji."

"Not at all," he said, and then winced. *That made no sense!* he thought. "What can I do for you, Creek?"

"I was hoping you needed to go to Davy today? I need a ride to the Kut N Kurl salon."

"You don't have your driver's license yet?"

"Dad has to take Connor to a doctor's appointment. I usually do that, but the doctor will want to talk to Dad. So he'll need the truck."

"I'll be glad to take you," Manfred said. "Do you have an appointment?"

"At three. Is that at all . . . ?"

"I'll stop by the service station to pick you up at two thirty."

"Thanks, M . . . Manfred." She'd been about to call him Mr. Bernardo. He had a lot of remedial work to do.

At two twenty-seven, Manfred pulled in at Gas N Go. There were no customers at the moment. Inside, Shawn was shelving motor oil. Creek was sitting on a stool behind the register, and she grinned when he came in. Shawn gave Manfred a grim look.

"Hey, Shawn," Manfred said, doing his best to sound casual and responsible. "I had to go to Davy this afternoon, anyway, so it's no trouble for me to give Creek a ride."

"All right," Shawn said heavily. He straightened up and looked at Manfred without much enthusiasm. "Teacher Reed's coming over to take care of this place. I'm leaving as soon as Connor gets home on the bus. His doctor is over in Marthasville. Be sure and have Creek home by six. She needs to watch Connor."

"She'll be back by then for sure," Manfred said. How much watching could Connor need? The boy was fourteen. "You ready, Creek?"

"Yeah, I'm ready," she said, sliding off the stool and walking around the counter. "Thanks for giving me a ride, Mr. Bernardo. Dad, see you later."

"Okay, Creek," Shawn said grudgingly. "You got enough money?"

"Yes, sir."

Shawn couldn't think of any other reason to delay Creek's departure, so Manfred held the door open for the girl and she flew out of the store.

Creek didn't wait for him to open the car door for her but scrambled inside as if she feared her father would stop her from going to Davy at the last minute. Manfred buckled up as quickly as he could, and looked both ways about ten times before he pulled out onto the Davy highway. If Shawn was watching—pretty much a sure thing—Manfred wanted to be sure he saw how responsibly Manfred would drive with Creek in the car.

"Relief!" said Creek.

"Relief?"

"Getting out of Midnight for a little while. Well, actually, getting away from my dad for a little while."

"You're at the age when most kids separate from their parents," he agreed.

"Okay, I won't call you 'Mr. Bernardo' again, and you don't call me 'kid.'"

"Deal. What I was going to say is, sorry you didn't get to leave for college like you were supposed to. Joe and Chuy told me about that."

She shrugged. Her dark hair swung forward to obscure her expression. "Yeah, I hope I can still get the scholarship. I was all set to go."

"What happened?"

She shrugged again. "It's a long, boring story. Some paperwork didn't make it on time. Is it true you're a telephone psychic?"

Manfred started to shrug and tell her that was a long, boring story, but he thought he'd come off as too sarcastic. "My grand-mother was a psychic, too," he said. "My mom . . . the talent skipped her. She became the polar opposite. She's become so down to earth and normal that it hurts to talk to her."

"So where does she live?"

"In Tennessee," he said. "I grew up in Tennessee. I lived with my grandmother a lot of the time."

"I haven't seen my grandmother . . ." Creek began, and then she trailed off. "I don't ever see my grandparents."

Manfred was not a mind-reader, at least not consistently or casually, but he'd been trained to be observant. Creek had not planned on ending the sentence that way. She'd almost said something completely different, something that would have revealed a lot about Lovell family life. Manfred was wise enough not to push, though. "Where's this hair place you're going to?" he asked. Visibly relieved at the change in the conversation, Creek gave him directions. Kut N Kurl was in an add-on structure attached to a house in a humble part of Davy. *Not that Davy has many grand parts*, Manfred thought. Until he pulled up in front of the house, their conversation was steady but impersonal. It was a start, he figured.

"How long do you think you'll be?" Manfred asked as Creek opened the car door.

"Usually takes an hour," she said. "Minnie might be running late. There are magazines to read, so don't worry if your own errands run longer. I'll be watching out the window."

Manfred could tell from the smile on Creek's face that getting her hair cut was a treat. That seemed a little sad. Maybe Creek just enjoyed the rare afternoon being in the society of other women? Maybe just getting out of Midnight and the ever-present grind of the convenience store was the real delight? "Okay," he said. "Message received. I'll be back in an hour or a little more. You've got my cell phone number, I know."

"Yeah," she said, embarrassed. "I hope you don't mind."

"Not at all," he said promptly, and in the interests of being as thorough as he could be, he walked her to the door marked KUT N KURL. As she pushed it open, a waft of the beauty parlor smell drifted out to Manfred and evoked memories he hadn't realized he possessed: taking his grandmother to her hair salon as she got older; smelling the salon incense of perm solution, hair dye, and wax; hearing the *snick* of scissors and the running water, the plastic crinkle of the protective capes . . . Suddenly, he had a mental image of Xylda so vivid that it almost brought tears to his eyes: this whole rush of past experiences, brought back by that one inhalation.

He knew he said something to Creek before he turned to walk back to the car, but he couldn't recall what it was a minute later.

He had to sit in the car for a while before he left to run his errands. He pulled out his list of errands from his pocket and pretended to be studying it until he was calm and composed again. He had to smile a little; Xylda would have enjoyed knowing she was the center of so much of his life.

Maybe she did know it. That was not a bad feeling.

Home Depot, Walmart, and Dairy Queen were his three ports of call. An hour and fifteen minutes later, Manfred pulled up outside Kut N Kurl again. Before he could turn off his engine, Creek was at the passenger door. "I was watching out the window," she said, climbing in.

"I brought you something," Manfred said. "Here." He handed her a cup with a spoon.

"What is it?"

"Butterfinger Blizzard," he said. "I just guessed."

"Oh, *boy*," she said, and started in on the ice cream right away. "This is great!"

"You've had one before, right?"

"No, never. Connor's on a very restricted diet."

She didn't explain why, and Manfred thought it would be pushy to ask. Manfred felt he might've undermined Shawn with the ice cream and that Shawn would not appreciate it. It felt strange to be on the parental consent side of things. "I hope I'm not in trouble," he said.

"Not with me," Creek assured him, and he felt better.

"I think it's great that he wants Connor to eat healthy," Manfred added quickly.

"He's got some health issues," she said, between bites of ice cream.

"Oh?" Manfred asked, "Allergies?" But when the pleasure on her face vanished, he realized he'd stepped over a boundary. "Sorry. Midnight people like to play things close to the chest."

Her smile reappeared. He felt a rush of relief. "That's one way to put it," she said. "Yeah, my dad is pretty strict about us eating in restaurants, especially Connor. What about your dad? Was he hard on you?"

"I don't know," Manfred said. "I never met him. I don't know who he was."

"Oh my God, I'm so sorry! Were you adopted?" She had flushed, which made her look even prettier, he thought.

"Nope. My mom was single, and she never told me anything about my dad."

"I guess you asked her a lot," Creek said, obviously feeling her way.

"Over and over, especially when I was little."

"I'm really sorry," she said. "I'm assuming you had to find ways to handle that. Were other kids mean about it?"

"I don't think it would be as bad now, but then, in a sort of rural area, it was pretty tough."

Creek obviously had a dozen things to say, but she seemed to be thinking twice about all of them. "Well, that sucks," she said finally.

"Yeah, it kind of did," he agreed, and they rode the rest of the way to Midnight in silence, working on their Blizzards. Manfred didn't think the lack of conversation was uncomfortable; he characterized it as thoughtful. He pushed aside his own childhood mystery with the ease of long practice and instead focused on Creek's.

What kind of father keeps two kids chained to a convenience store in a little town that's almost dead? And then has issues about them eating in restaurants? Manfred noted that was limited to out-of-town restaurants. The Lovells got takeout from Home Cookin regularly.

Manfred was beginning to wonder if there might be something sketchy about Creek's not getting her scholarship, too. He couldn't begin to imagine how he could tackle a line of questioning that would confirm or deny that suspicion, so he tucked the idea away for further examination.

He pulled into the convenience store parking lot before five o'clock. The old truck was back, parked over at their house next door, so Shawn and Connor had returned. Manfred debated going in to hand her over to her dad, then realized that would just be weird. She wasn't eight years old, and this wasn't a date. Plus, Shawn was probably watching.

"Thanks," Creek said. "I appreciate the ride and the Blizzard." She left the DQ cup in the cup holder, Manfred noticed.

"Glad to do it. Ask again," he said, striving to sound casual. "And by the way, your hair looks great. You get about an inch cut off?"

Surprise flashed across her face. "Yeah," she said. "I can't believe you noticed."

Not getting a lot of attention at home, Manfred noted. "My grandmother always wanted my opinion on her hair," he said. "That's what she said, but she really wanted me to tell her she looked great and not a day older."

Creek laughed. "So you're saying I shouldn't believe you when you tell me I look great?"

"I'm going to make a deal with you," Manfred said. "I'll do my best to always tell you the truth." He had no idea why he'd said that, but he knew instantly it had been the right thing to tell her.

"That's an interesting deal, Manfred Bernardo. Okay. I'll do my best to do the same." And Creek opened her door and walked swiftly into the store.

When the door swung shut, Manfred went home, but it took him an hour to settle back to work.

26

Manfred had had a civilized idea while he shopped in Davy, one he was sure his grandmother and his mother would approve. Late the next morning, he walked down to the Antique Gallery and Nail Salon with a bottle of wine. Chuy was in the salon part of the store. He was painting a design on some acrylic nails, which were on the fingertips of Olivia Charity, back from wherever she'd been on her trip.

After Manfred greeted both of them, he asked Olivia, "Can I look?"

"Of course," she said, and he bent over to see the design. Her fingernail pattern was dark blue and light blue chevrons.

"Really pretty," he said. And it was, but he realized he didn't know Olivia very well at all. He would never, in a million years, have believed this was her choice.

"Joe, Manfred is here!" Chuy called, and Joe emerged from behind a chest of drawers.

"Hey, man," Joe said. "How you doing?"

Manfred presented the wine to Joe, since Chuy was occupied. "Thanks for a great evening," he said. "Even if we did get in a fight afterward, the food gave us the strength to withstand the attack."

"Thanks, and have a seat," Joe invited. "I was just taking the old drawer pulls off the drawers and looking at the restoration hardware I could get to replace them. Nothing that can't be put off. I'd rather talk than work, any day."

Manfred hadn't planned on staying, but he found he welcomed the prospect of talking to other people in a different room. He sat down in the extra plastic rolling chair on the client side of the manicure table. Joe pulled up a folding chair that had been positioned looking out the window.

"That was quite a shock, to hear that you guys had been jumped," Chuy said, taking Olivia's left hand in his own. "I'm sorry we didn't hear you yell. Creek tells me she came to your defense. That Creek, she's a firecracker, huh?"

"We were glad to see her coming," Manfred admitted. "She can swing a bat, no doubt of that. I'm no street fighter. No big surprise there." He looked down at his thin body. "Maybe I need some bulk," he concluded.

"Nah, just toning," Joe said. "Or Bobo could teach you some karate." The conversation drifted to Jackie Chan and went sideways to Chow Yun Fat, while tangentially brushing on the injuries action stars incurred, and from that to doping exposés. Olivia threw in a comment from time to time.

Of all the citizens of Midnight, Olivia seemed the largest question mark. Even if he imagined that she had met and fallen in love or lust with Lemuel and moved here to be with him (and that was by no means a certainty), how could she resign herself to such solitude and isolation? Olivia was so clearly a citizen of a bigger world. Maybe that was why she traveled so often.

As Manfred walked home, he thought, *Every time I take a step forward in knowing these people, I end up with more questions.* How about Joe and Chuy? Granted, gay couples in a state like Texas wouldn't have too easy a time of it. But Manfred knew that in any large city—and Texas had a few of those—there were equally large gay communities. Why hadn't Joe and Chuy settled in one of those? Really, how many people were going to come to a hole in the road like Midnight to buy antiques? Or to get their nails done?

Once these questions had occurred to him, he thought the oddest thing of all was that he'd never set them side by side before.

Fiji had texted him this morning. "Tell Bobo about the vision," was all she'd said. He'd glimpsed her setting off with Bobo the day before, so she could have told Bobo all about what he'd seen; but Manfred knew it was his responsibility, as reluctant as he was to relay an emotional message.

He'd been wrong not to do it before.

There was no point in putting it off. He turned in at the pawnshop, went up the steps, opened the big door. Bobo emerged from the gloom of the back of the shop, like the Cheshire cat; first Manfred could see his smile, then the rest of him.

After they'd exchanged greetings, Manfred said, "I have something to tell you. When I went to Fiji's class the other night . . ." And he relayed what he had seen in the vision, though he didn't dwell on the grisly details of Aubrey's appearance. "So that's what she said, short and complete. She wanted you to know she really loved you," he concluded.

Bobo looked as if he'd been hit between the eyes. "You're not making this up?" he asked, and you could tell he was praying that Manfred was not.

"I would never lie to you about a vision," Manfred said. He liked and respected Bobo too much.

"Thank you," Bobo said, with considerable dignity. "Excuse me. I have to . . . I have to go do something." And he vanished. Manfred scooted out of the pawnshop as fast as he could, to leave Bobo alone to grieve. And maybe to recover a little.

Two people from Midnight decided to attend the funeral: Fiji and Creek.

"I must be some kind of masochist," Fiji said to Mr. Snuggly as she got dressed for the service. The cat, who didn't often engage in conversation, looked at her as if he agreed completely. "First I make sure Manfred tells Bobo that Aubrey really loooooved him. Now I feel like I have to go to the damn funeral. To be his eyes and ears. You know what, Snug? I could almost not go and pretend I had. All funerals are alike, right? Aubrey's funeral won't be different from any other." At least Creek was going with her. She'd have someone to talk to on the drive.

The service was being held in a town an hour's drive past Marthasville, in a largish place called Buffalo Plain. When Fiji pulled up to Gas N Go, Creek came out wearing a black short-sleeved dress and carrying a white cardigan. Creek's only jewelry was a large silver and turquoise cross. The simplicity suited her.

Everyone has a style but me, Fiji thought glumly. When she pulled on things she liked, Fiji was pleased with how she looked, but today she'd felt obliged to give her clothes quite a bit of thought. Black would be hypocritical, but she hadn't wanted to offend Aubrey's (presumably grieving) family by wearing something inappropriate, either. Dark brown pants and good shoes with medium heels had been her compromise, with a long-sleeved green sweater and the good gold chain and earrings she wore when she was dressed up. She'd worked on her hopeless hair a bit, but she caught Creek looking at her head in a startled way. Fiji felt like sighing. There were those to whom style came naturally, and those who didn't have a clue.

Fiji was sadly aware she was one of the latter.

She and Creek got along well enough on the drive. At first, they talked about Halloween and the upcoming decorating party. Fiji would be preparing her house for the holiday, and anyone who wanted could come over to help. This was the third year in a row Fiji had held an open house on October 31. And no matter when the schools or city fathers decreed children should go trick-or-treating, Fiji celebrated on the calendar day. After they'd discussed the plans for this year, an awkward silence fell. At least, Fiji thought it felt awkward.

"I'm glad you wanted to ride with me," Fiji said, too abruptly. "I guess I didn't realize that you and Aubrey were close." That was as close as she could come to saying, *Why the hell are you volunteering to go to this funeral?*

"Aubrey didn't have much to do after she moved in with Bobo," Creek said. "She cut back on her shifts at the restaurant so she could spend more time with him in the evening, when he was off work. So she'd come over to Gas N Go, buy some Corn Nuts, hang around. She'd talk to me and Connor."

"I didn't realize that. I'm sorry." For the first time, Fiji realized that Creek was lonely for female companionship, and Fiji knew instantly that she should have thought about that and done a little dropping by herself.

"She tried to be nice," Creek said.

That was damning with faint praise, if Fiji had ever heard it. She said cautiously, "But . . . ?"

"Well . . . she bragged about Bobo." Creek shrugged. "Like *all* the women in Midnight had been after him, but *she* was the one who'd gotten him—you know?"

Two spots of color began to burn in Fiji's cheeks. "Right. As if we were all panting after him," Fiji said, in a slightly choked voice.

"Yeah. Come on! He's a little old for me," Creek said with the sublime pride of youth. "He's got to be in his thirties, right?"

"Uh-huh."

"So *that* was silly. Madonna is married to Teacher. Olivia, well, she and Lemuel . . ." She did look over at Fiji then, and Fiji nodded.

"And you, well, you and Bobo are like best friends, right?"

"Yeah. We're buddies." Fiji was proud of how evenly her words came out.

"It bothered me that she couldn't help but flirt with every guy she saw. But she was nuts about Bobo."

"I believe that, too," Fiji said. "But she had some other reasons for going after him like she did."

Creek looked surprised. "I'm sure she did. Living in Midnight isn't every girl's dream. I mean, I understand that she was put into position to meet him and . . . and seduce him. But I know the love came later. She was basically a good person."

Fiji said, "She was a right-wing nut."

Creek said, "You think she couldn't love Bobo because of her politics?"

"I don't know how much you heard when the sheriff was telling us that she had a whole backstory she hadn't told Bobo? Creek, the only possible reason she could have for not telling Bobo the truth about her background when she decided she loved him is that she still planned on doing whatever it was they set her up in Midnight to do. And to me that's just nasty."

"I can't believe that. I know she loved him." Creek's jaw was set in a firm line.

"Okay, I'll concede the love. But if it had been true love, honest love, she would have told him her whole story."

"If you think she was so devious, how come you're going to the funeral?" Creek was on the verge of being angry.

Fair question, Fiji thought. *How to answer it?*

"I'm a proxy for Bobo," she said. "The family doesn't want him there."

This, too, was news to Creek. "Why not?" she asked, clearly indignant.

"They know he didn't have any part in her death, but they're still resentful," Fiji said. "I'm going so if he wants to know anything about it, I can tell him. He didn't ask me to do this," she added, in the spirit of absolute honesty.

"I understand," Creek said. She'd calmed down. "I think that's pretty nice of you."

They rode a few minutes in silence. Then Creek said, "What do you think about Manfred?"

Fiji was tempted to say, *Why do you ask?* But that would just be mean. "I don't know him very well, but so far, so good. He seems to fit into Midnight, and he seems like an interesting guy. What do you think?"

"I think what he does is kind of weird," Creek said, as if she wanted to be persuaded otherwise. "I can't decide if he really believes he's a psychic or if he's a con man. I don't know which would be worse."

"I'm surprised that's a problem for you, since you're so fond of Lemuel."

Creek was clearly taken aback. Fiji wondered what the girl had expected her to say.

"Well, Uncle Lemuel . . ." Creek began, and then faltered. "I do know what Uncle Lem is, but he's never been anything but wonderful to me."

"Then Manfred might be no different." Fiji struggled to keep her tone neutral.

"I guess my dad is so cynical it's rubbed off," Creek said, her voice stiff and resentful.

"Just think about it," Fiji said, sorry that they were not happier with each other, and wondering what else she could have said. Creek might be too young to take a direct conversation. Or maybe she herself was being a jerk. She felt that was all too possible. She said, "And there . . . that would be the turn to the left we have to make?"

Creek consulted the directions they'd printed off Fiji's computer. "That should be the turn, and then in three point four miles we make a right on Alamo Street. Then our destination will be on the right in half a mile. Solomon True Baptist."

Even the name of the church made Fiji feel gloomy when she eyed it on a large sign a few minutes later. The words were printed in Gothic lettering on a white background, and from the spotlight, it was illuminated when night fell. The overcast day depressed her even more.

Though they'd arrived thirty minutes early, there were already vehicles in the parking lot. They dawdled in the car for a few minutes, checking their phones and chatting very cautiously. But cars and trucks and vans began to fill the spaces on the graveled parking area, and Fiji and Creek sighed simultaneously and got out of the car to walk to the door. Solomon True Baptist was a low building made with yellow brick, sporting unnecessary white columns that were supposed to look as though they held up the porch roof. To make absolutely sure the building was identifiable, a short spire squatted on the roof. Some church member with time and talent had created beautiful flower beds around the building, though they were faded with the onset of fall.

Fiji stopped at a pew close to the rear of the church, and she and

Creek moved in after taking a program from one of the ushers. The pianist was playing a selection of somber hymns. Listening to the dark tones of the music, Fiji was terrifyingly, abruptly shocked—all over again—by the fact that a human being, a person she'd known, was gone forever. She hadn't liked Aubrey, and nothing she'd discovered about the woman after her death had changed that opinion, but purposeful eradication of another human being . . . that went against everything she'd been taught by Great-Aunt Mildred.

Great-Aunt Mildred had not believed in striking the first blow. She had believed in self-defense. Fiji found it impossible to believe that Aubrey had had a chance to save her own life.

Fiji glanced sideways at her young companion. Creek looked serious but not sad. Fiji thought, *She's been to a few funerals before.*

As the doleful music continued, for want of anything better to do, Fiji examined the cover of the program. Centered on it was a photo of Aubrey, with a sort of halo effect around it, as if she'd been snapped against a sunset. In a font resembling script, the obituary read:

> *Our sister Aubrey Hamilton Lowry, beloved daughter of Destin and Lucyfay Hamilton, sister of Macon, widow of Chad Lowry, will be sadly missed by those who knew her. For many years Aubrey attended church here, and she graduated from Buffalo Plain High School. She was a waitress in Oklahoma while she was married to Chad, and upon his death she returned to Texas. After working in Davy, she met her death by human hands, for reasons not yet clear to us.*
>
> *Praise be to God! All will be known on the Day of Judgment. For it is not for us to judge God's actions. "They went to bury her, but they found nothing more of her than the skull and the feet and the palms of her hands." (2 Kings 9:35)*

Fiji put her hand over her mouth. Creek, who had just read the same passage, turned to Fiji. For once, the two women were in accord. They silently grimaced at each other to manifest their disgust. But at that moment the music swelled, and the mourners followed a silent hand gesture from the man standing at the front of the church and rose to their feet. The coffin came in on its gurney, guided by two funeral home attendants, with Aubrey's family walking in behind it.

The couple at the head of the mourners must be the parents. To Fiji's faint surprise, they were only in their forties. Under ordinary circumstances, she realized they'd be vital and attractive people. Aubrey had definitely inherited her looks and charm from her father, who had his arm around a small, frail woman dressed in navy blue.

The other family members she could only guess about: the brother, Macon, was probably the big guy whose eyes were red with weeping. There was a man who (going on looks) must be Mr. Hamilton's brother, accompanied by his sturdy wife and their kids, who were in their early twenties. Cousins. There was one grandmother, tiny like Aubrey's mom. Once they were all seated, the funeral began.

To the fidgety Fiji, the service seemed to take forever. There were prayers and Bible readings and anecdotes. To Fiji's dismay, several people read poems or essays that described a very different woman from the one Fiji had known. Fiji noticed that even Creek looked uncomfortable as they listened to stories about how gentle Aubrey had been, how loving and thoughtful. And yet, if you listened with unkind ears (or as Fiji preferred to call it, "an open mind"), you could hear that all had not been well in Aubrey land. A careful listener like Fiji could hear that Aubrey had not communicated much with her parents or with her in-laws in the past couple of years, that she'd liked to party hard, that she'd been overly influenced by those around her.

There were more prayers, and the minister's well-constructed homily that was so touching even Fiji grew more solemn. She glanced at her companion to see that Creek was crying. Fiji fumbled in her bag for a tissue to pass to the girl. Creek gave Fiji a grateful look and used it to blot her cheeks and her nose.

By the time Fiji thought she was growing roots in the pew, after yet another prayer, the service was over.

When Aubrey had left her parents' church for the last time, Fiji said, "Do you want to go out to the cemetery?"

Creek, who had recovered her composure, nodded. "I guess so," she said. "It just seems polite."

Fiji joined the funeral procession, feeling like a fraud as the oncoming cars pulled off to the side of the road, and people standing on the sidewalks of Buffalo Plain took off their hats or stood at attention as the hearse drove by. About three miles out of town, the land began to rise again. They turned off the state highway to take a narrow road that jinked its way up a rolling hill. At the very top they entered the cemetery, the culmination of the road. The grounds were not fenced. There was a metal sign to the right of the entrance that read PIONEER REST. The graveyard was an old one; Fiji saw headstones that dated back to the early eighteen hundreds.

There were live oaks shading some of the older graves, and little brown leaves fluttered in the wind that scoured the hilltop. It was quiet and peaceful, or at least it would be after all the mourners left.

"It's like we're an interruption," Fiji said to Creek, who gave her a surprised look. Fiji wondered if she could come back on some other occasion, just to read the headstones.

She parked behind the other cars, all huddled to one side of the narrow paved path that made a lazy loop through the graves. In summer, attending an interment here would be a very hot, sweaty experience. In October, it was pleasant. The minute she got out of the car, Fiji's hair began its escape from the barrette she'd used to trap it.

Creek looked at the open grave as they drew near to the prepared site. It was hardly visible under all the funeral home paraphernalia, but it was there and it was waiting. In an attempt to comfort the girl, Fiji said, "She'll be here with frontiersmen and gunfighters and pioneer women."

Creek looked at her blankly, but after a moment she said, "All part of history. I see that."

Fiji had a moment's impulse to sing "The Circle of Life," but she suppressed it sternly. Her resentment of the dead woman was getting the better of her sense of appropriate behavior. *If I came as Bobo's representative, I'm sure not acting like it*, she scolded herself. She forced her face into strictly expressionless lines as they joined the small crowd around the tent erected over the open grave.

The earnest minister began to pray. Again.

Aubrey's mother, Lucyfay, who looked as though a strong breeze would blow her away, did not make a single sound during the long prayer. Destin Hamilton sat with one arm around his wife, one fist clenched on his thigh. He was visibly tense, about to explode with some strong emotion. Fiji couldn't pick what the emotion would be: grief, rage, impatience? It was painful to witness.

As the prayer went on and on, Fiji—and all the mourners—shifted and began to look around, because a sound was getting louder and closer. At first it reminded Fiji of a fleet of distant lawn tractors. Gradually, it became apparent that there was a procession drawing nearer: Motorcycles, all with the same flag attached, rumbled into the cemetery in single file. The minister gave up his attempt to be heard, and the mourners turned as one to watch the machines reach the place on the road closest to Aubrey's grave and then, one by one, park in a neat line facing in. Fiji counted thirty of them.

The riders dismounted and came to the grave site. Though it was impossible to read their faces, since all of them were wearing dark glasses and kerchiefs or helmets, Fiji thought their body language read self-conscious as they assembled in a group. After the noise of the motors, the appalled silence weighed heavily on the newcomers.

Two of them were carrying a folded flag. They handed it off to the leader in a clumsy bit of ceremony. The leader walked over to stand in front of the Hamiltons. He extended the flag to them. He was a tall man—broad, too—and wearing a black motorcycle jacket and jeans. He'd removed his helmet.

Fiji could see, from the ripple running through the mourners, that they knew him.

"Who is that?" she asked of the woman closest to her.

The woman, who was wearing a cross around her neck and a modest wedding band, said in an equally low voice, "That's Price Eggleston."

Fiji was not terribly surprised. Eggleston did not look stupid, but by interrupting a funeral he had to know he would offend an awful lot of people. She wondered what he hoped to achieve. She found out when most of the young people pulled cell phones from purses and pockets and began to record what was happening. They were taking photos or movies. Eggleston adopted a terribly solemn face. He held out the flag to the Hamiltons, who stared at it, appalled. They made no move to accept the triangular bundle.

"On behalf of the Men of Liberty, I present you with this flag of our nation in remembrance of our fallen sister," he said, his voice pitched to carry. "We will get vengeance for our fallen one. The man who killed her will not go unpunished."

There was no doubt in Fiji's mind that he meant Bobo. Before she could decide what to do, Macon Hamilton was on his feet and swinging at Eggleston. That was so exactly what Fiji wanted to do that her own fist clenched in sympathy. Unfortunately, Price Eggleston was quick on his feet for a big man, and he leaped back.

While Macon stumbled, Price Eggleston completed his mission by turning to the coffin and placing the flag on top of it. He then beat a quick retreat. The minister, trying to restore some decorum to the scene, said very loudly, "We now commend the body of our sister to the earth," and signaled the funeral home employee to lower the casket. As it began to descend into the grave, Lucyfay Hamilton finally snapped. She launched herself out of her folding chair as if she intended to descend, too. Or maybe her goal was to remove the flag from Aubrey's coffin. Only a quick movement by her husband kept her aboveground.

Everyone froze in place as they watched the casket. Eggleston took advantage of the situation to walk briskly back to his MOL posse and mount his motorcycle. All the MOL people followed and got ready to leave, and the motorcycles started back up with a huge buzz. The noise galvanized the mourners, some of whom began yelling at the funeral crashers. Macon Hamilton picked up a funeral home chair and threw it at one of the motorcyclists in the exiting procession. He missed the driver but hit the passenger, who tumbled off onto the grass. The passenger's helmet came off. Fiji recognized Lisa Gray. Bobo had been spot-on about Lisa and her veracity.

The girl scrambled up and climbed back on behind the motorcyclist, whom Fiji figured was her husband, Cole. Without further incident (aside from a lot of screaming) the entire motorcycle contingent roared away. Fiji saw one of the flags fluttering behind a rider detach and gust onto a nearby monument, and she scuttled over to rescue it. She straightened the cloth out to have a good look. The flag depicted a mailed fist clutching a rectangular banner in the middle. On one side of the banner was printed "Liberty" and on the other side was an arrow.

Fiji looked around and didn't see Creek anywhere. With a pang of guilt and worry she turned in a circle to survey the cemetery. People were milling all around, and the solemnity of the occasion was simply lost. Try as she would, Fiji could not find the girl.

She hurried over to her car, clicking it open as she walked. When the locks made their little chirp and went up, Creek popped to her feet on the passenger side. Fiji sagged with relief. "Get in, and let's get out of here," she called, and Creek scrambled in and buckled her seat belt. Fiji was equally hasty in her preparation, and before other mourners had gotten ready to leave, Fiji pulled her car out of the lineup and began going around the loop that would lead out of the cemetery and back to the road. She drove very slowly and carefully. Most of the people who'd come to say good-bye to Aubrey Hamilton Lowry were now bent over their phones, texting. The funeral was already viral.

When they were halfway down the hill, Fiji passed Creek the flag.

Creek said, "Stronghold. The mailed fist."

"That was what the guys said, right? The guys who attacked Bobo and Manfred? That they were citizens of Stronghold?"

"Yeah."

"So they're saying Aubrey was one of them? They're trying to make her into a little martyr?"

"Yeah. I guess."

Creek was looking tragic, Fiji realized. "Hey," Fiji said. "What's up, Creek?" *Surely*, Fiji thought, with more than a touch of exasperation, *surely this can't still be about her deep grief for Aubrey.*

Creek inhaled deeply. "Dad told me not to go to the funeral. But he never wants me to go *anywhere*, so I just blew him off. Why would people take pictures at a funeral? Well, normally they wouldn't . . . but when assholes show up on motorcycles and disrupt everything . . ."

"You couldn't know that would happen. No one expected that."

Fiji felt greatly at a loss. Most of her concentration was focused on driving through Buffalo Plain to turn onto the highway to Marthasville, but what thinking room she had to spare was occupied in (a) hoping they wouldn't catch up to the motorcycle group, (b) worrying about Creek, and (c) her curiosity about Creek's weird reaction when things went wrong at the service. "You're not supposed to be photographed?" she asked.

But Creek wasn't going to volunteer any more information. "Thank you," she told Fiji, a bit stiffly. "I appreciate your getting us out of there as soon as possible." The unspoken words "but not soon enough" hung in the air between them. After a minute, Fiji glanced over to see Creek's mouth clenched in a defiant line.

She's proud of being strong, Fiji thought, adding that to her growing fund of knowledge about Creek. "I didn't want to stick around, either," she said. She made an effort to smile, but she kept her eyes straight ahead. "Once I knew that was Price Eggleston."

"You know him?" Creek said. "You've met him? Who is he?"

"I know what he's been doing." She explained to Creek about Eggleston's militia, about his visit to the pawnshop and his sending the girl Lisa in to plant the camera.

"So he's a rich bad guy?"

Creek's been watching too many movies and not enough real life. "Well, he's better off than most people, I understand. I think it's his dad who has the real big money. But anyone who has to have a bunch of guns to achieve his ends, someone who doesn't mind beating up innocent people to get them, someone who's . . ." *Who's willing to hurt Bobo. Who's willing to send a young woman in to seduce a man to get his way. Who's willing to kill that young woman when she doesn't do what he wants.* "Yeah. He's a bad guy."

"So you think Eggleston's the guy who sent Aubrey to get close to Bobo, so she could do a Delilah and find out where the guns are?"

"That's my assumption."

"What do you think went wrong with that?"

Fiji hesitated for a moment. "I think Aubrey did really fall in love with Bobo. I think she refused to tell Price Eggleston what he wanted to know . . . the location of the guns. That is, she told him Bobo didn't have any, which he doesn't. Price didn't believe her, and he killed her. Maybe by accident. I don't know."

Creek stared at Fiji, her face inscrutable. This was the Creek Fiji knew best, not the girl who'd been panicked by a few cell phones. "So if he did that, you think he sent the guys to jump Manfred and Bobo that night?"

"Yes, that's what I think."

"Then he deserves whatever happens to him!" Creek said, with some ferocity.

Surprised by Creek's vehemence—and because she was curious to see what the girl would say—Fiji told her, "So far, a building he owns has been burned down, and two of his men have disappeared."

"You're not saying you feel *sorry* for him?" Creek's clear olive skin reddened along her cheekbones. "After all, he killed Aubrey!"

"I don't feel any pity for him," Fiji said. "I'm just saying, it's not like he's walking all over creation getting his own way."

There was an awkward silence. "He sure messed up Aubrey's funeral," Creek muttered.

"Yes, he did. I feel sorry for her family." Though she hadn't liked Aubrey in life or in death, Fiji thought it was awful that the dignified farewell service her parents had planned had been disrupted by an egomaniac who loved himself more than he respected the feelings of others.

"He should not get away with any of this." Creek was clear in her judgment.

"If he means to do evil to Bobo, believe me . . . he won't get away with it. And if he killed Aubrey, the police will arrest him."

"You think that Arthur Smith will arrest a rich man?"

"I do believe he will," Fiji said, and was a little surprised to find she meant it. Arthur Smith might be wily and perhaps he was politically oriented. She didn't know him well enough to have an opinion on that. But she did not think he was corrupt.

"And Price killed her."

Again with the killing. Fiji suppressed a sigh. Creek was very hung up on that point, while to Fiji, Price's biggest sin was the two attacks on Bobo. She was certain about Price's guilt in those. "I'm just guessing," she said a bit too sharply. "But that seems logical to me."

Creek nodded, seeming reassured, and they rode the rest of the way back to Midnight in near silence. "I'm just worried about the darn pictures," she said, when they got close to town.

Were the Lovells in the witness protection program or something? Fiji wondered. *What was the deal with the Lovell family and pictures? With being noticed?* But there was absolutely nothing she could do about the pictures that were surely all over the Internet now, and she was a bit tired of Creek's company; plus, there was the Midnight habit of respecting secrets. So she made no response.

27

The next afternoon, Bobo retraced Fiji's route to Buffalo Plain. He'd talked to Fiji that morning in her yard: she'd finally made a start at getting out all her Halloween decorations. She'd climbed down from a ladder to tell him about the funeral.

She'd looked preoccupied, and cold, wrapped up in the battered zip-up jacket she wore for yard work. He himself was wearing his old brown corduroy coat with the toggle fastenings, a relic from his college days. Fall had declared itself overnight. The sky was a brilliant blue with a cloud scattered here and there to emphasize how radiant the day was, but the chilling wind blew steadily from the west. It tossed the leaves through the air, forcing them to somersault before drifting to the ground.

Bobo stopped to fill up his tank and get a cup of coffee in Marthasville, and the grackles in the trees around the gas station were full of noisy conversation. One strutted on the ground by his truck and cast a bright eye up at him, as if wondering if he were a source of food.

"Not today, bird," he said, and the grackle flew away to tell its comrades. Most people hated grackles, but Bobo had enjoyed them since he'd moved to Texas. They seemed to tell each other everything.

Bobo's old Garmin got him to the cemetery with only a moment of uncertainty. He spotted the fresh grave right away; it was covered with withering flowers. To his dismay, he was not alone. There was another mourner. Since the cemetery was a dead end (*Yeah, pretty ironic, huh?*), there was no way for him to leave unobtrusively. He decided to accept whatever was going to happen. He got out of his truck. The small form beside the grave turned to face him, and he saw it was a woman. After a second, Bobo recognized her as Aubrey's mother. Aubrey had kept a picture of her parents on her side of the bed.

Though Bobo dreaded this encounter, it was impossible to back down. He walked toward her, doing his best to look as nonthreatening as a big strange man in an isolated spot possibly could appear to a lone woman.

The breeze picked up Aubrey's mother's short hair and ruffled it, and made the flowers rustle on their forms.

"I don't know you," she said after a moment. "I'm Lucyfay Hamilton."

"Mrs. Hamilton, I'm Bobo Winthrop. I didn't kill your daughter."

She stared at him wordlessly. She had Aubrey's eyes, he thought, but she was smaller all over than her daughter. She was only ten or twelve years older than Bobo, and if she had not been so sunk in grief, she might have appealed to him on a personal level, a realization he found shocking and confusing.

"That's what the sheriff in your county tells us," she said. From her tone and demeanor, he had no idea if she believed in his innocence or not.

"I heard you all didn't want me to come to the funeral, so I thought I'd come today to pay my respects," he said. "I didn't think anyone else would be here."

"After that man ruined the funeral yesterday, I wanted a quiet time to spend with my daughter," Lucyfay Hamilton said, turning back to the grave. "Did you hear about that?"

"Yes, a friend of mine was here. I heard. And I'll leave you to your private time." He turned to go back to his truck.

"You can stay," she said. "I've said everything to her I had to say."

Bobo had no idea how to respond to that. He shifted from foot to foot. "I really loved her," he offered.

"That's what she told me. 'Mama, he loves me, and he treats me better than anybody ever has,' she said."

"You were in contact with her?" Bobo said. "I'm sorry . . . somehow I thought that she was out of touch with you all."

"She was out of touch with her father and Macon," Lucyfay Hamilton said. There was a ghost of a smile on her lips. "Never with me."

"She didn't talk to her father because of her first husband?"

"And his really, really stupid death as a bank robber? And his scumbag buddies? Yes, that might have had something to do with it," Lucyfay said dryly. "We raised her the best way we knew how. She had to work on the ranch. She went to church. She wore nice clothes. Did she tell you my husband runs his family ranch, sits on the board of the bank?"

"No, ma'am." His bit his lip before he could say, *She told me you were dead.*

"And then she let his stupid friends talk her into 'avenging his death'—yes, that's the way they put it—by contacting you." Clearly, she was not able to say "seducing you." She turned away from him, to her car. "Well, she paid for her gullibility and her careless way with men. At least she had some happiness with you before she was murdered."

"Who do you think killed her?" Bobo blurted.

"Price says you did. I'd assumed it was Price's little militia, or Price himself. But I don't believe that any longer. Price is an underhanded young man. He's long on charisma and short on foresight. But I don't think he's capable of killing her and then putting on the show he did yesterday. Do you understand?"

Bobo nodded.

Lucyfay took a deep breath. "I think she insisted to the MOL that you were innocent of whatever they think you've done. I think she said she wouldn't inform on you anymore. And I think one of Price's goons killed her, though I don't think Price knows that. Then he ruined her funeral, with his damn stupid flag ritual."

Apparently she had had her say, because Lucyfay Hamilton got into her Lexus and drove off, leaving a dazed Bobo standing by the fresh grave. He felt so wobbly that he almost sank to his knees, before he was shamed by the melodrama of the gesture. He stiffened his backbone. *What's worse?* he asked himself. *To be accused of murdering the girl you loved or to be the cause of her getting murdered?* His misery swept him away and swirled him around like the leaves in the wind.

Weirdly, strangely—wonderfully—he knew this was the moment he was touching the bottom, and he understood that from now on, however gradually, he would begin to heal.

When Bobo looked down at the flower-strewn mound, he no longer saw through it to the decayed body of the woman he'd loved. He saw the opaque layer of dirt, the sealed coffin. He saw good-bye.

Bobo shifted uneasily, as if a long-carried burden had shifted on his shoulders. He closed his eyes. When he opened them, he was not any less sad, but he felt free.

28

Fiji said, "I've come to confess, Rev."

The old man stood before the bench where Fiji sat, his rusty black suit blending into the darkness of the church. It was late in the afternoon, but the chapel lights weren't on. The room was cold. Emilio Sheehan did not reply, but then, he was a man of few words unless the preaching was on him.

"There's a bad man who thinks Bobo killed Aubrey. Or maybe he's just pretending to think that; maybe he really wants Bobo accused of killing her because he wants to find out where Bobo's stashed a lot of guns."

"Hmmm," the Rev said. It was an experimental sound, as though he were clearing his throat before making a comment. She waited until it became clear he was not going to speak.

"So, I try to be a good person and a good witch, but I really want to do something awful to that guy," Fiji said. "Is it worse to sit back and do nothing while people plot against the . . . a good friend? Or is it worse to do something evil to them before they can hurt that friend?"

The Rev did not have to think long about this. "We protect the people we love, and we love the people of this community," he said, his expression stern and sure.

Fiji nodded to show that she accepted this as true.

"We must wait for the evil to come to us," he said. "But when it does, we can defend ourselves against it."

This was not the answer Fiji had been hoping for, and her face showed that.

"Otherwise," the Rev explained, "we rob the evil one of the chance to think better, to redeem himself."

"Human nature being what it is . . ." she said angrily, and then bit her lip to make herself be silent.

"Human nature," said the Rev. "Well, it's not good, that's for sure. But we have to give it a chance. I gave Aubrey a chance."

"What are you referring to?" Fiji said.

"She cared for Bobo."

"Yes."

"That was true. But for reasons best known only to her, she could not stop acting interested in every male she saw."

Creek had said the same thing. "They told you this? That is, the men she, ah, made passes at?"

"They would not tell me such a thing. I witnessed it. And Aubrey laughed about it when I spoke to her."

Fiji was astonished, and not a little disgusted. "You mean she flirted with, say, Chuy and Joe?"

He nodded.

"You?"

He nodded, a fraction of an inch dip of his chin.

"And Teacher . . . Shawn . . . Lemuel?"

Another nod.

Every adult male in Midnight. "I'm surprised Madonna or Olivia didn't *kill* her," she said in amazement, and then she froze. "Oh, golly."

"You may have the wrong murderer, you see," the Rev said. "Aubrey was daring the world to kill her."

"So she . . . her behavior led to her own death?" Fiji was scrambling to absorb this.

"Just because she threw out the dare doesn't mean someone should have picked it up," he said. Then he turned away to kneel in prayer at his little altar.

Fiji realized it was time for her to leave.

29

When he saw all Fiji's preparations for Halloween, Manfred looked around his own yard and found it wanting. He didn't know when he'd stop feeling the compulsion to work, so the next afternoon he walked down to Gas N Go to ask Connor if he'd be interested in cleaning up the outside of his house.

On the occasions Manfred went to Gas N Go—which Manfred had very precisely calculated could only be every third day, to avoid raising Shawn's hackles—Manfred had observed that while Creek was usually genuinely busy, Connor was not. Manfred didn't know if Connor was incompetent, or if Shawn had no faith in his son's ability, but either Connor was doing his homework or he was employed with some job a monkey could do.

Connor seemed profoundly bored. In Manfred's not-too-distant experience, a bored teenager was a teenager who got into mischief. And Connor seemed reasonably intelligent and likable, on Manfred's brief acquaintance. If there was no one in Midnight who was closer to Creek in age than Manfred himself, there was no one who even spoke the same language as the fourteen-year-old.

When Connor arrived at Manfred's house after school, Manfred led the boy through the room full of computer equipment. He looked back to see that Connor had stopped, transfixed.

"This is so cool," he said. "What do you do?"

Manfred tried not to sound embarrassed or apologetic when he explained his psychic online business, which was obviously not a hundred percent honest. But Connor didn't remark on that aspect at all, a little to Manfred's surprise. Instead, he was enthralled with the computers and Manfred's ability to make a living from them.

"We just have an old laptop," Connor said. "And Dad won't let us go on Facebook or anything."

Manfred tried not to look as astonished as he felt. He could not imagine two young people being without social media, especially when the Lovells lived in such an out-of-the-way spot. But given Shawn's aversion to his kids being noticed in any public way, it made sense.

"There are lots of ways to get into trouble with a computer," Manfred said, trying to hold up the flag for Shawn. He didn't want to undermine the man; that was not the way to win Shawn's trust, which was Manfred's current goal.

"Yeah, that's what Dad says," Connor muttered. He clearly didn't think the better of Manfred for having echoed one of his father's opinions.

Manfred felt about fifty years old. "Let me show you what I want you to do," he said, thinking a change of subject was called for. He led Connor out into the fenced backyard, which was overlooked by the pawnshop on the left and a dilapidated and empty cottage on the right. Bobo had told him that the empty cottage, even smaller than the house Manfred was renting, had been left by its previous owner to a distant cousin, and the cousin had never taken possession of the place. It sat in dusty silence with the curtains drawn and the doors locked, and its yard was a straggly mess. Manfred had realized that his own place very nearly matched it.

"What I want you to do," he said briskly, "is pull all the weeds that have grown up out here and pile them in that barrel. I'll burn them when they dry out." The old metal barrel, which had clearly been used for the same purpose in the past, was positioned just outside the overgrown hedge that encircled the backyard, just inside the chain-link fence. "Once the weeds are all up, the hedge needs trimming with these hedge clippers. Once those clippings are all gathered up and in the barrel, you can mow the yard. I've got an old-fashioned push mower right here." He still hadn't had a chance to get into the toolshed. The mower was parked under the eaves behind the house and covered with a tarp.

The hedge clippers were more exciting. He'd bought them at the Home Depot in Davy, and they were gleaming.

"At least they're sharp," Connor said. "But electric ones would have been better."

"This isn't that big a yard, and the manual ones are fine for the job," Manfred said, suppressing a scowl with some effort. "Also, this'll take you longer so you'll earn more money."

"All *right*." Connor looked a bit happier.

"You are on your honor, keeping track of your time," Manfred said. "I can't keep looking out here to police you."

"What does that mean—on my honor?"

"That means I'm trusting you to keep an accurate account of the time you work."

Connor brightened. "Okay. I can do that."

Though he prided himself on being able to read people, Manfred couldn't decide if Connor was excited about being trusted or if he was simply pleased at the idea of being able to hoodwink Manfred out of a few extra bucks. Maybe because the kid himself didn't know how he'd react? He definitely didn't give out a vibe that was easy to interpret.

Connor was apparently hard at work the couple of times Manfred went into the kitchen to get water or a cup of coffee. *The kid's going to be a good-looking man,* he thought, *but his social adjustment is going to be all off. I wonder what his dad thinks is going to happen when Connor and Creek are too old to keep at home, when he has to let them go out into the world? What did Shawn do that he has to keep them hidden?*

Not for the first time, Manfred wondered if the family wasn't in some witness protection program. After she'd taken Creek to the funeral, Fiji had run into Manfred when she was checking her mailbox, and she'd told Manfred the idea had crossed her mind. That scenario made sense to Manfred. It would explain so many things about the Lovells. But it also felt too TV-plot to be real. Besides, Shawn seemed so commonplace. What could he have done to earn him a place in the program?

Or was the man some kind of isolationist? Did he think he'd keep his children free from all modern influences if he raised them here?

Manfred added a little sugar to his coffee, shrugged, and went back to work. Though he was curious, Manfred was honest enough to admit to himself that Shawn Lovell's issues were only important to him because they affected Creek.

It was still light when Connor stopped for the day. He had done a lot of clearing. He told Manfred that he'd worked for two and a half hours and taken two breaks. The boy seemed very proud of himself. Shawn had come by to bring Connor some water. Manfred only knew this because he'd looked out the window to see Shawn walking down his driveway, bottle in hand. *I should have known Shawn would check up on him,* he'd thought, shaking his head, before he returned his attention to the screen.

Then Teacher Reed came by, just as Manfred was paying Connor.

"Hey, man," he called. "You taking my jobs out from under me?"

Connor looked startled, and a little flattered. "No, sir," he said, grinning. "I'm just weeding for Mr. Bernardo."

"I'd better watch my back," Teacher said with mock anxiety, and strode off about his business, whatever it had been. Manfred thought it was odd that Teacher was down this way, unless he'd been visiting the pawnshop and just happened to spy Connor working.

"I have to go home to cook supper," Connor said. "I'll come back tomorrow to finish."

"Good job," Manfred said, pleased.

"If you need that old stump pulled out," the boy offered, "I can tie a rope to it and pull it out with Dad's old pickup."

"Your dad might have something to say about that. Might damage the truck."

"It's a junker," Connor said dismissively. "He taught me how to drive on it. Course, I don't have a license yet. But I drive around town sometimes."

Manfred laughed, and said, "I guess I'd better check with Bobo before I do anything that drastic to the backyard." Pulling up a stump—in an area where graves had to be blasted with dynamite—might be a serious undertaking.

Manfred was just closing the door when he spotted Sheriff Smith parking his car in front of Fiji's place. The sheriff's visits were getting fewer and farther between. Apparently no new information had surfaced about Aubrey's murder. For the first time, the thought crossed

Manfred's mind that the mystery of her death might never be solved. It would hang over Bobo forever.

And *not* for the first time, Manfred was profoundly glad he'd moved here after Aubrey's disappearance.

30

The sheriff had been in Fiji's store before, but he looked around him like he'd fallen down the rabbit hole. It was clear that he was uneasy at being in a magic shop. Especially one that was being decorated for Halloween; in the absence of any customers, Fiji had started the ball rolling.

When he entered, to the jingle of the old-fashioned bell attached to the door, Fiji was up on a ladder in the middle of the room. She was hanging a full-size skeleton from a hook on the ceiling. More accurately, she was suspending a skeleton that appeared to have been hanged with a noose.

"Can I help you?" Arthur Smith asked immediately.

"Yes, that would be great." Fiji came down the ladder cautiously. "I seem to be an inch shorter than I need to be."

The sheriff smiled at her, and for the first time, Fiji thought of him as a man rather than as an instrument of her discomfiture. She estimated Smith was fifteen years older than she was, but he swarmed up the ladder with an impressive amount of ease. He completed the whole job in less than a minute. "Where should I put the ladder?" he asked.

"It goes in the extra bedroom," Fiji said. "The second door on the left." She hurried to open the hall door for him, which she'd had installed when she'd decided to make the living room her place of business. She didn't want customers wandering through the rest of the house as though they had a right to inspect it.

The first door on the left was the bathroom, and Fiji was relieved she didn't leave towels on the floor or clothes strewn around. She'd gotten in the habit of keeping it orderly since, on the rare occasion, a customer needed to use it. Across the hall, her bedroom door was shut, also a habit she'd acquired through experience. She scurried ahead of Arthur to open the second bedroom door, on the left after the bathroom. There was a double bed, but primarily she used the room for storage. It was obvious where the ladder went; the objects in the room were stacked as neatly as a Tetris game.

Since he'd been so helpful, Fiji felt she had to offer him some hospitality. "Coffee? Water? Sweet tea?" she asked.

"I'd sure like a glass of tea," he said. He retreated to the shop area. When she brought his drink, she found him sitting in one of the two armchairs facing each other across a wicker table in the center of the shop floor. The table was stacked with *Modern Witch*, *Texas Monthly*, and *Crafts for the Home*. She placed a coaster handy.

"So, how's the investigation going?" she asked, not knowing what else to talk about. She was not sure why he'd dropped in.

"I've interviewed more right-wing nuts than I thought there were in Texas," he said wearily. "And all of them are giving each other alibis." He picked up the current issue of *Modern Witch*. "This is a serious publication?" he said. "You regard yourself as a witch?"

"Yes, it is. And I do."

"You believe that you can affect the outcome of things?"

"I believe in the power of spells to affect events," she said, measuring each word before she added it to the conversation.

"Why did you dislike Aubrey Hamilton so much?"

She'd been pretty sure he'd get around to asking her that. She knew she wasn't hard to read, in some respects. "She wasn't telling the truth in her relationship with Bobo," she said. "I've been his friend for some time. I've seen him with other women. Aubrey was really opaque about her previous life, about how she ended up as a waitress in Davy. I thought it was a mighty big coincidence that she was working at Bobo's favorite restaurant, that she didn't have any sort of boyfriend to slow down the way their relationship advanced, that she seemed to agree with Bobo in every respect."

"Most couples have some differences."

"Exactly. But every opinion Bobo had, she had, too. Or so she said." Fiji shrugged. "It just seemed sketchy to me."

"And did you share these thoughts with Bobo?"

"No, I did not."

"If you're such good friends, why not?"

She stared at him, at a loss. *Why not? Because I have a crush on him the size of a boulder. If I'd really just been his buddy, I would have spoken up.* "Because his love life is none of my business. Since he's a grown man and he obviously liked her a lot, I wasn't going to butt in and tell tales. Especially since I didn't have anything concrete to tell him. What was I gonna say, 'She agrees with you too much'?"

"You didn't think of using your witch ability to expose her?"

Suddenly Fiji's interior alarm system went off. She was treading on eggshells now. "What do you mean?"

"You didn't cast a spell on her, or ask one of your witch friends to do something?"

"I don't have any witch friends," Fiji said. "Not any serious practitioners. Why?"

"When one of my deputies was going through Aubrey's boxed belongings, she found this. It had been in her night table drawer." Arthur pulled a plastic bag out of his pocket. In it was a fishhook, and tied to the hook were three silk threads. On the other ends of the silk threads were flat patches, the ones you'd buy at a sewing store or craft store to apply to a garment or pillow. One of them was a heart. And one of them was shaped like lips.

Though he hadn't exactly offered the bag to her, Fiji leaned over and took it. She looked down at it with some distaste. "I can only guess about the interpretation," she said. "I suppose the hook means the spell was cast so the person owning this could get their hooks into someone. The heart means the caster wanted to get the person to love her, and the lips are for physical passion. This is just my guess."

"Is this the kind of thing you do?" Arthur Smith looked at her with level blue eyes.

She was tempted, so tempted, to show him exactly what she could do, but that way lay disaster. It had taken her years to learn that lesson. "I would never create such a thing," she said. "And it doesn't come from any school of witchcraft that I know about. It seems . . . made up. By someone who really doesn't know anything about the craft."

He was good at staring, she found. "I just about believe you," he said finally.

She shrugged. "You do or you don't," she said, but she felt relieved. "This is not my work. I don't know if she bought *So You Think You're a Witch* or *Magic Is Us*, or if someone with a little woo-woo in her system made this for Aubrey. Frankly, I have a hard time believing Aubrey would be interested in making something like this. But no true practitioner would have created it." She handed the plastic bag to the sheriff. Mr. Snuggly appeared from behind the shop counter, where one of his many pillows was positioned, and came to look up at Arthur Smith.

"Nice cat." Smith's admiration seemed to be genuine.

"Sometimes he's not as nice as he looks," she said. Mr. Snuggly's head swiveled with uncanny abruptness as he gave Fiji what could only be described as a glare.

"Claws the furniture?" Smith asked.

"Ah, likes to wake me up in the morning," she said. "He's got to have his chow." The cat turned his broad golden-striped back to her in a pointed fashion.

"It's just like he knows what you're saying."

"It is, isn't it," she said.

Smith left a moment later. He didn't volunteer any more information, but Fiji saw that he was driving down to the Antique Gallery and Nail Salon.

In the remaining daylight, after the sheriff had driven back to Davy, the motorcycles roared through Midnight. They all paused outside the pawnshop and milled around in a threatening manner. The inhabitants of Midnight wisely stayed inside behind locked doors. The most proactive community members, Olivia and Lemuel, were not able to respond. Olivia was on one of her mysterious trips out of town, and Lemuel was dead to the world.

Fiji called Bobo. "You okay?" she asked when he answered.

"I've got my shotgun and I'm ready," he said. "I've called the police."

"Good." She called Chuy.

"You all right?"

"We're good. We're ready. You need us to come to you?"

"No, stay inside. Bobo's called the police."

In the next minute or two all the residents of Midnight had called each other, except the Rev.

Fiji asked for the help of several goddesses. She was too frightened to run out her front door and in the door of the chapel to check on him. After all, motorcycle gangs had a bad reputation when it came to women. She was ashamed of her own cowardice. Finally, she went up into her attic, a place she avoided normally, and peered out a window, the only place she could see into the pet cemetery.

To her surprise, the Rev was digging a grave, about half human size. He'd hung his coat on a tree branch while he worked. He was ignoring the loud engine sounds and the yells of the MOL. He didn't even seem to notice the noise.

She scrambled down the rickety folding ladder and closed up the attic, feeling a flood of relief. Though the MOL were buzzing and droning, Fiji could just hear the siren of an approaching police car. She ran to the front window, hoping to see them all being cuffed and thrown in the back of police cars. There was only a single patrol, but at the sight of it, the MOL group scattered like billiard balls when the break occurs. They fled in all directions across the landscape, not sticking to the roads, and the patrol car couldn't follow all of them at once.

In fact, it made no attempt to follow any of them.

Fiji dashed out onto her porch, her face flushed and furious, and she gestured from the patrol car to one of the fleeing motorcycles, her meaning as clear as if she'd had a blackboard behind her. But the officer inside only pulled up in front of the pawnshop and got out of the car.

The cop was a woman, and Fiji stormed across the road to her. Manfred joined her just in time to hear, "So you thought if you couldn't get them all, you wouldn't get any of them?" Fiji was livid.

"Car chasing motorcycle, the end's not going to be good," the cop said in a bored way. She was a chunky woman whom the uniform did not flatter. Her dark brown hair was pulled back into a tight knob on the back of her head, and her dark glasses were mirrors. Her face was hard and brown with crevices like a walnut's shell. "And they hadn't done anything."

"Hadn't done anything," Fiji repeated.

Manfred was afraid she was going to freeze the police officer. Now that he was close enough, he could read "Gomez" on her name tag.

"They didn't shoot anything, they didn't even throw rocks," Gomez said. "They didn't shout threats, even. Was I supposed to arrest them for driving in circles and looking scary?"

"That would have been a start in the right direction," Fiji said, and her hands twitched. Mr. Snuggly was standing at Fiji's feet, looking up at Gomez with an unblinking feline stare. Gomez noticed the cat. "He'll know me next time he sees me," she said, and laughed, but not as if she really found that amusing. "I'm not much of a cat person."

"Oooooh," Fiji said with faux sympathy. "Are you scared of my kitty? Well, Mr. Snuggly—"

"Hi, Officer," Manfred said smoothly, and Fiji felt like smacking him. But he kept on talking. "Thanks for coming so quickly. I don't know how much you know about what's been happening here lately, but we've been having trouble with people from this group coming into Midnight and attacking us." By the time he'd finished, Fiji had calmed down a bit.

"Not exactly the way I heard it," Gomez said.

That brought both Manfred and Fiji up short. "What do you mean?" Fiji said, holding on to her composure with both hands.

"Way I see it is you got some kind of dispute with Price Eggleston's political group. First the widow of one of them starts living here with one of you Midnight people, and she goes missing, turns up dead. Two of them come over here to talk to the guy she was living with, and they vanish. Poof! Then two of them come over here to find out why the first two vanished, maybe go a little overboard, and they get arrested. Then their little hunting club gets burned down. Now they come over here and let off some steam, and here I am and they've left. Having done nothing."

Fiji and Manfred darted a glance at each other. Fiji could tell Manfred was as shocked as she was at this interpretation of events. She left it to him to answer.

"But we don't know what happened to the two that disappeared," he said, looking flabbergasted. "And we didn't go set anything on fire."

Gomez's eyes went from him to Fiji. Her mouth pulled up at one corner in a distinctly skeptical way. "Right," she said. "Well, they're gone now, no one's hurt, and I'm going back on patrol."

"I'm glad Sheriff Smith doesn't share your views," Fiji said. She'd found her voice. Mr. Snuggly stood and stepped closer to Gomez, who took a step back.

"That's your assumption, that he doesn't," Gomez said, and got back into her car. "Better pick up your cat," she said out of the open window. "It would be a shame if he got run over."

Mr. Snuggly hissed. It was the most malevolent sound Fiji had ever heard from the cat. She was proud of him.

Gomez shut her window hastily and sped away. After her car was a cloud of dust on the Davy highway, all the people of Midnight came out of their houses and stores in the thick dusk. They gathered in front of the pawnshop, even the Rev—except for Bobo, the Lovells, Lem, and Olivia.

"I can understand why Shawn wouldn't want his kids to come out after that little invasion," Manfred said, though no one had said a word. Fiji raised an eyebrow at Manfred, who looked embarrassed. Just then, the door of Midnight Pawn opened, and Bobo came down the steps to join them.

He looks better, Fiji thought, *like he's put the worst behind him*. She noticed, all over again, that he still looked as though he'd lost an appreciable amount of weight, but he was clean and shaved, and his clothes weren't wrinkled. Overall, this version of Bobo Winthrop seemed more like the man she'd known than he had since the picnic. However, he was exasperated, as his first words proved.

"Why don't I just go to this Eggleston's house and turn myself over to the MOL," Bobo said to the silent gaggle of Midnighters. "Might as well get it over with."

"No!" said Fiji. "You better not, or I'll kick your ass, Bobo Winthrop!"

The rest of them said something similar, though in less passionate ways. Even the Rev (though he kept glancing at his watch) told Bobo that God helped those who helped themselves. Teacher said, "Man, you might as well hang yourself as do that," and they all nodded.

Manfred murmured to Fiji, "I wish Olivia and Lemuel were here."

"I think they've done enough," Fiji said.

"What do you mean?" Manfred said.

"Oh, use your brain!" she said impatiently. She turned her attention back to the conversation whirling around Bobo. Joe and Chuy were telling Bobo he could sleep in their guest bedroom, and Teacher was offering to install an alarm system. Manfred offered him a couch to sleep on, and Fiji said she had a guest bedroom. The Rev informed Bobo that he would pray for him and that the Almighty Father would protect the righteous.

At that, Bobo laughed. Then he apologized. "I'm sorry, Rev. I wasn't making fun of your religion. I was just doubting I was righteous."

The Rev said seriously—as he said all things—"Never doubt that you are a good man, Bobo Winthrop." Then he saw that a car had pulled into the driveway at the side of the chapel. "I have a funeral to see to," he said.

"This late? It's almost dark. Whose funeral?" Fiji was curious.

"I turned on the lights. Blackie the cocker spaniel," he told her, and crossed the street to attend to Blackie and his owner.

As Fiji had expected, Bobo was thanking everyone and turning down their offers. "Thanks, Chuy, Joe. Manfred. Feej. But I'll stay here at the shop. After all, I have to work during the day. Lem can't. And if someone threw a firebomb or set a fire . . . well, I'd have to get him out. If they come at night, he'd do the same for me. Teacher, I'll take you up on the alarm system. But you may not want to fill in here until this situation is resolved."

"I say yes to that," Madonna said instantly. She was gently swaying from side to side, Grady asleep on her chest, his head on her shoulder. "I'm sorry, Bobo, and you tell Lem we said so, too. But Teacher shouldn't risk his life to keep a store open."

"Absolutely," Bobo said, nodding.

Teacher looked as though he had his own thoughts on the subject, but he kept his mouth clamped shut. Madonna began to walk back to the diner, and after a second of looking very unhappy, Teacher followed her.

Fiji, frazzled and exasperated, bent and swooped up Mr. Snuggly, who nestled in her arms. "You crossed the road by yourself," she scolded the cat. He looked up at her with wide golden eyes. "Okay," she said. "Okay. I know you're a grown-up cat." He stared some more. She relaxed, smiled.

"If you're through communing with the cat," Bobo said mildly.

"Yeah?" She looked at him, still smiling.

"I'm gonna go clean a few guns," Bobo said.

Manfred stopped him. He said, "Bobo, I really think you should take Chuy and Joe up on their offer. Or sleep at my place. It's really your place, after all, and you'd be right next door to the shop. We'd know if anything happened."

"Or come to my house," Fiji offered. "There's not a lot of room in the guest room since that's where I store all my extra stuff, but there's a bed and it's made up."

"It wouldn't be so crowded if you had a storage shed," Bobo said, as if that were the most important thing in the world. "That'll be the next thing I work on, I promise. If I'm still around to work on anything." He smiled to take the sting out of his words.

"A storage shed is not at the top of my list of worries right now." Spots of color burned in Fiji's cheeks. She looked at Manfred, silently asking him to think of something persuasive to say.

Manfred tried. "This Price Eggleston is trying to spy on you and scare you in all kinds of ways. Are you sure it's the mythical arms of your grandfather he wants? Or is there something more personal in this?"

"I don't know him," Bobo said. "I only met him that one time when he came in the pawnshop. I can't think what he'd have against me unless he got involved with Aubrey at some point, either while she was married or after her husband was shot. Maybe he honestly thinks I killed her."

Mr. Snuggly opened his mouth, but Fiji looked down at him and the cat yawned instead of whatever he'd been about to do.

Manfred told Fiji, "It almost looked like he was going to say something."

"That's silly," she said.

The cat winked at him.

31

It rained the next day, torrents and buckets. The fierce wind drove the drops against the front of Fiji's place with more noise than she would have thought possible. She was so glad she hadn't finished her outside Halloween decorations; that was scheduled for Saturday.

Only two customers came into her shop all morning, and she spent most of her time dusting and rearranging the merchandise. She managed to break two glass figures in the process, which effectively erased her profit from the two customers. She had to warn Mr. Snuggly to stay in his cushioned basket while she swept up the glass. To be doubly sure she'd gotten every tiny glass splinter, she vacuumed. Later that afternoon, she went back to the kitchen, leaving the hall door open so she could hear the shop bell, and started a pot of soup. It was a day that cried out for soup. She put on an Enya CD to work by.

While she chopped up vegetables and leftover chicken, Fiji thought about how to resolve the town crisis. The death of Aubrey was no longer Bobo's tragedy—or at least, not only his. Aubrey's murder surely tied into the legend of the missing guns. Fiji feared that bad men would keep showing up as long as Bobo lived, in search of the mythical treasure trove of death.

Fiji heard the shop doorbell tinkle, and she dumped everything on the chopping board into the pot of chicken broth. As she washed her hands, she thought of having corn bread with the soup tonight. As she was drying them, she told herself how much better the soup would be without the corn bread, and failed to convince herself that could be so. As she hurried down the short hall to the front of the shop, she called, "I'm coming."

She was already smiling when she stepped into the front room. The smile vanished when she saw a tall man in a cowboy hat standing in the middle of the display cases. He was draped in a cheap yellow rain poncho, dripping water all over the boards and throw rugs. She was not a psychic or a telepath, but she knew bad intentions when she saw them, and Price Eggleston meant her no good. She spun on her heel to run down the hall and out the back door, but in three big strides he went around the chairs and table, seized her by the shoulder, and wrapped one arm around her middle. Then he clapped the other hand over her mouth.

Fiji struggled with all her might, using her elbows and kicking and squirming, but he was a strong man. She caught a glimpse of Mr. Snuggly. He'd jumped out of his basket and was hiding in the shadows under the shelves. She fought all the harder, hoping her assailant would not notice the cat and do him harm.

"Keep still, you bitch!" Eggleston growled, and she kicked backward to strike his shin. He was hampered by the plastic poncho and by his instinctive avoidance of the furniture and fixtures of the shop. But when he let her down a little, enough so her feet could touch the floor, Fiji planted them on the floor and pushed backward with all her might. She succeeded in causing Eggleston to slam into a clear case full of small glass ornaments and sun catchers, and the case went over. Fiji was trying to leave a record of what had happened, and when she heard the crash as the case hit the floor, she knew she had succeeded.

But the struggle had exhausted her, and she had to catch her breath. Eggleston took advantage of her weak moment by dragging her out of the shop into the rain, leaving the shop door open. There was no traffic, no one in sight, as he wrestled her out to his truck, pinning her against it while he pulled her hands behind her and clicked her wrists into a pair of handcuffs. Even then Fiji did not quit fighting entirely. She tossed her head from side to side when he tried to place some silver duct tape across her mouth, but eventually he timed it right and sealed her lips shut. He stuffed her into the front seat before running around to the driver's side. He looked both ways behind him, backed out across the empty road to face west, and drove off toward Marthasville with the angriest woman in Texas sliding around on the bench seat, unable to stop herself, her hands cuffed behind her.

In the store, now silent except for the drumming of the rain on the roof, Mr. Snuggly considered his options. He could go back to sleep in his basket (he liked that idea very much), but that didn't seem a noble reaction. He could chase after the truck in the rain . . . he discarded that option instantly. It required too much action on his part, and though he was a very fast cat, he could not keep up with a truck. He licked his paws as he gloomily settled on the most becoming option.

He would have to go next door.

If cats could sigh, he would have, when he stepped out onto the porch and looked at the rain. But since the bad man had left the door open, he really had no excuse to linger. Mr. Snuggly glared at a cat's version of hell. But he gathered himself and dashed in a blur of marmalade to the cover of the nearest bush, where he took shelter. He got drenched instantly with the water that had been clinging to its leaves.

"Curse the man," he muttered, and prepared for his next sprint to the doors of the chapel. The small eave provided no cover for Mr. Snuggly at all, and he began to caterwaul. He leaped up to scratch at the wooden doors. The Rev responded almost immediately. He had to look down to see who was making such a noise at God's door, but when he realized Mr. Snuggly was his visitor, he stepped back and the cat shot through the aperture and into the relative peace of the chapel.

"Brother," said the Rev. "What has happened to Fiji?"

"A man came," Mr. Snuggly said. "She fought and cursed like a madwoman, and I was proud of her, but he was too big and too strong. He took her."

"Miss Fiji has been abducted?"

"Yes, indeed." Mr. Snuggly, his errand complete and his duty discharged, began to clean his fur. He paused long enough to say, "You must do something about it. She has left the cooking thing on, which she will not do if she is not remaining in the house." Mr. Snuggly was proud to have remembered that detail.

"Thank you, Brother," the Rev said, and it was his turn to consider options.

After asking one or two more questions, the Rev went next door to see the chaos in Fiji's normally orderly home (though the old man disliked rain almost as much as the cat, whom he carried tucked under one thin arm). Somehow the broken things on the floor made him much more anxious.

The thud of feet on the rock sidewalk leading up to the porch announced new arrivals. Bobo hurried into the room, closely followed by Manfred. Manfred had taken a moment to pull on a hooded plastic poncho, but Bobo had come as he was. His shirt was soaked with rain, and his hair clung damply to his scalp.

"I saw a truck hauling ass away from here. What happened?" he asked, every line of his body tense. "Where is Fiji?"

"She's been taken," said the Rev.

"Little Timmy fell down the well," said a tiny voice, and the two men looked around wildly to find the source.

"Who said that?" Bobo asked.

"Don't even ask," the Rev said, with a kind of tired exasperation. "Let us pray for our sister, for she has been taken, and we must recover her."

"What are the cops doing?" Manfred demanded.

"I haven't called them. This is something we have to do. The man who took Fiji has had enough time to switch vehicles or possibly to reach his destination."

"Have we heard from Fiji at all?" Bobo asked.

"She's handcuffed and gagged," the Rev said.

Bobo made a shocked and angry noise, as if someone had poked him with a hot needle.

"We need to go across the street to the pawnshop, Bobo," the Rev said. Manfred wondered why. "We'll take the cat with us." The cat in question raised his head and looked at the Rev with his eyes slitted in indignation. "Manfred, if you would put the cat under your rain poncho, it would protect him on our way across the street."

Manfred felt almost as unhappy as Mr. Snuggly, but he lifted the poncho, scooped up the cat, and pulled the yellow plastic down over him.

The second they were inside the pawnshop, Manfred set Mr. Snuggly on the floor. The cat stretched and began inspecting all the chairs he could choose to sit in. Naturally, he selected the one Bobo favored, and in a second he was curled into a ball in the middle of the chair, purring loudly.

Bobo hardly seemed to notice but drew three chairs together around that one so that they could talk. They all sat, and the Rev told them that he had been alerted to Fiji's plight—and he used the word "plight"—by the cat.

If the Rev had had much of a sense of humor, it would have been highly gratified by the expressions on Bobo's and Manfred's faces.

"And what's so funny about that?" said the same small, bitter voice they'd heard in Fiji's store.

They both turned to look at the cat.

Mr. Snuggly said, "I can talk. Woo-hoo."

Manfred filled his lungs with an audible gasp. It appeared he'd forgotten to breathe. "I thought so!" Bobo said triumphantly. "From that day I dropped the gardening fork on my toe. I *knew* I heard someone laughing. So, cat, you were the one who actually saw someone take Fiji?"

The cat nodded and then closed his eyes, intending to resume his nap.

"Wait a minute," Manfred said. "You have to tell us all about it."

"The man came in the front door, and when she came from the kitchen, he took her." He put his head back down and closed his eyes.

"She fought?"

"Oh, yes," said the cat, opening his eyes a little, very reluctantly. "The case got broken, and some of the glass landed *very* close to me. I could have been cut! But he hustled her out into the rain and handcuffed her. I saw him when I got up on the counter to watch. He put something over her mouth and shoved her into his truck. Then I ran over to the chapel, because I knew she would give me permission to leave the grounds under the circumstances. I roused the Rev by an almost supernatural effort."

"Almost supernatural," Manfred repeated.

"Yes. He heard me and listened to me, and now here I am, warm and almost dry and in a good chair. When I wake up, you can give me some salmon." Mr. Snuggly's eyes drifted shut and he relaxed into sleep.

"Somehow I thought a talking cat would be friendlier," Bobo said. "Ah . . . more caring?"

"He might talk, but he's still a cat," the Rev said, as if that were explanation enough.

"Setting aside the talking cat and the fact that he doesn't seem too concerned about his owner, which I know is a lot to set aside, this is about Fiji," Manfred said.

"Yes, and I will say two things here," the Rev told them. "Bobo, though God tells us not to judge, you have taken the easy way out two times in a row, or your friend down below has."

For a wild moment, Manfred thought the Rev's downcast eyes meant Bobo had a connection with the Devil, but he understood after a long second that the Rev meant Lemuel.

"What do you mean?" Bobo looked bewildered.

"Did Lemuel not settle your problem with the first two thugs this Eggleston sent?"

Bobo flushed deep red. "Yes," he said. "Lemuel and . . ."

"Lemuel and Olivia," the Rev said. "And do you not suspect that it was Lemuel and Olivia who went over to Marthasville and burned down Eggleston's house?"

Bobo became even redder. "I don't *know* that," he said.

"But you believe it's so."

Manfred looked from the wizened old minister to the big blond man, trying to absorb all these new ideas. "So," he said cautiously, "you're telling Bobo that Eggleston wouldn't have resorted to kidnapping Fiji if Lemuel and Olivia hadn't been so drastic in their reaction?"

"I am saying we'd have a much better chance of getting her back unharmed."

"Okay, point taken," Bobo said. "But what now?"

The Rev looked almost approving. "Good. The right spirit will lead you into the paths of righteousness," he said. "We must find where he has taken her, and we must rescue her, because the police will not be able to do this."

"But won't we have to take measures as drastic as the ones you're condemning?"

The Rev said very patiently, "Now is the time to take measures. Her welfare is at stake. It's not the answer to every problem. It is the answer to *this* problem."

"If you're a hammer, every problem looks like a nail," Manfred said suddenly. He'd just caught on.

"Exactly. And Lemuel and Olivia are hammers." The Rev nodded, glad now that he felt they were all on the same page.

"Lem will be up soon," Bobo said, glancing at a clock.

"It's too bad you're not a tracking creature," the Rev said. "But Lemuel will do his best."

"Olivia's not here?" Manfred was looking all around him in furtive glances, worried that Lemuel would pop up out of nowhere and scare the shit out of him.

"No, she's gone." The Rev looked sad, whether because he missed Olivia, thought she would be useful if she were here, or regretted whatever cause had taken her away, Manfred could not decide.

"Should we get Chuy and Joe?" Manfred said.

"No, they need to stay here," the Rev said, without any hesitation.

"Teacher?"

"No, he would not come," the Rev said. "Better not to ask him."

Manfred wondered how the Rev knew all this, and how the oldest resident of Midnight had been tacitly acknowledged leader of the Fiji rescue expedition—but since Manfred himself was not qualified to take control, he was not about to ask out loud.

"What are we going to do?" Bobo asked impatiently.

"We're going to find Fiji and get her back."

"Great. How?" Bobo snapped.

The Rev looked up at Bobo, but Bobo didn't relent.

"As soon as Lem is up, we'll go. We'll take the cat."

Both the younger men looked at the Rev as if he'd lost his mind, and so did the cat, whose eyes sprang open. Manfred thought they were lucky Mr. Snuggly's outrage made him speechless.

"Mr. Snuggly, Manfred will hold you. He is a psychic, and that will help you focus."

"Oh, all right," the cat said sullenly. "I must get my feeder back."

Bobo looked a little punchy. "All this time, he's been able to talk," he whispered. "And he calls Feej his *feeder*?"

"You have a vampire living in your basement, and you're stunned by a talking cat?" the Rev said, with some asperity.

"Good point," Manfred said. "Catch up, Bobo. Okay, so we take the cat out with us, and because he's . . . what, her familiar? . . . he'll be able to tell where Fiji is?"

"Yes," said the Rev. "He is a lazy cat, but he must do that for her."

"What's all the palaver about?" Lemuel said behind them, and Manfred couldn't help it. He jumped. Everyone except Mr. Snuggly politely ignored that.

Lemuel had come up through the trapdoor. "I could tell there was trouble up here," he said, moving to stand beside Bobo. Lemuel was wearing starched khakis and a button-down shirt. He made it look like a costume. His pale hair was slicked back, still damp from a shower, Manfred assumed.

"Fiji has been stolen," the Rev said. "We think the man who took her was Eggleston. If you had not burned down his hunting lodge, we would know where she was, but since you have done that, we must look for her elsewhere. We have the cat."

Lemuel absorbed all this quickly. He didn't respond to the Rev's rebuke, and he didn't waste time raging against the kidnapper. "We must start now, then. How long have they been gone?"

The Rev looked at his watch. "Less than an hour."

"We can all get in your station wagon," Bobo said, and that was another surprise for Manfred. He'd never seen the Rev drive.

"Do you need to change?" Lemuel said to the Rev, and Manfred wondered why the Rev would need different clothes.

"Not now," the Rev replied, and he left the shop, running faster than Manfred would ever have believed a man his apparent age could move.

In three minutes, he was parked in front of Midnight Pawn in an ancient station wagon. It was dark and rusty and huge, and probably steered like a boat, but in this weather, that was about what they needed. Manfred had not removed his rain poncho, and he scooped up the cat again. They scrambled out of the store and into the station wagon, and without a word the Rev drove west.

32

The rain did not slacken as they drove toward Marthasville. It beat against the road and the station wagon as if it were trying to pound them apart.

From the rear seat, Manfred, who'd been tapping on his phone, said, "Price Eggleston has a home address on Rolling Hills Road. Someone named Bart Eggleston, I'm assuming that's his dad, has a phone listing on the same road. From the addresses, they're next door to each other."

"Your computer told you all that?" the Rev said.

"My telephone told me all that. You really should try it sometime."

"I have a telephone," the Rev said. He was bent forward to peer out the windshield. "It stays on the wall in my house and takes messages if I don't want to answer it. That's all I need."

Manfred could tell from the limpness of the warm bundle under his poncho that Mr. Snuggly had gone to sleep again. So far, he was not a fan of the cat. But he would rather think about the cat than

Lemuel, who was sitting beside him and behind Bobo. The vampire seemed more stone than flesh. Manfred could not imagine what Lemuel was thinking. The vampire could be lamenting the absence of his lover, he could be angry at the Rev, he could be planning revenge on Fiji's abductors, or he could be trying to remember if he'd flossed that night. He could even be considering the scolding the Rev had given him.

The Rev drove as fast as he could, considering the age and size of the vehicle and the terrible weather, but there was no way they were going to catch up with the pickup truck. When they'd gotten close to Marthasville, the old man said, "Manfred, wake the cat."

Manfred said, "Okay, I'll give it a shot." He gave the cat a gentle shake and lifted up the flap of yellow plastic that had covered him.

"I'm awake," said a peevish voice. Mr. Snuggly looked up at Manfred through slitted eyes. "I will know when she is close," the cat said.

"You'd better," said the Rev, very quietly.

"No threatening the cat!" Mr. Snuggly said.

No one spoke after that. They all concentrated on finding Fiji.

33

Fiji was scared, and she was angry. It was impossible to say which emotion was stronger. Just after they'd left Midnight, a moment of hydroplaning on the slick road had left her down on the floor-board, since she had no way to catch herself. Fortunately, Eggleston steadied the truck and calmed down. Fiji was glad the road west was mostly straight and the hills were gentle. She had so many thoughts running through her head that she couldn't seize any one of them to develop. She had wept a little (out of sheer anger, she told herself), and her nose was stopped up in consequence. Since her mouth was sealed shut, she had to concentrate on her breathing. Finally her nasal passages cleared, and she was getting oxygen in a regular amount in the normal way. It was amazing how much that helped to clear her mind.

She had a few thousand things to say to Price Eggleston, but by necessity they were bottled up inside her. *That doesn't mean I'm powerless,* she told herself sternly. *I can still work magic without a voice. Or hands. Or the cat.* Great-Aunt Mildred had told her that spoken spells and hand gestures were only tools to the witch, that what mattered most was intent. "Focus and intent," she'd said.

So this is like a test, Fiji told herself. *I can do this.* She could see Eggleston's foot very clearly, in its cowboy boot. She concentrated on the boot. She imagined it getting hot. Suddenly she realized the left foot was the one that needed to get hot; if the right one caught on fire, the truck might crash with her helpless inside it. *Idiot,* she scolded herself, and rubbed her cheek against her shoulder to wipe off a tear. Shoshanna Whitlock had been easy; she hadn't been expecting any resistance and she'd been standing still.

This separates the witches from the wannabes, Fiji thought, and she focused on the heel of the boot. She made it hot. She thought of heat, of fire, and she sent it all into the boot. She didn't let herself blink, and she held herself still, and she was glad that the big man at the wheel did not seem to want to talk to her. In the movies, villains always wanted to explain themselves. It was her luck to have been captured by a villain who wasn't of the chatty variety.

His left foot stirred. He rubbed it across the floor mat. "What bit me?" he muttered. Instantly changing her tactic, Fiji imagined a big snake, though she wasn't educated enough about snakes to make it a particular pattern. She figured with the gathering darkness that Eggleston couldn't see down by his boot very clearly, and in this she was right. He could see the coiled shape and feel the intense heat she generated in his heel, and that was enough to make him yelp, swerve violently onto the shoulder of the road, throw the truck into park, and leap out.

Here she had a choice—if the snake flowed out after him, would he run? Or should she "keep" it in the truck with her? When he drew a gun, Fiji's choice was made for her. She didn't want him firing into the truck. So out the snake went, slithering right for her abductor.

The man made a sound that combined fear and incredulity, and he shot at the imaginary snake.

Fiji congratulated herself and began thinking of ways to keep him out of the truck, but she wasn't able to come up with anything good while her abductor was frantically searching the ground to find the corpse of the illusory serpent. This was made nearly impossible by the pouring rain and the dark sky. *Lemuel will be rising soon*, she thought, and though some of the feelings she'd had for Lemuel lately had not been kindly, she looked forward to seeing him now with a passionate longing.

She tried to build an illusory wall between the man and the truck while he was still searching for the snake, but she was too uncomfortable with her wrists strained behind her, and too upset, to concentrate properly. *I should have made the snake bite him*, she thought. Perhaps he would have been upset enough to manifest the symptoms of snakebite. Perhaps the "venom" would have killed him.

Fiji's wall did not manifest successfully. All too soon, her abductor became convinced that he'd either wounded the snake or frightened it off. He holstered the gun, and after a few more seconds of looking around—during which she prayed *someone* was making progress in tracking her—he pulled her up onto the seat and buckled her in. He went around to his side and climbed in, and the truck lurched back onto the road.

"You're lucky that ole snake didn't bite you," he told her. "I got no idea how the damn thing got in here."

I don't feel too lucky right now, she thought, leaning forward as far as the seat belt would permit to relieve the pressure on her arms. She began to focus on his boot again. She thought of heat. She wanted him to become convinced he'd been bitten, somehow, and was just now feeling the full effect. She doubted his cowboy boots would even permit fangs to penetrate, but maybe he wouldn't believe that. In a second, he moved his left foot restlessly.

"Ole snake," he said, trying not to sound anxious. "Don't worry, lady, you're going to be okay."

She didn't answer. She was too busy staring at his foot.

"Goddamn," he muttered. "That hurts."

Yay! She was doing the right thing. Mildred would be proud of her.

And then his heel began smoking and burst into tiny flames.

He yelled and the truck left the road. This was maybe more success than she'd planned on, because they careened down into a slight ditch and jolted up the rise on the other side, smacking into a barbed-wire fence. She did not let the accident break her focus this time, and the flames grew hotter. He threw the pickup into park and ejected himself from the cab of the truck again. Out in the downpour, he began stamping around on his foot. Because he'd panicked, he didn't rip off the boot but stomped down into a puddle to extinguish the flame. It worked just as well, and she almost shrieked in frustration when her work again came to nothing but a delaying tactic.

Plus, this time he figured it out. "You did this," he said, and he wasn't screaming at her and he didn't sound angry with her, which somehow made his voice all the more frightening. She thought her brain was going to pop with the effort she was making to shrink back against the seat of the pickup, imagine some way to protect herself, and rub the edge of the duct tape against the seat belt. Since he'd only slapped it on and her face had been wet, she succeeded in removing enough of it to allow her to speak.

"Why did you take me? I haven't done a thing to you."

"Blame your friend Bobo. He's got something I want. He killed two of my soldiers. He got two others arrested. He burned down our meeting place. And he murdered a woman who was part of my movement. Lisa tells me you're real close to him. Maybe you've taken Aubrey's place. So I've taken someone of *his*, until he steps up to answer for his crimes."

"Oh, bullshit. None of that is true. He doesn't have this cache of arms, he didn't kill your so-called soldiers, and your buddies deserved to be arrested. He thought the sun shone out of Aubrey's ass. He did not harm any of those people, and he doesn't have any of that stuff."

"But my soldiers disappeared after I sent them to talk to him."

"You mean, after you sent them into his own place of business to beat him up. Be man enough to say it." She could not twist her head enough to see him well, but she hoped she was shaming him. Being diplomatic would be wiser, but she was mightily pissed off.

"Why not? He's got what I need, what I want. He's not part of the cause. He should give up the arms that were so important to his grandfather, a real patriot. Those guns were meant for people willing to fight to sustain our liberty. Don't you know how close we are to Armageddon here? Don't you understand how fast we'll go under? The Mexicans will drown us. The tide will come across the border, and that'll be all she wrote. Unless we're armed and ready."

"So the answer to everything is to kill people."

"We gotta defend ourselves! You're just being a damn liberal if you don't see that. Aubrey understood."

"Then why did you kill her?"

He came closer to the open door. He was hopelessly soaked now. She saw that the torrent had abated to a slow but steady pelting of drops. "We did not kill her. He did, your boyfriend Bobo."

"He did *not*," she said again. "He grieves for her every day. He had no idea when we set out on that picnic that we would find her body. I was there. I know."

This time he did slap her, an openhanded smack to the cheek.

"You're wrong, bitch. You are so wrong, and he is so guilty. I liked you better when you weren't talking. Shut up, now, or I'll tap you on the head with the gun," he said, as he climbed into the truck.

That was an effective threat, because Fiji had recently read an article about how thin the skull could be. It had creeped her out. She was terrified that his "tap" could put her in a wheelchair for life. She had no idea if she had a thick skull or a thin skull, and she didn't want to bet on it one way or another.

He managed to get the truck back on the road after some maneuvering. She'd hoped the tires were stuck, but no such luck. They resumed their rain-drenched trek to Marthasville . . . or wherever they were going.

"How'd you set my foot on fire?" he said suddenly.

Uh-oh. She said immediately, "That's ridiculous. I got no matches and I'm handcuffed."

"Midnight's got a reputation for funny people," he said. "I think you're one of the funny ones."

"Funny ha-ha, right?" she said.

"Funny crazy," he replied. She shut her mouth. But her curiosity couldn't let her keep quiet forever.

"Where are we going?" she asked, after an interval.

"To a place your buddies will never find. A place behind my parents' house." He laughed. "My mom and dad ain't been in it in ten years."

"A bomb shelter?" she asked.

"Hey, how'd you know?" He was immediately suspicious and indignant.

I figured it out, idiot. "Not too many basements in Texas, so I figured it was a separate building. Marthasville isn't on a lake, so it couldn't be a boathouse."

She could almost feel his suspicious eyes dart over her vulnerable skull. She held her breath until the moment had passed when he would have hit her.

She prayed to the Goddess and her consort to get her through this mess alive, and she prayed her friends were looking for her now . . . if the damn lazy cat had done his job.

"Did you see my cat?"

"What?" She'd definitely surprised him with that one.

"My cat. Did you see my cat in the store? Did you shut the door?"

Her heart was sinking as she realized that Mr. Snuggly might be stuck in the shop with no way to get out. "No opposable thumbs," he always said, smug as a cat could be, when she asked him to do something the least bit difficult.

"I don't know," Price Eggleston said with massive irritation. "You worried about your kitty? You should be worried about yourself. Your own pussy!" he said, proud of his own wit.

She had to admit she was more than a little worried about every part of herself. She wanted her friends to come after her, and she had no doubt that they would . . . if they knew she was in trouble. But that was far from certain. And Eggleston had a gun. If anyone (and *anyone* meant Bobo) was hurt in rescuing her, she would feel terrible forever. "Save me, save me!" had morphed into "Help me . . . without getting hurt."

Far too soon to suit Fiji, Eggleston slowed down for the first traffic light on the outskirts of Marthasville. Fiji saw the well-lit parking lot of the Cartoon Saloon shining through the downpour. She spared a thought for the handsome bouncer, who had never called her. After another light, the truck turned right. They were still not in the town, but Fiji realized they were in an older and affluent suburb. The trees were all well grown and the houses set back from the road. After they'd driven past three homes, Eggleston turned right into a driveway that seemed very long but was probably only a quarter of a mile. The truck stopped. Her captor got out and came around to pull her out of her side.

"Now, you shut up. Don't make a sound."

It was a huge mistake for him to tell her this, because it implied that whoever heard her would want to help her. It was also a huge mistake on his part to think his threat would be enough to silence her. She drew in a huge breath and then let it out in one ear-ripping scream. And she made it a word, so none of the people she imagined might hear her could write it off as an owl or a train or anything but a human. "Heeeeeelp me!" she shrieked.

The rain stopped.

After a second's shock, he backhanded her, but she drew in another breath, keeping her feet with some difficulty, and she yelled, "Help! Help!" She fell.

Lights came on maybe ten yards from where the truck was parked, and there were sounds, and then a man dashed out the back door, a thin man, with a rifle in his hands. In his other hand he held a big flashlight, and he shone it on Fiji, now sprawled on the wet ground, and her captor, who was bending over her with his fist raised.

"Price! What the hell you doing!" the man barked. She could tell he was older by his voice and the way he walked.

And she heard a woman's voice, too, calling, "Bart? Who is it?"

"Mamie, it's Price, and he's hit some woman." The older man shone the light directly in Price's face. "Son, this is low, even for you." He drew closer.

"Here, young lady, let me help you up." The new arrival bent over to assist Fiji, who felt ridiculously embarrassed to have a man of his age helping her. She felt the reflex of shame that she was a round woman and not a skinny one, and therefore harder to get off the ground. But Bart Eggleston was stronger than he seemed, and soon she was on her feet, mud and grass plastered to her clothes, her hair soaking wet. And still handcuffed.

Price Eggleston was ominously silent while this was going on. Fiji had not known him long, and she'd evaluated him as being not too bright. But he'd been leading a pack of men, and she should have factored that in, she realized.

He said, "Mom, Dad, this doesn't concern you. This woman is not a Christian and she doesn't support our cause. There are certain things I have to do that I'm not proud of, and this is one of them."

"You have to throw a poor young white woman into the dirt and keep her out in the cold?" his mother said caustically. Price's mother had very black hair and dark eyes, but she was a pale woman. *Probably doesn't tan because she thinks she might be taken for a Mexican*, Fiji thought.

She felt ashamed as Mamie added, "Don't make any difference if she's a Christian or not, we are, and we got to treat her right."

"Wait a second, Mamie," her husband said. "Price, what are you trying to do here?"

"Her boyfriend is the one who killed Aubrey, Dad, and I took her so he'd come looking for her and I could get a shot at him."

The older Egglestons paused.

Fiji said, "I'm sorry, but your son is mistaken. If he's thinking my boyfriend is Bobo Winthrop, he's not right. But Bobo is a friend of mine, and I have to speak up for him. Bobo never killed anyone. He's a sweet man, and he loved Aubrey. Up until this moment, we believed that Price killed Aubrey."

Bart and Mamie looked at each other. "Come on in the house," Mamie said at last. "Let's get out of this damp. Price, loose the poor girl's hands."

Price, looking very young now with his hair plastered to his head under his cowboy hat, pulled a key from his pocket. After some fumbling—during which Fiji almost shrieked with frustration—her wrists were free. She cried out with the relief of being able to put her hands in front of her. Her wrists had ugly chafe marks on them, but she was ready to disregard them since she had her hands back.

"Thank you, Miss Mamie," she said, because she would have shot herself in the foot rather than thank Price.

"You're welcome, sweetie," said the older woman. Now that she could spare a second to look, Fiji could see that Mamie Eggleston was wearing an expensive peach velour tracksuit studded with gold metal stars. She'd slid her feet into plastic mules, which was practical, though her feet must be cold by now. Bart Eggleston was still in his jeans and a flannel shirt. What time was it? Now that Fiji could look at her watch, she realized it was barely six o'clock.

She had a host of thoughts that wanted to be recognized, but she snapped out of her musing when she realized there was an awkward silence among the Egglestons.

"I hope I can call my neighbor to come get me," Fiji said brightly. "I left some soup on the stove, and my cat needs to be fed." Better to know than to be kept wondering, she figured. Her answer came almost immediately.

"Well, young lady," Bart said slowly, "this is right awkward. We don't want our son to be arrested, and you seem like the direct kind of person who would want to take him to court for acting impulsively."

"I'm not sure how impulsive his act was," she said, still trying to keep her voice even. "He had the handcuffs for my wrists and the duct tape for my mouth. He waited outside until there was no one in the store." She was guessing on that one, but it was a pretty good guess. "I assume he's ready to call my friend Bobo to tell him what he has to do to get me returned. That pretty much seems like kidnapping, right?"

The Egglestons looked even more uncomfortable, and the look Mamie cast on her son was not an admiring one or a loving one.

Fiji's heart sank. She'd said exactly the wrong thing. They'd understood that she was not going to forgive and forget. She didn't believe she could have convinced them otherwise, though. Of course they didn't want to see their son taken to jail, especially if they shared his political and social beliefs. Of course he hadn't wanted them to know he was hurting a woman. But now that they knew, and they'd met the woman, they were going to give him a pass. She dared not go into the house.

For a brief second, she tried to imagine what kind of woman they would have taken into the house, given dry clothing to, called the police for. She could not come up with such a woman, not when their son's freedom was at stake.

I have to freeze them all, she thought. That was a spell she knew she'd mastered.

Her fingers began making their small movements, clumsily because of the cold and the stiffness from being confined. Since Price was nearest to her, it affected him first, and in a matter of seconds he became very still. His dad said, "What the hell . . ." before he, too, turned to (frozen) wood. Mamie was smart enough to realize that something Fiji was doing was causing this extraordinary reaction in her menfolk, and she tried to cut and run, but her clogs slid in the mud of the yard, and Fiji seized her arm—both to stop her from going down and to get her attention. Once Mamie looked into Fiji's face and Fiji repeated her hand gestures once more, Mamie was still as anyone could want.

This was so much better than using only her intent, as she had in the truck.

Fiji didn't know how long she had until the spell wore off; not long, she figured. She didn't want the Egglestons to send the police after her for theft, so she couldn't take Price's truck. Instead, she ran for the road. Fiji was not much of a runner, but she fairly scampered down the paved driveway.

When she'd reached the road, which seemed twice as far away as she'd remembered, Fiji turned left. That was the direction from which they'd driven in. There were enough trees and bushes planted close to the road to afford her a place to hide if the Egglestons came after her. She ran as long as she could, and when she was all stove up, as her great-aunt would have put it, she walked as fast as she could. Every time the cold, the pervading damp, and the emotional exhaustion threatened to bring her to a halt, she thought of Price Eggleston's pussy joke and kept on moving.

When she brushed up against any plant, water coursed from it to soak her even more. Tendrils of mist drifted across the road. The air was turning colder, and she had no coat, no money, no cell phone. She wondered when she'd reach the highway. She knew she could not walk all the way back to Midnight. Maybe someone would take pity on her and let her use a phone. Maybe she could find a convenience store, and the clerk would call the police.

She saw some headlights. It couldn't be the Egglestons, who'd be coming up from behind her. It might be reinforcements they'd called for, though, she realized abruptly. Should she hide, just in case? But by that time she was too tired and befuddled to make herself plunge into the dripping undergrowth. She was shivering, and her teeth were chattering. She had her arms wrapped across her midriff, trying to hold in a little warmth. When the station wagon slowed down, her highest hope was that whoever was inside didn't want to kill her.

Fiji didn't expect that she would hear a nearly simultaneous shout of "FIJI!" that would almost knock her over with its enthusiasm, or that people would pour out of the station wagon to hug her. After a long moment, she understood that she was safe and that she would have a chance to get warm and dry. She burst into unheroic tears.

When she was in the station wagon, crammed into the backseat with Manfred and the Rev, a little voice said, "See, I found you! And I got wet!"

34

So you left them standing in the rain?" Manfred asked, twenty-four hours later. He, the Rev, Bobo, and Lemuel—and Olivia, who'd returned that day—were in Fiji's shop. They'd set up the folding chairs, and it was snug. She'd spent the day sweeping up the remains of the display cabinet and cleaning the floor, in between drinking bowls of hot soup (what she'd left on the stove had been salvageable) and taking hot showers.

"It had stopped by then. For all I know, they're still there. I really don't care."

"And why should you?" Olivia said. She leaned forward to put her beer bottle on the wicker table. Fiji had made sausage balls and a dip for the carrot sticks. It had been comforting to cook, and also pleasant to be close to the warm stove.

It had taken her all night and day to feel that she was the right temperature inside and out.

Bobo had offered to close the pawnshop to come to sit with her, in case the Egglestons showed up, but she had told him she had to be by herself sometime. And she doubted Price Eggleston would show, not with the story she could tell the police.

"Which I didn't tell them," she had pointed out to Bobo. "As they can be sure by now, since the cops haven't shown up on their doorstep. So they won't come after me again."

"After all," said a little voice from the basket under the counter, "I am here to save you again."

"Thanks, Mr. Snuggly," Fiji said for perhaps the twentieth time. "How'd that chicken go down?"

"You should cook chicken for me every day," the cat said. "Now I'm going to sleep."

"Thank God," Bobo whispered.

"I heard that!" said Mr. Snuggly. "You just watch it, I'll sit on your face someday when you're . . ." and the cat fell asleep.

"He really makes me glad that most cats can't talk," Bobo said, which pretty much expressed the feelings of everyone gathered in the room.

"He has his moments," Fiji said. She cast a fond look in the direction of the cat's basket.

"Ahhh . . . none of us knew Mr. Snuggly was speech-capable," Olivia said, trying to sound nonchalant.

"Well, he doesn't talk very much. But once he gets going, he seems to want to get his two cents into every conversation." Fiji shrugged apologetically.

"I heard that," said the little voice sleepily, before trailing off into silence.

Fiji gave Olivia and Lemuel a very particular look. "Price Eggleston told me and his parents that he kidnapped me not only because he believes Bobo killed Aubrey, but also because two of the men they sent to beat Bobo up have vanished for good, and that Price Eggleston's hunting lodge has burned down."

Olivia looked away. Lemuel didn't flinch. Bobo looked acutely uncomfortable.

"All right, don't admit it," Fiji said. She shrugged.

"But why you?" Olivia asked. "Why not one of the rest of us?"

"You remember Lisa Gray, Rev? The girl who got married over in your chapel not long ago?"

The Rev nodded.

"This Lisa told Price I was Bobo's best friend," Fiji told the group, "so he figured Bobo would cough up the mythical arms if I was grabbed."

"How could he think I killed Aubrey?" Bobo said. "Price killed her, maybe because she wouldn't betray me."

"I don't think so," said the Rev.

"But if not Price, who? It's not like we have a lot of killers running around Midnight," Fiji said.

Another uncomfortable moment of silence had all eyes trying not to turn to Lemuel and Olivia.

"Not me," Lemuel said, raising his white hands. "I didn't touch Aubrey. Olivia didn't, either. You can look at us accusingly till the cows come home. I would tell you how and why, if I had done anything untoward to Aubrey."

"I would, too, just to stop Bobo from wondering," Olivia said. She looked a bit sad. Fiji could not decide if Olivia was unhappy because all her friends in Midnight thought she was capable of murder or because the idea of losing Bobo's friendship made her sad.

"But it must have been someone from Midnight," Fiji said. "How could it not have been? Bobo was gone, but the rest of us would have noticed her going off with someone else, right?"

"She was in the pawnshop that day?" Manfred asked.

"I forgot you hadn't even moved here then. You fit in really well," Fiji said. "And that was intended as a compliment."

"Yeah, I registered it as one," Manfred told her. "So, Bobo was gone. It was over two months ago, so it was still summer, huh?"

"The weather was good," the Rev said. "It was sunny and mild, and I had a funeral that day. The Lovells' puppy."

"Creek had a puppy? Sure, someone mentioned that. It got run over?"

"Hit-and-run," the Rev said. His demeanor was always the same, but if Manfred had had to characterize the Rev's face at that moment, he would have said the Rev looked . . . grieved.

"So the kids drove the body over, and we had the funeral," the Rev went on after a moment. "Then they left. Creek said she was going for a walk. She was upset."

"So Shawn was at work in the store. Creek was going for a walk, and Connor was going back to the store?" Bobo asked.

"I assume," said the Rev.

"Madonna had taken the baby to his checkup in Davy," said Fiji. "She reminded me of that at the picnic."

"Where were you, Olivia?" There was nothing accusatory in Bobo's voice, but Olivia looked away nonetheless.

"I slept in that day because I'd gotten in from Toronto late the night before," she said. "I was up by about two, I guess. I caught a glimpse of Aubrey as she walked west from the pawnshop."

"Wasn't she supposed to keep the store while Bobo was gone?" Manfred asked.

"No, Teacher kept the shop that day," Bobo answered. "At least, he was supposed to. And he must have. I found two computer entries from that day."

"Then who came in the shop?" Fiji sounded eager. "Maybe they had something to do with—"

"No," Lemuel said. "Of course I checked the shop records, as soon as Bobo told me Aubrey was gone. There were two transactions—but one was before you saw her, Olivia, and the second one . . . August Schneider pawned his mother's silver again. He does that three times a year, at least."

"This August, he's an okay guy?" Manfred was returning from Fiji's kitchen with another beer.

"August is eighty-seven if he's a day," Bobo said. "I don't see him being able to harm Aubrey."

"But what if he hit her with his car?" Olivia said suddenly.

"No!" Bobo said, protesting, but there was a sudden burst of enthusiastic conversation. The tenor of it was one of relief. The culprit would not be one of them, it would not be one of the Eggleston warriors, and August would hardly know about it.

Olivia leaned over to take Bobo's hand. "I know you don't want to even think about that, but what if he did? You know August ought not to be driving. But he's got no one to take the keys away from him. And he's got that big old Cadillac."

"We've already looked at the Caddy, and there's not a speck of blood on it," said Arthur Smith. The bell had tinkled when he entered, but no one had paid attention.

There followed a moment of total silence. No one wanted to ask what he'd come for.

"I had a strange conversation with the Eggleston family this morning," Smith said. He'd taken off his hat, but now he put it back on, as though that signaled he was conducting business. "All three of them were coming down with a cold because they'd been standing out in the chilly air last night. I asked them why, and they couldn't say. Bart was mad at Mamie for telling me that much. But they did seem to chalk that up to you, somehow, Fiji."

"Oh, boo hoo hoo," said Lemuel, sounding like the very embodiment of cold himself. "If they were foolish enough to stand out in the rain, it's hardly Fiji's fault, Sheriff."

"Only if she held a gun to their heads."

"The other way around," said Bobo unwisely. But then the glares of everyone around him reminded Bobo that he was not going to tell the law what the Egglestons had done, and he subsided.

Arthur Smith said, "If you're not going to tell me, I could haul you all in and keep you until you told me what happened. But if you're all right, Fiji, and no one is going to file a complaint against anyone else, there's not much I can do about it. I was looking forward to an excuse to get that asshole into jail, but if you won't talk . . ."

Fiji looked at him with a bright smile. "I wish your staff wanted to get him in jail as much as you do. Any other news, Sheriff?"

"Yes," Smith said. "I do have news."

His voice was so grave they all hushed and turned to him, even Lemuel.

"It's strange you should have brought up August Schneider's car. Because we've determined Aubrey Hamilton was, in fact, hit by a vehicle."

"I thought I saw a bullet hole," Olivia said quietly. "But you told Bobo she wasn't shot."

"You saw a roundish hole. But the pathologist says it's not a bullet hole, but a puncture where something on a vehicle—probably a truck, from the height—pierced the bone. That hole enlarged as tiny pieces of the bone flaked away during the time she lay there."

Bobo said slowly, "She was hit by a *truck*."

They all turned to look at Smith, who nodded. He looked from one to the other, quizzically.

"Oh," said Manfred, finally understanding what they'd all pieced together. He lowered his face to his hands.

"You all know something I don't know," Smith said. "I think you'd better tell me."

There was a long moment, a moment when the room fell absolutely silent.

"I don't guess we know anything you don't already know," Fiji said finally.

An unhappy sheriff left a few minutes later, after threatening them all if they didn't tell him what he'd overlooked.

"He was so mad," Fiji said unhappily. "And he seems like a nice guy."

"That nice guy thought I'd killed Aubrey," Bobo reminded her.

"That's his job."

"All that aside," said Olivia, "what do we do now?"

"When we're sure he's gone, we've got to go talk to the Lovells." Fiji sounded sure but still unhappy.

"Will you explain to me what's going on?" Manfred said. He had that note to his voice, the one that tells the listener that the speaker knows he is going to receive very bad news in a very few minutes. He suspected he knew what that news was; he wasn't certain.

But no one enlightened him.

Lemuel glided out the door to return after a few minutes. "Sheriff's gone," the vampire reported.

Olivia looked at her watch, a slim silver thing that looked expensive to Manfred's uneducated eyes. "It's time for the gas station to close," she said. "We might as well go now."

The Rev said, "I'll go prepare." And he went over to the chapel.

Manfred trailed along, feeling left out and apprehensive. No one specially invited him, but no one told him not to come, and all the others seemed to be going.

They walked in a group, their steps mysteriously matching, and Manfred found himself walking beside Olivia, who turned to look at him with something like pity. But what she said was, "It's good you're here. You're a good citizen for this place."

"There are bad citizens for Midnight?"

"Yes, a few." And she said nothing more.

35

They filed into Gas N Go, one after another, the electronic chime on the door sounding steadily, all of them but Lemuel, who vanished into the dark. Shawn was behind the cash register, clearing it out. Creek was cleaning the women's bathroom and had the door propped open to dispel the fumes of the cleaner. Connor was mopping muddy footprints from the floor.

"Hey, guys," said Shawn, giving every appearance of genuine surprise. "What's up?"

Creek stood, peeled off the rubber gloves she'd been wearing, and stepped outside the bathroom, looking at them doubtfully.

Connor propped the mop against the wall and grinned at them, happy to be interrupted. "Is it time to put up the Halloween stuff, Fiji? Doing it at night would be awesome! Want me to go get the Reeds?"

"No," said Fiji.

"Then what's up?" He looked from face to face, but there was an awareness, just below his smile, that something more important than seasonal decorations was up for discussion.

"The sheriff just came to tell us that Aubrey died from being hit by a truck," Fiji said. Though her voice was neutral, every word felt like a stone thrown at the Lovells.

"Oh, I hope they're not going to arrest Bobo?" Shawn said. He looked genuinely upset.

"No," Fiji said curtly. She took a deep breath. "So here's what I think happened. I think the truck chased Aubrey down and hit her on purpose. I think whoever drove the truck loaded up her body and dumped it over the bluff by the Roca Fría. Or maybe the truck pursued her across the open ground to the river and knocked her over the edge."

"Not in front of the kids," Shawn said with what seemed like genuine indignation.

"The kids," Fiji said.

"What?" Shawn demanded. He'd gotten up, come down from the platform on which the counter was built. He faced Fiji directly. "You mean . . . what?" But there was a terrible awareness in the way he stood, as if he were bracing himself to take a blow.

"I'm saying that she disappeared the day *the kids* took Creek's puppy to the pet cemetery."

"So?"

"How'd they get the dog's body there?"

"They . . ." Shawn's face froze. Manfred could see the man's throat move as he swallowed. "They drove it over there," Shawn said quietly. "I couldn't leave the store, so Connor drove the old truck with the dog in the back wrapped up in plastic."

"And then?"

"Creek came back by herself. She said she'd been for a walk, because she was so sad. It was only a stray, but it was a nice dog. We'd never had one."

"And why hadn't you had one?" Fiji asked.

"Because . . ." Shawn said hoarsely, and then could not finish the sentence.

"Because of *Connor*," Creek said.

She threw her brother's name out like a stone into a pond, and the ripples spread and spread. Connor himself still stood by the mop, and he was still smiling, but it was like his face had frozen in that position and he didn't know how to change it.

"Because he's killed things in the past," Fiji said with certainty. "And you knew he would in the future. That's why you're here, why you don't want anyone to take pictures of you and your kids, why you try to limit their exposure to the world. But you had to let Connor go to school in Davy. You couldn't homeschool him, not and work full-time here at the gas station."

"He promised," Shawn said. The man's shoulders slumped. "He *promised*. We took him to therapy. We . . ." He looked at his son. "Connor?"

Creek's mouth was partly open, and her eyes shone with unshed tears. She was so young, but Manfred didn't think any life experience could have prepared her for this moment. She'd been facing the cluster of Midnighters, but now she turned to her right to face her brother. "You killed my dog?" she said. It sounded almost conversational.

Connor's smile became genuine. This smile was the worst thing of all. It was broad and white and delighted, with no hint of shame or remorse or feeling.

"Well, I gotta say, you caught me fair and square," the boy said. "Creek, sorry . . . but it had been so long." His expression morphed into a strange mixture of rueful regret—he'd been caught misbehaving—and an honest appeal for understanding. "It was only a stray. You can get another one, right?"

"You promised," Creek said, in an eerie echo of her father. She looked ten years older.

"Well . . . yeah, I know I did. But the urge comes on me, and I gotta do *something*. It was better killing the dog than a person, right?" He said that, but Fiji could tell he didn't feel it. He was making an effort to seem like a boy with genuine human responses.

"But you killed a person, too," Bobo said, and there was only silence.

Until Connor bolted for the back door. But that was where Lemuel had stationed himself.

There was no breaking Lemuel's grip.

In the end, Connor enjoyed telling them about Aubrey.

The streets had been empty, as they so often were. He'd even seen Fiji drive off toward Davy, though she'd seemed preoccupied and hadn't appeared to notice him.

"I didn't," she said quietly. "I don't know what I was thinking of, but I didn't notice him at all. Just so used to seeing the old truck."

"But you said you saw Aubrey that day." Bobo looked at her quizzically. "The sheriff told me."

"I thought I was lying. But apparently, I did see her, after all."

Connor grew impatient at Fiji's interruption. "So I pulled up beside her and asked her if she wanted to go for a ride. She laughed, said she was tempted since it was a cute guy like me asking. She said she was going to hike to the river and back, so she could surprise Bobo when he came home. She was going to tie a scarf on a tree out there to prove she'd done it."

Bobo's head fell on his chest and his face twisted. He was squeezing back tears, and it was painful to watch.

Joe and Chuy slipped through the door and stood to either side of it, like sentinels. No one remarked on their coming or explained to them what was happening. The tingling of the electronic chime sounded weirdly commonplace in the pervading tension.

"What happened then?" Fiji asked Connor.

"So, she always flirted with me. Like that 'ordinarily I'd love to take a ride with a cute guy like you,'" Connor said, his voice high in imitation of the dead woman. "Bobo, I want you to know that I just wasn't interested in her that way." Bobo did not acknowledge his words, but Connor went on, "I'm not one of these guys who kills women for sex." His voice was laden with contempt. "But it was like she wanted my attention, she *had* to feel like I was interested in her," Connor said. "I didn't get it. But she said, 'Don't you dare follow me, now!' in this chirpy voice, and she switched her butt as she walked, like she was saying, 'Yes, follow me,' so I drove after her in the truck."

Aubrey's pathological need to be admired had met up with another pathological need.

"She started out across the bare land to the river, and I bumped along behind her. She looked back once and laughed, and then I got a little mad, so I speeded up. She started running." And Connor smiled again. "Then she wasn't laughing."

He stopped. He smiled. He said nothing.

"And you hit her with the truck?" Shawn said, as if he were still holding out some hope that there had been a huge mistake.

"She made a bigger thump than the dog, that's for sure! She actually went up in the air."

Fiji could not stand that Bobo was hearing this. But he would not leave, and she would not ask him to.

"And she came down on the slope down to the river," Connor said, in a matter-of-fact way. "I went down there to check."

"Because you wanted to see what had happened?" Fiji said, having to struggle to get the words out of her throat.

"Yeah, well . . . yeah. Because that's the moment, you know, the great moment. She wasn't quite dead."

"Did you kill her?" Fiji said. Tears were streaming down the witch's face.

"We keep an old poker in the truck for dealing with snakes," he said. "Not the same one I used on Mrs. Ames," he added in a careful aside.

No one spoke.

"Her chest bones were all cracked. I poked a hole in one of the cracks," he added, by way of explanation. He seemed lost in his reminiscence of the big moment. "But it did look like she'd been shot."

"So you got the gun Bobo had used for target shooting," Fiji said.

"Well, he'd left it in his truck, and the truck wasn't locked," Connor said. "But that was days later."

Creek squatted down as if her knees could not hold her any longer.

"I washed the truck," the boy said. "That same day."

"Who did he kill before? This Mrs. Ames?" Fiji asked Shawn. But Shawn did not answer. He'd looked at the Gorgon's face; it was his son's.

But Creek answered. "Three-plus years ago he killed our next-door neighbor," she said. "My mom had just died. Connor was really not talking to anyone, and we were pretty worried about him. While Dad and I were in the backyard raking leaves, Mrs. Ames came over with yet another casserole. Connor had got it in his head that she wanted to marry Dad and replace Mom. So he hit her with the fireplace poker. She must have had a thin skull."

Fiji thought, *I knew it. Thin skull.* Connor had a bad history with fireplace pokers.

"And you covered it up." Bobo was angry; not as angry as he would be later on, probably.

"No, we called the police!" Creek said, and she was a little angry, too. "Since he was a minor, they never tried him. The court psych evaluation said he was mentally disturbed, and his mother had just died, so they put him in a home for kids like him. He got therapy," she added defensively. "I mean, we tried."

"But then when he got out, he killed a cat," Shawn said, finally finding his voice. He might have been a million years old. "We found it. We knew he'd done it. So we had to move. We thought if we moved to a really quiet place, if we limited his exposure to other people . . . if we were careful to stay out of the news, all of us . . . then none of the past publicity would catch up with him, no one would know about his juvenile record, and he'd have a chance to straighten out."

"Are you happy with how that worked out?" Creek said to her father. "All that we did, coming to live here, no friends, no family, no money, we did all that for Connor, and this is what it's come to. I almost got to college and got away, but no, the paperwork went missing." Her hands were clenched in fists.

"I got the paperwork out of the mailbox and ripped it up," Connor said.

"What?" She looked at him blankly, as if his words made no sense.

And his father was looking at him the same way. "Connor . . . why? Why didn't you want your sister to go to college?"

"I'd be lonely, and you'd make me do every damn thing around here," Connor said. "Wouldn't you?" And he actually sounded accusatory.

There fell a stunned silence. Until Connor began shifting around, looking bored and antsy. Lemuel had let go of him, but he moved a little closer as Connor fidgeted.

"What will we do?" Shawn asked, as if to himself, his voice despairing. Fiji did not know if she wanted to slap him or comfort him. He looked around at the small crowd in the store, meeting their eyes in turn. "What will *you* do?"

Fiji could not think of what to say.

"He should die," Olivia said.

None of the others offered an opinion.

"But I'm *me*," the boy said. He gave a shrug, smiled. "I'm just a boy."

"There are plenty of boys," Lemuel said. "As you said about your sister's puppy."

"Uncle Lem," Creek said. It wasn't clear what she was pleading with him to do. Maybe she didn't know herself.

"Don't kill him," Shawn begged. "We've gone through so much with him."

"But what has that gotten you?" Olivia said. "No gratitude, no obedience, no change in his behavior. Just your own lives ruined. And wherever you run, it'll be the same."

"He's got the taste for it now," Fiji said, almost inaudibly.

Connor didn't plead for his life or offer any rebuttal. He waited, with a calm face, for whatever would happen next. He could not conceive of the world going on without him, Fiji could tell.

"What is your judgment, Bobo?" Olivia asked. "Creek lost her dog, but you lost your lover."

"I wish he could understand," Bobo said. "I wish he could be cured. But if he were, how could he live with himself?" He stared at the boy and seemed more puzzled than furious. "I don't think Connor will ever understand. He'll keep killing people as long as he's alive. I know Shawn and Creek will be better off without him."

"But he's my son," Shawn said. "He's my son. I can't bear to lose him."

"Do you deny that he'll kill again?" Olivia said, oh-so-reasonably.

"No." Creek sounded sure.

"Do you think any help you can get him will stop him? Cure him?" Fiji asked.

"No," Creek said again.

"You're condemning more people to death if you let him live," Olivia said flatly.

"Being a parent isn't about being logical," Joe Strong said. Those were the first words he'd spoken since he and Chuy had entered. "Shawn, what Olivia says is true. He will kill again. He'll leave a trail of death behind him." Joe didn't sound as though he were making a judgment, but reporting the future.

"But I can't consent to you killing my son," Shawn said, his voice shaking. "What do you expect me to say? 'Put him down, like a dog'?"

"Funny you should put it that way," Lemuel said, and quicker than the eye could follow he stepped forward and snapped Connor's neck.

36

Fiji and Manfred and Bobo walked back to their homes together, in a cluster, with Bobo and Manfred supporting Fiji. She was not crying, but she was clearly very shocked, if not in shock.

"Was that justice?" she said. She sounded as though she honestly wanted to know.

"More justice than he gave Aubrey," Bobo responded.

"But isn't that what separates us from . . . I don't know . . . barbarians?" Manfred said. He was deeply troubled, and he didn't know how to turn off the memory of Connor's neck snapping.

"Barbarians." Fiji laughed. The thin sound floated up through the cold air. Tonight felt like winter, and Manfred shivered. He'd come out without a jacket, as they all had. "I guess we are. That was justice. He couldn't be cured."

"You don't know that," Manfred began, only to be cut off by Bobo.

"Don't try to defend him, not now, not in front of me."

"Sorry," Manfred muttered, glad they'd reached the pawnshop

entrance. "Well, I'll walk Fiji home. You going to be okay? You need me to do anything for you?"

"I'll be better by myself," Bobo said. "Thank you, Manfred." He forced himself to look Manfred in the eyes. "This is a lot for a newcomer to absorb."

"Yeah, well. Okay, we're off." He steered Fiji across the road, with their usual careful look both ways. "I don't know why we always do that," he said.

"Because the time you don't look is the time you'll get flattened by a truck," she said, and he could feel her shudder.

"Fiji, I can't even think how I feel about what we just saw," he said.

"You don't need to know right now how you felt about it or how you're going to change as a result of having seen it," she said. She shuddered again. "It's a good thing that everything's settled."

"What about the sheriff? Do you think he knows about Connor's past?"

"He shouldn't, because Connor was a juvenile when he killed that Mrs. Ames, so he shouldn't be able to find out. Right?"

"If he does suspect Connor, what's he going to do when he finds out Connor is dead?"

"He's not going to know that." Fiji sounded a bit astonished at the notion.

"Why not?"

"His dad's not going to tell anyone what happened, for Creek's sake," she explained. "Did you see Creek's face? She was glad Connor was dead. Of course, she'll have a hard time, but she could see the truth of what Olivia said, and she was so angry with him for so many things."

"But the sheriff will want to know where Connor is."

"Yeah, he will. But kids Connor's age run away all the time. And he may read a confession into Connor's absence. Which, after all, is accurate."

"We didn't help the Lovells . . . do anything." With the body, he meant.

"Joe and Chuy stayed. Do you really think they'd want our help?"

They'd reached Fiji's front door. Mr. Snuggly was there. He looked up at Fiji reproachfully. "Kept me waiting," he said.

"You could have gone around the house and gone in the cat flap at the back," Fiji pointed out. "Tonight, Connor died."

"Good," said Mr. Snuggly. "I was tired of hiding from him."

"He tried to catch you?"

"Yes. He liked to kill things, you know." By then Fiji had opened the door, and the cat padded in.

"Well," she was saying as she closed the door behind her, "you could have told me."

37

Manfred (looking both ways) went back to his own place. He turned on the heat, a step he'd been putting off. It came on instantly, with that burned-air smell. But the gush of warmth was a relief. Manfred went into his bedroom and wrapped up in an old quilt of his grandmother's before he went into the kitchen. He would not have thought he could be hungry, but apparently his stomach thought otherwise.

Though it seemed ludicrous, almost disgusting, he turned on his television. He couldn't bear to think of what might be happening at Gas N Go. Creek and her father had to be going through another hell, as if they hadn't suffered enough. And what would happen to Connor's body?

While he ate a peanut butter and jelly sandwich, Manfred tried hard not to think of the terrible night the two remaining Lovells were enduring. *Surely there must be some relief mixed in there,* he thought. *They're free from the prison he put them in.* And then he remembered he was supposed to be watching television, and he made himself concentrate on a rerun of *The Big Bang Theory*. For the first time, he saw Sheldon's narcissism as monstrous, rather than amusing.

He settled back on the couch and presently sank into a kind of nearly sleeping dream. In this fantasy, Creek came to his door, told him she couldn't handle being with her father anymore, asked him to take her in and make her his . . . and said that she forgave him for standing by while her brother was executed. When he made himself get up and stumble to his bed, it was past midnight.

He found out the next day that at about that time, Creek and her father had loaded everything they had of value into the old truck and had taken off.

He discovered they'd fled when Sheriff Smith stopped by. Shawn Lovell had left the sheriff a letter. At some time during the night, Shawn had dropped the envelope, inscribed "Arthur Smith," into the old mail slot in the front door of the Antique Gallery and Nail Salon. Chuy had given it to Smith an hour previously.

"Now I'm going to tell you what he said," Smith told Manfred. Manfred could only sit in his work chair and try to look relaxed.

"In this letter, Shawn Lovell tells me that he just discovered his son killed Aubrey Hamilton Lowry. He tells me that Connor had a terrible back history of mental problems. He asks me not to blame them for leaving after Connor ran away."

"What?" Manfred said, startled. Whatever he'd expected, that wasn't it. "He ran away?" Manfred said weakly. "Wow, that's unexpected."

Smith raised his thick blond eyebrows. "He says he doesn't want his daughter to be tainted by the fallout from the crime and that Connor's confession shocked them as much as anyone else. Shawn enclosed a note from the boy. Connor says he's sorry for everything he's done. He says he's leaving because he couldn't stand being around people who cared for Aubrey."

In Manfred's opinion, this was a mighty fine letter for having been written from beyond the grave. "And do you believe Connor wrote that letter?" It was clear to Manfred that he was not putting an idea into Smith's head that wasn't already there.

"Handwriting experts are comparing it to the boy's signature, but so much schoolwork is done on computers now." Smith shrugged. "Since we've got a confession that fits all the known facts and I found the boy's killed before . . . I called a detective in the force where they used to live, and he remembered the case very well."

"Are you going to look for him? Or for them?" Manfred asked. He made sure his face was composed.

"The answer would have to be, yes, we are going to look for Connor real hard. He'll always be a threat to others unless he has a lot of serious therapy, and probably even afterward. For Shawn and Creek Lovell? Realistically, they're not going to be our priority. We've got actual bad guys to catch."

The sheriff rose to take his leave. "I guess I won't be coming back to Midnight as often," he said. "I had never had to drive out here before Aubrey went missing."

"I hope you won't ever have to again."

"If you don't mind me saying so, you don't look too good."

Manfred was certainly willing to believe that. "Yeah, I didn't sleep well last night. Nightmares."

"Every last person I've talked to here today has said the same damn thing," Smith said. "You seem to be having some kind of epidemic."

"Maybe because it's the beginning of winter," Manfred said

absently, letting his gaze flicker over to the screen that waited for him. SandyStar521 was waiting to find out what her future held in store.

"I'll let you get back to work," said Smith, taking the hint. He moved, a little stiffly, toward the door. He seemed to be feeling the onset of winter himself. "You got a visitor." Smiling, the sheriff nodded toward the front window. Mr. Snuggly was looking in, precariously balanced on the narrow sill.

"Let's see," said Manfred. "Maybe he wants to talk to you."

The sheriff looked at him oddly, and Manfred realized there hadn't been any touch of levity in his own tone. When Smith opened the door, Mr. Snuggly leaped down from the sill and arranged himself in front of the sheriff: looking up with his great golden eyes, tail wrapped neatly around his paws.

"What do you need, cat?" Smith asked, smiling.

Manfred held his breath. But his hope was dashed when Mr. Snuggly did not answer Smith out loud. That would have been pretty amusing, and Manfred needed to see something amusing.

Instead of speaking, Mr. Snuggly turned to start back to Fiji's house. He looked over his shoulder to make sure Smith was following, and when Smith did not, the cat stopped to look back. Manfred didn't know if the invitation included him, so he waited until Mr. Snuggly gave a tiny jerk of his head, a gesture that seemed to include him as well as the sheriff.

As they walked up to Fiji's front porch, Manfred was sorry to see that the formerly abundant flowers were all but gone. Instead, there were pumpkins set out on either side of the door, carved into grotesque faces with considerable skill. Fiji had put out a sign reading, PUMPKIN CARVING WORKSHOPS! $25 INCLUDING PUMPKIN AND CARVING KNIFE!

She was working off her unhappiness.

When they entered the shop, Fiji had moved the two armchairs and the wicker table into the back of the house somewhere. She'd set up four card tables with folding chairs, covered the tables with orange plastic table coverings, and put cloth aprons and the pumpkin carving knives at four spots on each table. Since the glass case had been broken and not replaced, there was just enough room.

"I've got fifteen minutes before my class comes," she said. "Else I'd ask you to sit and have a cup of tea or some soda."

"That's all right, I need to get back to Davy," Smith said. "Ms. Fiji, I've got a few things to tell you." He explained the content of the letters to her, much as he'd done for Manfred.

"Manfred, I'm sorry," was the first thing she said.

Manfred shrugged. "They had to do it."

"Why sorry for Manfred?" Smith asked.

"He was a friend of Shawn's," she said, without missing a beat.

"We both liked to fish," Manfred said off the top of his head.

"Really?" Clearly, Smith did not think it likely from Manfred's appearance that he'd ever been in a boat, much less put a worm on a hook.

"Sure, me and my grandmother went fishing all the time," Manfred said truthfully. "She loved to be out on the water. Said it helped her clear her head. Of course, we ate the fish, too. Didn't have a lot of money. What do you do for fun, Sheriff?" he asked, from sheer curiosity.

"As a kid, I liked to fish, too," he said. "After I got into law enforcement, time for that got scarce. But I got interested in cold cases, and I belonged to a club that met once a month to talk about famous cases from the past. That was kind of relaxing. Now I work jigsaw puzzles." He paused for a moment and returned to being the guarded, serious sheriff. "Ms. Fiji, is there anything you want to say to me about the Egglestons?"

Fiji opened her eyes wide. "I can't think of a thing I want to say about them. Why?"

"I'm still curious about them all catching cold simultaneously. And they mentioned your name."

"Mentioned me? That's strange. I don't think I've ever met the older Mr. Eggleston or his wife. I did see Price riding his motorcycle at poor Aubrey's funeral. At least, I guess that was him."

"All right. Sheer curiosity, I guess. Were you out that night? The night it rained so much?"

"Only an idiot would voluntarily go out in weather like that."

He looked at her, taking her measure. He didn't seem totally satisfied with the conclusions he drew. "Eggleston and his buddies did make quite a scene at the funeral," Smith said. "I understand he went to Mr. and Mrs. Hamilton yesterday and made an apology. Said it was just a tribute gone wrong."

"Hmm. Well, he did the right thing."

"I'll be on my way. I'm glad I got a chance to talk to you, Fiji."

"Same here, Sheriff."

He left, putting on his hat the moment he stepped outside. After the door shut behind him, Manfred said, "Give the guy a break, Fiji. You could have called him Arthur."

"Yeah, well, I'm not in the mood to make stuff easy today. You want to help me carry in the pumpkins?"

"Sure." He needed to stretch. Too much time at the computer desk.

"I really am sorry about Creek," she said, when they'd finished. They both sighed when they heard a car pull into Fiji's driveway. "They're already starting to come."

"Yeah, I'm sorry about Creek, too. But I guess this way is better for her. Where is Connor?"

"Where the two guys who came to beat up Bobo are, I guess," she said, which was no answer at all.

"And that is?" He was impatient.

"If I can figure it out, you can," she said, and then her first class member came in the door.

The following week, after everything had seemed to fall back to normal and the papers had stopped putting Connor's school picture on the front page every day (due to his confession, the district attorney charged him as an adult), Manfred got a phone call. It was a number he didn't recognize, but he got a lot of those, and he answered it without any expectation.

"Do you know who this is?" the voice said.

"Yes," he answered, just as guardedly. It was Creek.

"We're okay," she said. "We're north of where we were. It's a lot colder! Hard to get used to."

"Are you really okay?" He didn't know what else to ask.

"As much as we can be. Dad got a job. Me, too. The same kind of work I did for Madonna."

She was waiting tables.

"They treating you right?"

"Yeah, it's okay. I miss you."

"Same here."

"I'll try to call again sometime."

"I want to hear from you."

"I'm glad to hear your voice. I really am. Okay. Bye."

"Bye."

And then her voice was gone, and he believed he would never talk to her again. He thought again of the way her hair swung around her face, the smooth olive skin of her cheeks. He did not know if he should share this call with his neighbors or not. Somehow, he thought not. It seemed too personal and private.

Connecting Creek's call with loss, he suddenly found himself punching in his mother's number.

She was glad to hear his voice.

38

Kids didn't trick-or-treat in Midnight. It was too remote, too spooky. But there was kind of a local tradition in Davy to take the less anxious kids to the Witch's House. This had begun in Mildred Loeffler's time, and Fiji had happily continued the celebration. She and other inhabitants of Midnight worked on her house and yard for two days, to the disgust of Mr. Snuggly, who thought Fiji's time would have been better spent brushing him and stroking his fur and feeding him good things.

Fiji had pressed some of her neighbors into further service this Halloween. Joe and Chuy were wearing silver jumpsuits and huge white wings, and they stood on either side of the steps up to the porch, like patient gleaming angels. They were both wearing long blond wigs, which looked far more natural on Joe than it did on Chuy.

They took turns saying "Enter" to each child, in a deep, forbidding voice. If they'd been dressed like devils instead of angels, it would have been a rare child who had the nerve to claim his or her candy.

All of Fiji's bushes were draped with fake spiderwebs. She'd positioned huge spiders on each one. Fiji had said a few spells over them, and the eyes of the arachnids gleamed and sparkled and moved in a thoroughly disconcerting way. There was also a huge kettle smoking over a smoldering fire, all of which Fiji had under careful (and magical) control. Parents always thought it was done with batteries, but children somehow knew better.

Prodded by his mom and dad, who'd thought his question was really cute, one boy asked Fiji (dressed in a Morticia dress and a pointed hat) if she weren't "afraid bad kids would come egg your house someday." Fiji leaned down to look in his eyes, and he found he was more intent on those eyes than on her cleavage. "I don't think anyone will ever do that to me," she said gently. "Do you?"

After a moment of paralyzing fear, he said, "I sure won't."

She straightened, with a slight smile, and his parents were proud of him. But for the rest of his life, he dated that as the moment he realized the world would not always think he was as adorable as his parents did.

Manfred had been called into service, too. He made a great devil, somewhat to his own surprise. He was dressed in black jeans and a black silk turtleneck. He'd grown his goatee out and colored it black for the night, he wore heavy eye makeup, and he had a black hoodie drawn up around his face. He would have looked even more striking, but he refused to wear the stretchy outfit Fiji had suggested when they'd gone to the costume store. "I'd look like Gollum," he said, "but in black."

"You're not that skinny," she'd retorted, disappointed, but he'd kept his ground. She'd asked the Rev to play a part, but he had told her that he intended to spend Halloween in the chapel in prayer for the souls of the dead. He'd stuck to his guns, no matter how she begged. However, in compensation, Bobo had agreed to participate for the first time.

Bobo was the most handsome Perseus anyone had ever seen. He carried a remarkably lifelike Gorgon's head, and he wore a sort of toga and sandals. In the hand not clutching the head, he carried a large shiny sword from the pawnshop.

"It ought to be curved," Fiji had said. "And you ought to have *winged* sandals."

"Well, no one's pawned any winged sandals, or sandals of any kind," he said.

Bobo was not much of an actor—he got upset when children found him genuinely frightening—but when he held out the loathsome snake-covered skull and proclaimed, "Behold the head of the evil Medusa," it was a showstopper. The least sensitive children wanted to touch the "head," which was disgustingly slimy and slithery. Every now and then, when Fiji had a free moment, one of the snakes seemed to writhe a bit.

When the second hour of Fiji's open house was almost at an end, a mother from Davy said, "How on earth do you get it to look like the cat is talking?"

"Oh, did it look realistic?" Fiji had to struggle to keep a smile on her face.

"It was so cute! It said, 'Get off my tail or I'll smother you in your sleep.'"

"Just some batteries and a CD!" Fiji said. "And isn't that just what a cat should say?"

They both laughed heartily. When the mother left, Fiji turned and glared at Mr. Snuggly, who yawned.

At nine o'clock, Fiji went out onto the porch. The house had emptied of outsiders, but in the yard a few families and some teenagers were still enjoying the Halloween decorations. She adopted a dramatic pose on the porch, Manfred pressed "Play" on a CD player, and a fanfare rang out. When she had everyone's attention, Fiji proclaimed, "This ends the celebration of the season at the Witch's House!" She made a few grand passes in the air with her hands. The spiders' eyes dulled, the cobwebs stopped moving, and the two angels bowed and retreated into the house. Fiji herself took a deep bow, to a smattering of applause, and straightened to say, "Have a safe drive home, y'all, and I'll see you next year!"

She wasn't spoilsport enough to turn off all the lights in the front yard, but she did lock the front door and draw all the curtains to make sure visitors knew the show was over. Fiji kicked off her high-heeled boots and collapsed into her rocking chair with a groan of relief.

"Good job!" Manfred said. He pulled down his hoodie.

"Thanks, all of you," she said. "Anyone who wants a beer, there are plenty in the refrigerator. And there are some trays back there, if you wouldn't mind bringing them out. I'll get up in a minute. My feet are killing me."

Soon all the food was assembled on one card table, folding chairs were up and in use, and everyone had a beverage. Chuy and Joe were glad to get out of the silver jumpsuits and into their normal daywear.

Those wings had to be heavy, thought Manfred, who'd been curious about their feathery appearance. He saw the jumpsuits, neatly folded in Fiji's storeroom/guest bedroom, but the wings were nowhere in sight. Across the hall, Bobo retired to Fiji's bedroom to pull off his tunic and sandals, and put on his jeans and flannel shirt and sneakers. The golden sparkly stuff Fiji had put in his hair was coming off everywhere. He stepped out to see Mr. Snuggly crouching before his dish in the kitchen, eating some chopped beef for his Halloween treat.

"Though," Fiji said, raising her voice, "he doesn't deserve it! After talking to that woman!"

"She stepped on my tail," a muffled voice called back, and Bobo laughed.

Manfred reflected that all the inhabitants of Midnight had accepted the news that Mr. Snuggly could talk with remarkable equanimity. Even Bobo, who was the most unmagical person Manfred could imagine, had come to take the cat's conversation for granted after a day or two of expressing wonder. And the death of Connor had become part of the life of the town. It was never mentioned. Only the Reeds had expressed shock and amazement at Connor's confession and the vanishing act of Shawn Lovell. Teacher was working full-time at Gas N Go, according to written instructions left by Shawn, until he could sell the convenience store. And Teacher seemed very happy with that, though Madonna was predictably grumpy.

The town had closed over the Lovells' sudden absence.

All in all, Manfred realized as he sipped a beer, he'd had an amazing time of it since he'd moved to Midnight. He felt more and more at home. As the beer took hold, Manfred found himself wondering if his selection of Midnight had been predestination? Fate? Chance? Manfred couldn't decide and wasn't sure he needed to. But he still regretted Creek's abrupt departure. He withdrew into himself a little as he thought of her, letting the conversation of his new friends wash over him.

Bobo stood up, so quickly it startled everyone in the room. The silence that fell jolted Manfred out of his reverie.

"What's up?" he asked, thinking he'd missed a cue.

"I have no idea," Joe said. "Bobo?"

"I have something to show you all," he said. "And I'm going to do it now while I still have the courage."

"Where?" Fiji said. "If it's far, I'm going to put on my sneakers."

"Across the street. In the shop."

"Okay, just wait a sec." Fiji hauled herself up, wincing as she walked back to her room carrying the boots that had given her such grief. Very shortly she returned, still in her black costume but with battered Pumas on her feet. "I'm ready," she said, and they all got up. Manfred didn't know how the others felt, but he was kind of worried and kind of excited.

They trailed after Bobo as he crossed to Midnight Pawn. Instead of going up to the door to the stairs to his apartment, he went through the main door to the pawnshop. Olivia was sitting in Bobo's favorite chair, and Lemuel was behind the counter reading a tattered book. They both looked very surprised that Midnight was coming to the shop.

"We've had no customers," Lemuel said. "And it's been a slow night in every respect."

"Looks like you had a crowd over there," Olivia said to Fiji. "Did everyone have a good time?"

"Yes," Fiji said, but not as if she were paying attention to what she was saying. "Bobo says he has a surprise for us."

"Really?" Olivia stared at Bobo. "I thought we'd kind of had our fill of surprises."

He laughed. "You may like this one. I don't know."

He walked toward the back of the shop, pulling some keys out of his pocket as he went. When he got to the storage closet, he unlocked the padlock, then the dead bolt, and opened the door.

Manfred first noticed all the televisions on the shelves, maybe thirty—plus a small locked case full of guns and jewelry. And there was a shelf of power tools and appliances.

"That's a lot of TVs," he said. "But surely that's not the surprise?"

"That's not the surprise. Those are just the first things people think of pawning." Bobo went down the narrow corridor between the shelves to arrive at a wall at the back. It would have been a good place to put some extra shelves, now that Aubrey's boxes were gone.

"What are you doing?" Lemuel said.

To Manfred, the vampire sounded not only surprised, but unhappy.

"I found this," Bobo said, looking over his shoulder at them. He was not-quite smiling. "It made me feel like the shop was the right investment." He reached up high—he was the only one of them who could stretch that far—and lifted up the corner of an old heat register. It was in a dark corner, and it had looked for all the world like it screwed firmly into the wall. Bobo's fingers, fully extended, pressed something inside the aperture, and there was an audible mechanical noise. Somewhere, parts had worked together.

Bobo pressed the wall, and it folded back.

"Jesus God," said Chuy. Bobo reached in to pull a chain hanging from the ceiling, and a bare bulb lit up the closet, which measured about four feet by three feet.

It was full of guns, rifles, grenades, ammunition. Those were the things Manfred could recognize. There were things he couldn't.

"You had them all along," Olivia said, after a shocked silence.

"You had them all along," Fiji echoed.

Olivia sounded admiring. Fiji sounded angry.

Manfred had to bite his lip to keep himself from saying the same damn thing.

"Well," Joe said. He took Chuy's hand. "I guess we didn't know you as well as we thought we did."

39

Bobo felt terrible. He ran his fingers through his hair and looked down at the floor for a minute, gathering his thoughts. "I never wanted anyone to use them," he said, trying to explain. "And I never wanted law enforcement to have them, because that would mean it was for sure that my grandfather had done more terrible stuff than he was even charged with." He sighed, and the big intake and exhalation of breath helped him steady his voice. "Mostly, I didn't want any right-wing militia types to use them, and I didn't want anyone else to know about them. I'd rented a storage unit under another name in Oklahoma. I left them there for a long time, making sure to keep my payments up. But when I came here, and it felt so—so doable . . . I knew I could learn the business, and Lemuel didn't throw me any . . ."

"How did you find the secret closet?" Lemuel asked, and he didn't sound happy.

"I just held my hand up to see if warm air was coming out. You remember, I moved here in the cold weather, in November. I was taking inventory in here, and I thought it felt kind of cold, and I thought it was strange since there was a heat register in here, and then I thought it was strange that it was way up there, and then I started fooling around with it . . ."

"What was in here, instead of the guns?" Olivia nodded her head toward the guns.

"Just some old books. I carried them up to my apartment and hid them in that old TV console that I have under the front windows."

"Old books," Lemuel said, as if he couldn't believe it. "The old books I've been looking for, all these years."

"Seriously? If I'd known, I would have told you," Bobo said, honestly surprised. *I found something a vampire didn't find,* he told himself, and tried not to smile.

"And you went to get the rifles?" Joe said.

"Yeah, I took a Sunday and Monday and drove over to load them up. I sweated bullets all the way back, thinking a state trooper would stop me and find all those guns." He looked at Fiji. "Hey. Sweated bullets?"

"I got it," Fiji said, with half of an unhappy smile.

He was used to Fiji giving him the full smile, all the wattage. He knew he'd screwed up. "Okay, I get that I should have told you all either before this or never," he said. "I just couldn't take the secrets anymore. My grandfather was a shitty human being. I hate that the world knows our family as the kind of people who think bombing a church is a good idea. I hate having a secret to keep. Since I realized what a—what kind of person he was, I've lived to refute that."

"I understand," Joe said. He turned to look at his partner. "You, Chuy?"

"I'm having to rearrange the way I think about you," Chuy admitted. "But I understand why you hid all this stuff. This is what everyone's looking for?"

"Yeah. This pile of rifles and guns and the other stuff. This is what everyone is looking for."

"Hard to believe," Manfred said.

Bobo wasn't sure what he meant. Did his tenant mean that the fact that Bobo had the guns after all was hard to believe? Or the fact that people would go to such lengths to acquire a secret cache of weapons that wasn't nearly as fabulous as it was reputed to be? "I think it was just . . . these aren't any different from rifles and guns you can buy anywhere," he said hesitantly. "It's just the legend around them. And the fact that they'd be hard to trace, or at least not as quick to trace as guns stolen from Walmart or Jack's Outdoor Center." Looking around, he didn't see any faces that weren't displeased or outright unhappy.

His back straightened, and he lifted his head. "So, if you're going to come back at me on this, say so now."

The little crowd in front of him looked back at him. Fiji said, "Bobo, you did what you had to do, and it's a family matter. I'm not telling anyone. It's none of my business."

He'd known he could count on her. She'd never let him down.

Olivia said, "I'll sleep better knowing that I can bring down Armageddon if I have to." She smiled at him.

"I would only like to see the books," Lemuel said next. "I have to recover my pride somehow. I was too short to reach the grille and too dated to ask myself why the room wasn't warmer."

Chuy said, "Joe and I will not tell anyone." But he didn't add anything else, and Bobo knew they were both disappointed in him.

Manfred said, "I'd much rather they were here than in the possession of assholes like that Price Eggleston. And I'd like to know how you feel, Fiji. About letting Price off the kidnapping hook."

Bobo blessed Manfred for diverting attention away from him. Everyone had had his or her say on the matter, and his secret was safe. And now, if something happened to him, everything in the closet would be taken care of in some way. He knew his friends would dispose of them wisely.

Fiji leaned against Chuy's free side, and he put his arm around her. "It's the price I'm going to pay to keep the sheriff from coming to my door, asking how I came to freeze three people in position for an undetermined amount of time. I got away. They won't do it again. Mamie and Bart weren't a part of my abduction, though they would have covered for their son . . . but I get that. Price is the dangerous one, at least to me, and I'm pretty sure he won't be back. Especially now that I know he didn't kill Aubrey."

"But will he start up his group again?" Manfred said.

Bobo shrugged. "I don't know. That's beyond me. I think we've done all we can. We can't stop extremists from spreading their propaganda. We can't kill everyone who attacks us, as much as we might want to." His eyes slewed to Lemuel and Olivia. "And, as Fiji says . . . we know he didn't kill Aubrey."

"And none of us figured that out, either," Joe said, his voice very sad. "I should have seen it."

There was a long, hushed moment, as they all looked back, trying to think of some signal Connor had given, some wave he'd sent off, that they should have been able to receive and decode.

"Well, I'm a witch," said Fiji briskly. "And I didn't pick up a damn thing. Great-Aunt Mildred would be ashamed of me. My guess is that Connor never thought of what he did as wrong, so he gave off no guilt. I'm giving myself a pass on that one. And now I'm going home to put away the food and fall into bed." She did not look at anyone as she left, and Bobo knew he had fences to mend.

Olivia and Lemuel resumed their seats in the pawnshop waiting for whatever business would come. Olivia usually retired about one in the morning, leaving Lemuel to have some alone time. "Tonight it might be later," she murmured to Manfred. "Lem will want to talk about the books, I suppose."

Joe and Chuy left after murmuring, "Good night," to everyone. Once they were outside, Joe slung his arm around Chuy, and the two walked home together in perfect harmony. They saw the Rev walking to his own home across the street, and they inclined their heads to him.

Once Bobo was up in his apartment, he looked out his front window, standing at the old console he'd rescued from the back of the pawnshop. He'd sanded it down and refinished it before installing some shelves inside for the books he'd planned on reading when he'd moved to such a very quiet place. Instead, he'd begun downloading what he wanted to read onto an e-reader or ordering special favorites from a bookstore in Houston. And that had worked out fine, because the space in the console was perfect for the books he'd removed from the secret closet. They were an unappealing lot. He was sure that if Lem was interested in them, they were not wholesome novels.

For the first time, as Bobo squatted to open the door and look inside, he wondered if he hadn't exchanged one secret for another. But the musty old books were so worn you couldn't even read the titles on the spines, and he had no desire whatsoever to open one of them. He shut the door and stood, looking out the window once again. As he watched, Fiji's yard lights went off and then the lights in her big front room. After a moment, the only light showing was shining softly onto the ground at the right rear of the house, Fiji's bedroom. All the lights at the Wedding Chapel and Pet Cemetery were off. The Rev had gone home to bed in the little house no one had ever entered.

If he leaned into the window and looked right, he could just see the glow from the trailer where the Reed family would be doing whatever they did at night. Putting the baby to bed? Watching television? Bobo could not see what was happening at the Antique Gallery and Nail Salon, but he figured after standing all evening in their wings and silver jumpsuits, Chuy and Joe were crawling into bed. (They were in bed, but they were indulging in some fooling around.)

Manfred's front light was still on, and Bobo wondered if his tenant had gone back to work. The boy—the young man—did seem oddly compelled to work until he dropped. He had told Bobo that there was some reason that was pushing him, some drive that he didn't understand.

"But I will," Manfred had said. "Someday, I'll know what it was all about."

Bobo hoped that someday, he'd understand what it was all about, too.

Till then, he was staying right where he was, in Midnight.